The PRO

Also by Mike Shropshire

The Ice Bowl
Season in Hell

The PRO

Mike Shropshire

THOMAS DUNNE BOOKS
ST. MARTIN'S PRESS
NEW YORK

THOMAS DUNNE BOOKS.
An imprint of St. Martin's Press.

www.stmartins.com

ISBN 0-312-24231-X

First Edition: June 2001

10 9 8 7 6 5 4 3 2 1

To the late Donald I.Fine,
patron saint of the marginally unbalanced

My greenskeeper presented himself as many things to many people. According to the personalized license plates on his burnt orange 1977 GMC pickup truck, he was "Ol' Sarge." To me and most of the members of this golf club, he was Doublewide McBride, aka the Old Scotsman. In the peculiar town of Immokalee, where the phantom apparitions of Seminole warriors prowled the streets at night, they called him the Snake Man.

No man could uphold such various identities unless he maintained an early-to-rise, early-to-work ethic. So when the pelicans began to squawk just before sunrise, Doublewide had been up and at it for about an hour and a half. First stop, always, was the police station where, thanks to connections, Doublewide would buy a thermos of coffee powerfully enriched with a secret energy-boosting agent.

By the time I arrived at the club around seven, Doublewide would have already toured the course and captured various species of the serpent family that crawled out of the rough and into the sand traps. Some alligators the size of submarines occupied the lagoons that abutted the 14th and 15th fairways, but even a man of Doublewide's tenacity left those guys alone. "This place gives you a pretty good idea of what it's like to play golf at Jurassic Park," Doublewide declared one morning. He spewed out an endless barrage of profundities like that, revved to the gills on that cop-shop coffee. After his daily pre-dawn snake patrol, Doublewide went to war against the forces of Indonesian root rot and Nicaraguan screw worms, the unseen co-conspirators that threatened to annihilate our fairways.

Caloosahatchee Pines graced the outskirts of Punta Gorda, Florida, and it had to rank as the oldest golf course in the United States. That would be my educated guess. In the category of oldest, I am talking about the average age of the club members who played there. Most of my players—I was the club pro—were older than the League of Nations. Nobody would have ever confused the pink stucco club-house there with the Royal and Ancient at St. Andrew's, although the course itself was not entirely void of a kind of idiosyncratic charm. In order to reach the third green, you had to hook your approach shot around a long-abandoned lighthouse. Nobody knew why the lighthouse was out there, since this golf course was seven miles inland from the coast. "That at least explains why it's abandoned," reasoned Doublewide McBride.

In his relentless curiosity, Doublewide was the only person who ever asked me about my full name: Franklin Delano Bonnet. My mother named me after FDR because I was born the day he died. I do not recall why I became known as Del in junior high school. But Del Bonnet sounded like one of those singers on *American Bandstand*, and I didn't resist the change.

By the time Doublewide McBride ventured off on his tractor to spray the grass, the first foursomes had already arrived, ready to tee off. By noon, from the window of the pro shop, I noticed that Maureen Henry's approach shot to the 18th green had rolled past the hole, down a small embankment and nestled into a poor lie next to the cart path. I confidently predicted that Mrs. Henry, who had the bone structure of a parakeet, would chip up to within one foot of the hole. I was familiar with her game. I was familiar with *all* their games.

I also knew that Mrs. Henry, a native of Fort Wayne, Indiana, was the first woman ever to skydive in that state. That was before she met Mr. Henry. She never related any of that to me personally. But when you work at a golf course every day, you hear all kinds of things. There is something about a golf course that brings out the conversationalist in most people.

Maureen Henry tapped in the short putt, finished with a round of 81. That was a damn good score for a couple of reasons. First off, that 81 was only five shots over this woman's age. Second, she played in conditions that were hardly ideal. With one of those tropical disturbances that churned through the Gulf to the southwest and winds on the golf course that gusted to 40 mph, the flags on all the pins were horizontal. For me, that was a harbinger of unrest.

Most of my life, the winds of destiny had carried me to various locations and circumstances. Customarily, these were turbulent breezes. I came to take it for granted that things would always be that way. Then one day I drifted ashore, so to speak, here at Caloosahatchee Pines, and the wind suddenly died down.

That was nine years before. I am not going to imply that those years had been hugely productive. Part of my employment package at Caloosahatchee Pines was to have included bonuses from the sales of Max-Fli golfballs and Foot Joy shoes and all the rest of that stuff at the pro shop. The members there were hardly destitute. Most of my male membership were comfortable because they belonged to the junior levels of the "Maybe I can't cut the mustard, but I can still lick the jar" generation.

They maintained that fixed income mentality and bought most of their golf essentials at places like Wal-Mart, and who could blame them? And apparently I wasn't excessively endowed when it came to powers of persuasion. As my ex-stepfather used to say, I couldn't sell pussy in a lumber camp. So I wasn't getting rich there. But I was anonymous and, to maintain that status, one must often sacrifice lofty financial goals. It could not accurately be said that I was running from my past. But the fact that my past kept lurking around was a source of constant annoyance.

A couple of career lowlights, insignificant ones that had been magnified through the passage of years, followed me around at Caloosahatchee Pines. The membership remained under the impression that the trouble had been more egregious than what actually happened. They thought I had held up a drug store. Not me. But in 1970, I became the first and only contestant in a PGA tour event to be led off the course in handcuffs. Prior to that, I'd demonstrated what somebody might have called a "natural affliction" for the game of championship golf and was one of about a dozen and a half young tour hotshots who rated at the next tier down from Nicklaus, Palmer, Player, Casper, and one or two others. I beat Ray Floyd in a playoff at the Cleveland Open and finished in the top five at the U.S. Open at Rochester in 1968, the one that Lee Trevino won to become an instant superstar.

Then came New Orleans. We have confirmed that the House of the Rising Sun wasn't the only place in that town where young fools could land in embarrassing circumstances. After the third round of the New Orleans Open, I was just two shots off the lead and decided to celebrate prematurely at Arnauld's Restaurant on Bienville Street in the French Quarter. It was at that place I was introduced to a friend of a friend with brown eyes the size of hubcaps. Her name was Miranda, which was appropriate as later events would demonstrate.

After the restaurant, Miranda decided that she wanted me to drive her car back to her place because, by then, she could barely stand but neither, unfortunately, could I. And her goddamn Cadillac Coupe de Ville had an alignment problem and refused to stay on the road and then, well—I got distracted by something that was happening in the front seat and drove into the little Trosclair grocery store off Magazine Street. By into the store, I mean right through a plate glass window and back into the produce area.

The place was closed, thank God. It was after midnight. I made a quick decision. "Miranda," I said, "I've gotta take a leak." So I climbed out of the wrecked Caddy, picked my way through the rubble and out of the store and, once on the street, started running like Seabiscuit until I waved down the cab that took me back to the hotel.

It was by the dawn's early light that Naomi Trosclair, the woman who owned that grocery store, turned out to be something other than a turn-the-other-cheek Christian. Let me tell you something about those Louisiana people. They are impetuous. Dead set on retribution, they are quick to attempt to right the things that they perceive as wrongs.

Miranda didn't remember my name, only that I played in the New Orleans Open golf tournament at the Lakewood Country Club. Too bad for me that I was conspicuous among the other golfers on that unforgettable Sunday morning because, with all the little shards of broken windshield glass still stuck in my hair, I glistened like fake diamonds in the bright bayou sunshine. On the third fairway, I lined up a 6-iron to the green when this cop crawled through the ropes and told me all about my right to remain silent.

The PGA demands, of course, that the contestants on its tour maintain an ambassadorial posture when it comes to behavior on and off the golf course. So, naturally, they handed me my ass in a bag. According to the certified letter they sent me, "Abandoning the scene of an accident can only be deemed as conduct unbecoming to a PGA representative."

An incident like that customarily might have qualified as minor league trivia, at the maximum, and soon forgotten. In the eyes of First Amendment libel law specialists, I would have barely qualified for "public figure" status. Unfortunately, that New Orleans episode got amplified and dramatized into a posture of absurdity, way out of hand, because of something Miranda said. This total stranger, Miranda, given her once-in-a-lifetime opportunity to talk to a reporter, said that the wreck happened because she had performed what the newspapers of that era termed "oral copulation" that distracted me enough to drive into a goddamn grocery store.

I could have stood, holding a bullhorn on the courthouse steps, and truthfully announced, "Miranda, you handed that reporter a pack of lies." But I was defenseless. Why? Because the people of this country maintain a historic and long-standing fascination with blow jobs. In some distant time, far into the future, perhaps anthropologists will be able to explain the reasons why so many Americans become so mesmerized about blow job stories, particularly when a semi-celebrity and a moving automobile also become part of the plot.

They kicked me off the tour for a year, and when I came

back, the needle that I took from my touring colleagues was longer and sharper than I could stomach. "The Skullmeister," they called me. I teed off at the Bing Crosby Pebble Beach tournament, playing with a guy who had won some Grand Slam events and was therefore well known, and I heard this golfer tell the gallery, "I also hit one of Del's balls by mistake the other day, but then I recognized it. Had lipstick all over it. Haw-haw-haw." That crap became relentless. When you were drawing laughter instead of cheers from the galleries, the professional athlete should perceive that he or she suffers from a skewed image. Eventually, I did what any sane person would have done under the circumstances and quit the tour forever.

An episode that we would label Public Fiasco II happened years later when the University of Illinois at Cicero, where I was coaching, became the first and only golf team ever to get an NCAA death penalty. This happened during the height of all of those savings and loan scandals so when Henry Dugan, the columnist from the *Chicago Sun Times*, called and asked me to explain how in the hell something like that could happen to a golf program, I knew how to say, "My only crime is that, deep in my heart, I care about people and sometimes I trust them too much."

So then the sportswriter wrote this column where he said, "When Del Bonnet wasn't arranging payoffs for his players, he was busy offering private lessons to the coeds. Some of those lessons even included golf." The part about the coeds was pure fable. The coeds at Illinois (Cicero) didn't need lessons in *anything*. So when it came to ink, I could have still lived without it, and that was why the anonymity of long hours at Caloosahatchee Pines maintained its appeal. Last winter, Greg Norman passed through to play an exhibition sponsored by some shoe company he represented. Somebody mentioned to Norman, "The club pro here, Del Bonnet, used to play on the tour."

"Really?" said the Great White Shark. "Never 'erd of 'im."

For the first time since that Black Sabbath in New Orleans, the stigma seemed to have gone away.

The good people at Caloosahatchee Pines largely agreed that I was a pretty good teacher when it came to the basics of setting up a golf swing. The employment of word pictures worked pretty well, particularly with the beginners. A big problem with the mediocre players, the predominant one really, was that they came off the ball, or looked up, just as their club head met the golf ball. "So concentrate on this on every shot: Pretend that there is a string attached to your nose and at the other end of the string there's a fishhook, and that's stuck ever-so-slightly into your nut sack. So if you yank your head up in the middle of your swing, visualize what will happen." That's what I told them, and it was a teaching device that worked well. So what did I tell the women beginners? Well, I didn't tell them anything because women usually tended to stay down on the ball.

But in the modern world, the simple ability to communicate no longer remains sufficient. That lesson came with the unexpected arrival of Tyler LaGrange. Tyler was elected president of the board at Caloosahatchee Pines six months before, and he thought the golf pro needed to provide monthly projection charts for all of the golfing members. Like if Arlene Portwood, age eighty-eight, was shooting 130, Tyler wanted me to get her down to 127 whether Arlene wanted to or not and, if she didn't, then Tyler LaGrange wanted me to appear before the board and explain why.

LaGrange was a young guy, not a day over sixty, and still active as the regional marketing director for some brewery, and that partially explained his fetish with sales projections.

LaGrange disagreed with my marketing strategy, that consisted of a sign in the pro shop that read, THERE'S NOTHING SPECIAL ABOUT OUR GOLF BAGS, BUT YOU CAN'T LICK OUR BALLS. He wanted to get rid of the sign. In fact, Tyler La-Grange wanted to get rid of me. How come? Because he thought I had a "thing" for his wife, Jerri, that's why. Or even worse, LaGrange thought that Jerri might have had a "thing" for me. The club president pictured me as somebody who appeared in his wife's masturbation fantasies. The fact was that Jerri, while gifted with a cheerful personality and fine soprano voice, had the torso and legs of Sam Huff. I wished that somebody would tell Tyler LaGrange that according to the teaching professional's code of ethics, fooling around with the female clients or patients or whatever the hell you call them ranked as a cardinal transgression. We were like preachers in that regard and, yes, sometimes we strayed, although I never did. Now tennis pros, they were different.

Those guys would hit on their own grandmothers. A classic example of this tennis pro syndrome pranced in my very presence at Caloosahatchee Pines. Antonio Paez. Somebody ought to have writen a song about Antonio: "You Light Up My Wife."

Another thing I wished somebody would tell Tyler La-Grange was that I was a self-declared nonsexual. That was different from being asexual in that there was still an arousal factor lurking around down there in the ash pit of my emotions. But after a couple of busted marriages and some other partnerships that wound up like my evening with Miranda, which was to say not on the best of terms, I thought I might have been better suited for noble isolation. If I was not any good at something, then why bother?

OK. I lied. I was not nonsexual, but at that time was between opportunities and, when a single male of the species reached my age, a hiatus in the area of the love life loomed as something of indeterminate longevity. Within the previous three months, I had considered entry into a matrimonial compact with Carla. Owned her own travel agency. Young widow, but hardly famished for companionship. Was active in the Presbyterian Sunday school. Gifted with a body like that of a little rubber monkey. It was nine-year-old Crockett, the fellow who was then scheduled to become my red-headed stepson, who capsized that deal. Crockett liked to conceal himself in Carla's big hibiscus plant with a pellet gun and wait for the postman. "One of these days, you're going to put somebody's eye out with that thing," I told Crockett one August morning. I'd waited forty years to use that line on somebody and, not four seconds after I'd uttered it, I felt a deep and fiery sting in the back of my neck.

I have never said that I'm proud of what happened next. I could not say that I was not ashamed of it either. However, the understanding that Crockett and I accomplished that morning rendered any further fellowship with Carla impractical.

I was explaining all of that to Doublewide, a man capable of understanding that plot line but who chose not to sympathize with it. Doublewide, who had been fired by Ronald Reagan during the great air traffic controller purge, contended that he had either been romantically involved, or was about to be, with every reasonable candidate on the West Coast of Florida.

Doublewide conceded that his secret lay simply in the fact

that he had big feet. "For every woman, that's the ultimate turn-on," he said. "It might even be subliminal. And the hell of it is, my feet ain't *that* big. I wear shoes six sizes too big. Of course, one of the negative side effects there is the appearance of poor posture, but that's part of the price I have to pay." Doublewide chain-smoked Kool cigarettes. Zero body fat percentage, probably. He was emaciated (people called him Doublewide because he resided in an oversized trailer home) and, year-round, kept what he called a "Sumatran gold" suntan.

Just back from a quick run over to Immokalee, the Gateway to the Swamp, where he'd sold forty dollars' worth of live golf course water moccasins to the Wildlife Park tourist trap, Doublewide pontificated on life's hidden meanings in the Leader Board Lounge, which was what they called the bar at Caloosahatchee Pines. Ordinarily, Doublewide was not allowed to drink in there. But that evening, the place was deserted because the club had chartered two buses off to St. Pete where Perry Como and the Ames Brothers were giving a concert.

Aside from his duties as superintendent of the grounds, Doublewide also worked infrequently as a licensed private investigator. Like myself, he had experienced his share of occupational adversity. After I explained the details of my potential adversary at Caloosahatchee Pines in the form of Tyler LaGrange, he shared my intuition that conflagration might lie just ahead.

For the last year, Doublewide had bugged me to try out for the Seniors Tour. "Now it sounds like you might not have an alternative. Fellows like Tyler LaGrange, they come from a job background where they'll just go and screw somebody in the ear because they have the authority to go and do it. No reason for it. They just can't help themselves, so don't take it personally. But it *is* time to go," he insisted. I explained a mitigating and major impediment to the Seniors scheme, and unfortunately, it involved finances. Doublewide, product of a lifetime of playing angles, offered a solution. "I am sure," he suggested, "that you are acquainted with Dorothy Ridge."

Of course I was acquainted with Dorothy Ridge—from afar. She never required any professional golf instruction. With a sweeping backswing, Mrs. Ridge got terrific topspin on her tee shots. She could poke a drive ninety yards down the fairway, and then it would roll ninety more. If I'd had her short game, I would have won that U.S. Open at Rochester. Mrs. Ridge was about the only woman on our golf course who consistently beat Mrs. Maureen Henry and, since people at golf courses *do* talk, I knew some other poignant facts about Mrs. Ridge, too.

Dorothy, a former Rockette, was married (and was undoubtedly a trophy wife when they hitched up) to what might have been described as an older man, and in these parts, that meant around triple digits. Colonel Barclay Ridge owned a considerable estate thanks entirely to his late father, a chocolate baron. For the previous five years, Colonel Barclay had not known his own name, or his home planet, although that condition was regarded as much as an infirmity of old age as it was the man's close and long-time friendship with Comrade Smirnoff.

So—according to the country club information circuit— when the family gathered for the Colonel's birthday party at the nursing home, he recognized nobody, but kept staring curiously at Dorothy Ridge and then finally intoned, "Didn't I fuck you in France?" Yeah. That story was the talk of the club, largely because Dorothy herself was the person who told the tale. She took it all in stride. In fact, she walked into the courthouse with the same purposeful gait that she demonstrated on the golf course, told her story and, when the judge ordained Colonel Barclay a legal vegetable, she assumed executorship of his $11 million estate.

That much remained everyday news at Caloosahatchee Pines. Doublewide McBride, private eye, supplied additional data. "I have been employed by Dorothy Ridge's stockbroker to do some investigative work into his own domestic affairs, and in casual conversation, he mentioned that—against his counsel—Mrs. Ridge cashed in about $3 million worth of IRAs and T-Bonds and reinvested those in some higher risk stocks, such as Alliance Gaming and Speedway Motor Sports, and she's goddan near doubled that money. That's what the stockbroker says, and now she's in what he calls an acquisition mode so . . ."

Present myself and my Seniors Tour ambitions to Dorothy Ridge as a potential growth stock. Amusing fellow, that Doublewide McBride. If only that bottle of chardonnay I was drinking was as inspired as Doublewide. One thing I did know. I was well into the third quarter of the game of life, I was 14 points down and my point guard just picked up his fourth foul. The time had arrived to call "time out" and devise some new strategies.

Golf club technology might not have advanced that much since I played on the tour, but that was not because nobody had tried.

If you watched as much late night trash TV as I did, you'd have noticed that the golf gimmicks outnumbered even the vegetable slicers after 2 A.M. They sold them by the ton. That Big Bertha driver. Why hadn't I invented that thing?

Gimmick merchandise might have gone well enough in

the Baby Boomer golf market, but the limited patronage of the Caloosahatchee Pines pro shop maintained a traditionalist buying formula. So when a sales rep who worked out of his station wagon announced "the most monumental advance yet" in driver design, I encouraged him to look elsewhere. The new club looked typical enough. Titanium club head the size of a football.

"Not titanium," corrected Jerry Coluccio, the sales rep and patent owner, in a conspiratorial whisper. "Kryptonite. I call this driver the Enola Gay. Revolutionary aerodynamics. Extra weight in the club head *and* the grip. It'll increase your distance off the tee by fifty yards."

"Go away, Jerry," I said.

"I'll go, but I'll leave an Enola Gay. Try it and call me."

Jerry left both his business card and his golf club with its little mushroom cloud etched into the top of the clubhead.

My prejudice against the New Age drivers stemmed mostly from the sound that resulted when the club struck the ball. With my old set of Spaulding persimmon woods, there was always the familiar stimulation of the pristine, bullwhip snap that suggested the ball had been hit harder than it really was. With these new clubs, the "snap" you got was like the one a plumber hears when he bangs on copper pipe with a rubber hammer.

When Arlene Portwood's doctor called to cancel her 6:00 P.M. golf lesson, I was left with some idle time and carried Jerry Coluccio's magic driver to the then-deserted practice tee. And in the deep twilight of the following afternoon, before an audience of varied bird life, I played a solitary round on the back nine at Caloosahatchee Pines, and used the driver.

"Tunk!" That sappy metal driver noise. I watched with supreme curiosity as my drive landed not in the 10th fairway but disappeared across the highway to the right. Then I cringed and awaited the sound of a shattering windshield and when that didn't come, I hit a second ball. Same results, different direction. Deep, deep into the Caloosahatchie rain forest where only Doublewide dared to venture.

Although my drives sailed away to outlandish destinations, I sensed a forceful unity with this, this Enola Gay thing. I began to tinker, modifying my stance and my grip. That's a tactic that I would NEVER recommend to an average player—restructuring your game to accommodate the golf club. But this Enola Gay demanded radical tactics.

After an hour's worth of experimentation, I tamed the Enola Gay. Or maybe the Enola Gay tamed me. In either case, we channeled our energies into stunning results and attained an accord. In this arrangement, I, the golfer, would not function as the boss, but rather in a 50-50 on-the-course partnership with the Enola Gay.

We played the last four holes of this twilight abandoned Caloosahatchie Pines golf course in five-under. Jacked up by a sensation of unprecedented rejuvenation, I flipped through the club directory, and attempted to locate the home number of Dorothy Ridge.

2

No matter how vigorously most people labor to arrange modest control of their destinies, the natural laws of coincidence and chaos eternally prevail. I had frequently marveled at how a single external event... Richard Nixon's famous ass-covering Checkers speech... could so profoundly impact the itinerary of my lifetime and my personal fortunes, or lack of same.

That all happened when I had just started grade school in Topeka where my father, Gene Bonnet, enjoyed some prosperity in a small business that sold truck tires. My mother Connie helped out as a part-time bookkeeper at a well-known psychiatric hospital in the same city. Connie, a brunette bantamweight and intensely prideful of her multitudinous opinion base, frequently said, "The only reason they use that shock treatment in the clinic is because it weeds out the fakers."

So, after the would-be vice president Nixon concluded his historic, live-TV Checkers performance, Connie delivered what the track and field people refer to as a personal best. "That fuckin' little pin-headed, lying freak!" Because this politically funded appearance had preempted *Dragnet*, the steam had already mounted to alarming pressure levels and, when Nixon delivered his parable about the dog, Connie's boiler exploded. Even though I was just a kid, I later visualized the episode so vividly because I had feared Connie was going to wreck the TV set.

Truck Tire Gene, which was how my old man was fondly known around the community, refused to be upstaged. "Goddamn it, Connie, listen to me. I served under Ike—you didn't. And I can tell ya for sure that Ike would never have brought that Nixon guy on board unless he knew for sure that he was a first class troop."

At that point, I retreated to the bedroom and can recall having thought, "You better watch it, Gene," when I heard the debate suddenly punctuated by a thud, then a moan, and finally the rather terminal quality of the slam of the front door. Gene moved out for good the next morning and, to this day, if you look closely enough, you can see where his entire nose had been moved about a quarter-inch to the starboard side of its original mooring.

While the inevitability of Gene's eventual departure remained beyond dispute (the McCarthy hearings would have done that marriage in for sure), that Checkers incident clearly provided a potent catalyst for instantaneous change. So in my reasoning, the Nixon family pet could assume the delightful responsibility for having brought Doyle Getzendeiner into my life.

Connie married Doyle, who reminded everybody of Don Ameche, about the time I started high school, and it was Doyle who taught me how to grip and swing a golf club. There was an entire galaxy of additional material that Doyle could have taught me, had my aptitudes been so inclined. Doyle maintained the perpetual ability to sell products to customers that they neither needed nor desired. A Dodge-Plymouth dealership provided Doyle with the ideal platform for the demonstration of his enormous skills in the art of human persuasion. From my perspective, the man served as the ultimate living emancipator because he allowed me what he termed "the pick of the litter" from the junk heaps on his used car lot that bore the big orange and black sign that read EASY TRADIN' DOYLE.

One of Doyle's sales gimmicks included handing out baby chicks to any potential customer who wandered into the showroom with a kid in tow. And what was the source of the chickens? Truck Tire Gene, of course, who had bought a farm over near Emporia. He'd also married Lorraine. If Doyle could have doubled for Don Ameche, then Lorraine offered at least a casual resemblance to an emerging film starlet of the time, Miss Sophia Loren. One summer morning when I fetched some chicks out of their coop, Lorraine directed me into a nearby alfalfa field. "I wanna show ya somethin', kiddo." Then she dared me to deny that an exact likeness of Jesus Christ wasn't floating overhead in a cloud formation.

Throughout my teenage years and as a young adult, I used to envision a circumstance where Lorraine and I then proceeded over to the hayloft and this envisioning sometimes was enacted in shameful detail. What did happen was that a gust of wind came along that pressed Lorraine's sundress into the anterior contours of her physique, and I understood at that moment that Gene had a good life working out there on the prairie and that made me happy.

And . . . back in town . . . Doyle, who had the good sense to never address political topics at home, got rich from a local TV commercial that he dreamed up himself, where he dressed up in a Man from Mars costume, climbed out of a hokey spaceship and said, "Plymouth's for me in '63!" Connie quit her job at the hospital—"Most of those folks aren't crazy at all. They're just a bunch of drunks"—and she and

Doyle began going on a lot of cruises. So, thanks to Checkers, matters apparently turned out nicely for everybody. Or at least that's what I thought until a few more short years down the calendar, when that golf swing that Doyle taught me generated some serious implications in my own life.

What happened was that I won a basketball scholarship at Will Rogers State University in Sapulpa, Oklahoma, where I maintained a solid C-plus average in WRSU's internationally acclaimed college of municipal recreation and parks supervision and an equally acceptable 11.8 scoring average on a team that called itself the Fighting Tumbleweeds. Unfortunately, the already limited co-ed population at WRSU remained devotedly indifferent to the exploits of the Tumbleweeds and I concentrated my off-duty leisure hours at the public golf course.

The lyric of a showtune goes, "Oh-OAK-lahoma, where the wind comes sweeping down the plain . . ." Jesus Jones, did it ever, usually about 60 mph on a calm day. So my golf game soon adapted itself to adverse conditions, and when those Apollo astronauts started whacking golf balls around the lunar surface that time, they got better lies then anything available in the fairways at Whistling Creek. The course record there belonged to me and that was one that would never be broken—the reason for that being that the course itself now lay under the waters of Lake Ma Barker, one of the largest resort developments in the entire state.

After graduation, four of the five starters for the Tumbleweeds took advantage of their education, went out and became deputy game wardens, working for the state. There was a job for me there, too, but I was never all that enthusiastic about life among the small-mouth bass and wild goose set. I agree that a constant vigil needs to be in place that warns the public about the possible consequences of an untended campfire, but I had higher aspirations. My goal, since I had been encouraged by Tumbleweeds hoops coach Hoppie McBee, was to reach for the stars, and in my circumstance, that meant returning to Topeka and going to work for Easy Tradin' Doyle. But, like Coach Hoppie had reminded us after the big upset loss to the Sacramento Institute of Cosmetology (SIC) in the quarter-finals of the NAIA tournament, "There *will* be those days in life when the champagne turns into mule piss." But no disappointment from the arena of athletic competition could have prepared me for the paralysis of spirit that accompanied the news that Connie, suddenly and without warning, had given Doyle the heave-ho. So Doyle had sold the dealership for cash and vanished.

"What happened? Did he convince some old lady that he actually *was* Don Ameche and then close the sale?" I was on the phone with Connie and needed an explanation.

"No. Nothing like that. I just got sick of watching him on those TV commercials, jabbering away about rebates and his big pre-Christmas sale and his big post-inventory sale. What next? A pre-fire sale? Then he goes on Channel 14 last week in an Uncle Sam costume, pitching his All-America Memorial Day Special. Every time I went to the grocery store, I felt like people were staring at me and whispering, 'Look. There she goes. *Mrs.* Easy Tradin' Doyle.' There's got to be more in life than just . . ."

I didn't let Connie complete her sentence. "Right now and for the rest of my life, my biggest regret will always be that I came one year short of being old enough to vote for Goldwater!"

Connie, as usual, was quick with a counterpunch. "Well, I suppose I *am* partially to blame for that, since I knowingly made a decision to breed a child with a card-carryin' idiot."

Then the operator came on the line, said my three minutes were up and that I needed to deposit another $1.30. So I hung up. But this was one of those occasions when Madame Fate was shuffling and dealing the cards at a world record clip. The very next morning, I wandered into the Sapulpa Post Office, just about to mail off my credentials to the employment office at the Oklahoma Game and Fish Commission, my heart heavier than watered-down biscuit dough. Then I heard a ringing baritone: "Hey yew!"

The man who introduced himself as Carl Mayes didn't know my name, exactly, but he remembered having seen me score twenty-two points—my greatest game ever in the green and gold of the Fighting Tumbleweeds—against Tishamingo Baptist College two years earlier, an event that I had already just about forgotten. Carl invited me to join him for a cheeseburger. I went along, but was wary, mindful of the teachings of Coach Hoppie McBee. "Watch out for these old jock sniffers," Hoppie used to tell us. "Most of 'em are queer as a three-peckered goat."

Right away, without saying so, Carl Mayes, dressed in the first polyester suit that I had ever seen, made it evident that his sexual preference was bourbon and 7UP. He'd drained three of those before the counter girl at the Char-ko Grill could bring out the fried onion rings, and by the time the Wahooburgers arrived, Carl had offered me a position as sales rep for Burning Arrow Petroleum.

"I've had good luck with yew ath-uh-letes," Carl said. "To be perfectly candid, most of y'all aren't exactly Phi Beta Whatever-the-shit-ya-call-it, but you show what I like to call 'nitiative. Plus, there's that name identification factor that gets your boot in the door with a lot of these *po*-tential *in*-vestors. Particularly in this state."

"Well, with all due respect, Carl, the WRSU Tumbleweeds

aren't exactly the Oklahoma Sooners," I said, wondering at once what Easy Tradin' Doyle's reaction would be to a comment like that. Carl, whose build, thick brown hair, and rustic cranial features suggested that he might be one-eighth buffalo, shook his gigantic head. "Hail," he said, meaning, of course, hell. "Most all these sons-uh-bitches dunno the difference between the Oklahoma Sooners and the Sears catalog when it comes down to it. All that matters is that they believe you're *somebody* and that's your edge. 'Sides. The awl bizznizz is jist like any other bizznizz. Truth is a secondary commodity."

The deal that Carl Mayes presented, I thought, was a little top-heavy in commission compensation. Beyond that, all I got was meal money, use of a company-owned, butt-sprung '65 Pontiac station wagon with sawdust in the transmission that Burning Arrow Petroleum probably bought as a Labor Day demo special from Doyle, and, as a lone perk, a membership to the Midwest City, Oklahoma Country Club. "Ever play any golf?" Carl asked me. "Lotta these *in*-vestor guys—they like to play golf." Now, the ghost of Checkers and the shadow of serendipity emerged hand-in-hand.

By midsummer of 1967, the fund-raising strategy of Burning Arrow Petroleum had shifted from a get-ridiculously-rich-from-one-of-our-wells theme to a tax-write-off-from-one-of-our-dry-holes posture. Four-star dusters. That's what Carl called his dry holes, and his recent inventory had become ample.

Carl was marginally pleased with my on-the-job efforts. I'd set the hook for a couple of mid-level deals on which Carl had been able to reel in the line—even though I had absolutely no clue as to what I was talking about. In retrospect, I believe the technical term for what Carl had underway was and still is securities fraud.

Again in retrospect, the federal pen, probably Leaven-worth, was wistfully beckoning when another mystic navigator, quite unexpected as usual, materialized to rechart my course. The customary post-round chatfest was underway at the Midwest City Country Club, where it appeared the mutual goal of everyone involved was the eventual mass extermination of the human liver.

My job was to entertain another potential client, Maxie Pearl from Junction, Colorado, and somehow interest him in the prospect of placing about sixty grand into an energy-producing project in Manitoba. I did not know that night that the lease I was proposing no longer belonged to Burning Arrow, but by then, I *should* have known.

Ever so fortunately for me, Maxie Pearl had already probably figured that out, and he didn't care. Maxie was one of those Western outdoors guys, he owned a bunch of quarter horses, and you couldn't tell for certain whether he was thirty-five or fifty-five. In Maxie's case, the size of his gut seemed within a reasonable state of containment, so I would have guessed him closer to thirty-five. I'd made a couple more putts than usual that afternoon and had stiffed Maxie to the tune of about $150, which equalled my weekly salary at Burning Arrow. Not good strategy in courting investors, but I was only an apprentice.

Maxie sat there in the country club bar, not saying much and listening to George Jones on the jukebox singing "The Race Is On" when he got a peculiar, almost distressed look on his face. Then, out of nowhere, he said, "How often do you do that?"

"Do what?," I said.

"Shoot sixty-six," Maxie said.

"Every fuckin' time," I said.

The next morning, I phoned Carl Mayes with the big

news. Maxie Pearl had agreed to throw in not sixty, but ninety grand.

"No shit?" said Carl.

"No shit," I said, not bothering to add that the ninety grand did not involve Burning Arrow Petroleum but rather a speculative venture that would finance me for a year on the PGA tour.

3

This morning on the practice tee at Caloosahatchee Pines, the teacher, as usual, was learning from the pupil. I was being paid to recommend some alterations in the golf swing of Hayes Clark, a golf swing that could best be described as terminally brittle. Clark, who made a fortune by manufacturing signs for the post office department that read NEXT WINDOW, really didn't seem to care that much about the golf swing. He simply wanted to vent. Specifically, he wanted to talk about an epidemic of what he called "the fifty-five-year-old white American male syndrome."

Clark, armed with his 5-iron and one of those big Roman statue noses that some women associate with other sizable body parts, smacked yet another 90-yard worm burner and detailed his dilemma. "I've got me this trophy wife and a set of trophy twins—over there at the private grade school. Tuition's eatin' me alive," Hayes said in his Pittsburgh accent. Don't ask me how I know it's a Pittsburgh accent. I just do.

"And . . . (whock—another two-hopper out toward second), I got me this other previous wife, this old stegosaurus up in Myrtle Beach. There's a whole colony of bitter exes up there. They could chop wood with their faces. Arnelle and her lawyers—Arnelle's Army, I used to call 'em—can't bleed me any more, but I know that she's lurking around out there. She E-mails twice a week bitching because I lavish all this attention on the trophy twins at the expense of 'our' boy in Atlanta. 'Course, she knows that Patti reads those E-mails, and it really pisses her off. 'Why don't you tell the old bitch to go jump off a bridge?' That's Patti talking. I tell Patti that that'll just make it worse, but she won't listen. So finally, I E-mailed Arnelle back and said, 'Look. He's your kid and he's my kid but he's no longer *our* kid.' So what do you know? Two days later, 'our' kid, who's still trying to find himself in the hedge fund business, sends me this phone bill. Twelve hundred and eighty bucks. Several calls to Singapore. And across this phone bill, he's written the word 'Help!' So I send him a copy of this book: *The Seven Habits of Highly Successful People*. Or *The Habits Of Seven Highly Successful People*. Some shit like that. Anyway, I haven't heard from them lately. But I will. And then there's Pop. He's eighty-nine. I got a letter from the rest home that says he's been confined to his room for flashing a nurse and if it happens again, he gets the heave-ho. 'Well, he damn sure ain't movin' in with us!' That's the trophy wife talking. But, all bullshit aside, here's the part that really has me worried. When Patti and me got together, that was ten years ago, and I was forty-five and she was like—nineteen or something— back then she called me her 'blue-steel Viking.' Now, as of last week, I'm her 'adorable little clown.' And she says she wants to go back to school. I ask her, 'What kind of school?' and she says, 'I dunno. Maybe polo lessons.' Maybe I'm nuts. But I feel threatened."

Amazing how a golf course can draw out the inner soul, even if it's on the practice tee. "Think positive thoughts and try hitting one cross-handed. It couldn't hurt," I tell him, the creative instructor at work again. Whack. A sharp liner to deep left center. All this venting seems to be paying off.

"But you know what I'm talking about," Clark says to me. "Everybody I know is paddling the same lifeboat. You go outside, look up, and the buzzards are circling."

No. I don't know what he's talking about. There are no trophy wives in the life of the golf pro at Caloosahatchee Pines. Not a dog, not even a parakeet. No ex-kids. Technically, there might be an ex-wife out there somewhere, but she married a chiropractor about fifteen years ago and then sort of vanished. As for the part about the aging problem parents, well, I talked to Connie on the phone last Mother's Day, and she told me that she'd been sending death threats to the White House on a regular basis and that the "secret police" wrote back and said that she shouldn't waste her money on postage and should invest it in a good laxative because they don't take her seriously.

"I wrote 'em back and told 'em I wouldn't be so sure," Connie said.

So, yeah, I worry about my mother some, but in a way that's different from most folks. Suddenly, all of this seems sensationally emancipating.

My pupil, Hayes Clark, whiffed completely on his next swing while an assembly of seagulls strutting around the roof of my pro shop made chuckling sounds. "Ya know what?" says my pupil. "Congress ought to pass a law where every five years, you have to switch families and you have to switch jobs."

On the last five swings of his lesson, Hayes fanned on four attempts and hit one vicious liner that missed the left ear of Mrs. Gorski, way over on the practice green, by about three inches. She never saw the ball. At the risk of getting fired, I'm surprised that more people don't get killed on the golf course. But this has to have been one of the most successful golf lessons of all time. Last week, in the magazine for retired people that they call *Golden Alternatives*, there was a story about some guy who was raising emus in some place like Cheap Suit, West Virginia, and he decided to try the Seniors PGA golf tour, and he didn't win a single tournament and still collected over a million dollars. Now, without realizing it, Clark Hayes convinced me that now is the time to leave the past behind and abandon this shit heap forever.

Life is simply a matter of checks and balances and in my case, unfortunately, this has been a life more checkered than balanced. But before I can blindly embark on this last final excursion into the abyss of the great unknown, it has been written that it is best to align oneself with a support mechanism. That was written, in fact, in the same issue of *Golden Alternatives* that contained the article about the man who traded six emus for a new set of Ping irons and made a small fortune. This other article said no matter how wise and mature a person might think that he or she is, you can't have enough mentors. So where in the hell does somebody at my age locate a mentor? Well, that used to be the sticky part. Mentors are like angels, the article said. They're all around us, but you needed a special intuition to pick one out. Until now. Thanks to an outfit known as *A Word from the Wise*, you can call a 1-900 number and rent your own mentor. The advisory panel listed a retired lieutenant general, a former head coach of the Houston Oilers, a former LA police chief, Miss Universe of 1977—persons of that ilk. But no golf pros. Still, the article made some good points, and I decided to attempt to contact the only worthwhile mentor I had ever known—Doyle Getzendeiner, my ex-stepfather. He had vanished from my life about a quarter of a century before, but memories of the faint aroma of his Brylcreme lingered yet.

Late in the afternoon, I approached greenskeeper Double-wide McBride, who was loading a barrel containing that day's serpent haul (three mocassins and some moss-coated creature with little mean teeth that he identified as a cesspool mermaid) into his green Chevy pickup, to solicit aid. Doublewide, never daunted by the concept of change, had made a career out of changing careers. His resume would read like the Yellow Pages. Once, he recounted that between tenures as city manager of Bleeding Gums, Missouri, and Deputy Commissioner of Lakota Sioux Lottery and Gaming in Discouraging Word, South Dakota, the big man had been self-employed as a tracer of lost persons. "I need to locate my mentor," I said, then provided the very few clues that might somehow lead to the whereabouts of Doyle. In my last conversation with Connie, she assured me that he was alive. "I can't prove it, but I just *know* it. I can sense that he's out there lurking somewhere." Connie had her quirks, but it was never wise to argue with her instincts.

Not two hours later, while I sat on the balcony of my condo in the Aspen Villa development, eating a container of Stouffer's Linguini Bolognaise and listening to the ill-tempered yak-yak-yak of the bird life that occupies the sinister foliage along the banks of the Caloosahatchee River, the phone rang. It was Doublewide. My off duty sleuth had already made a hit. A web site—www.easy_tradin_doyle.com. "That might be your guy. He's sellin' bumper stickers. 'Show Me An Okie And I'll Show You A Hard Luck Story Getting Ready To Happen.' Material like that," said Doublewide. "I ordered about fifty."

That's it! There could be no doubt that was, indeed, my

guy. From somewhere in the nearby swamp, this long-forgotten recollection of Doyle appeared on the condo balcony. Doyle's only debacle. We'd encountered Gene, my zoological father, outside the Safeway and he'd politely mentioned this knee-slapper that nature occasionally springs on rural folks. One of Gene's cows had hatched a two-headed calf. Gene hadn't thought much of it. In Gene's thinking, this was a minor note on the larger scale of nature's knee-slappers. "That's just farming," he said.

But you should have seen Doyle's eyes light up. He had to have that calf for his Dodge showroom, and Gene was all too happy to provide the thing. Doyle announced the display of the thing in a fire-engine-red headline of a big ad that ran every Saturday in the car section of the paper. Come and have your picture snapped with the eighth wonder of the world, and we'll knock another 6 percent off what's already the best deal in Kansas on a '58 Dodge Lancer. Doyle had a lot full of those Lancers because the '58 Chevy Impala was the rage of the industry.

A promising crowd was already assembling in the show-room when Gene delivered the calf out back in the paint and body shop. He had tied two ribbons around both its necks. What Gene hadn't told us was that the calf also had seven and a half legs and a couple of features that tended to confirm that either God isn't quite as all-knowing as He thinks he is or that He's got one hell of a twisted sense of humor. This collective gasp went up when Doyle dragged the creature into the showroom.

The crowd had been fairly slow to gather at the Dodge dealership on that overcast Saturday but it quickly dispersed when some hay shaker said, "Look, Sarah. That thing's got two assholes!"

Doyle just stood there and grinned and said, "Well, I guess that makes three of us." At closing time, he had just as many Dodge Lancers on the lot as there had been when the place opened that morning. "But the important thing is that I had half a plan and tried to work it," he'd said on the way home. I'll have to remind Doyle about that when I talk to him. That's what this Seniors tour thing is—a half a plan. Except that if that Enola Gay driver keeps on working, this is more than a half. I dialed the 1-800 that Doublewide gave from Doyle's web site.

"Welcome to the Trader's Village," said this recorded female voice on the phone. The person talking was obviously moonlighting from her day job, which was phone sex. I had never done any phone sex—that's for tennis pros, remember—but this was how they must sound. She had one of those lusty "you know how to whistle don't you? Just put your lips together and b-l-o-w" types of voice.

"For English, press one," she said. "For Latin and (exhaling tantalizingly) Greek, press two"

I pressed 1. "To order from the Trader's Village Road Rage Kit, press one," she said. "To order from the Hickory Nut Scented Soap gift catalogue, press two. To purchase a Mother's Day Mammy-gram for that special gal in your life (sigh), press three. Otherwise, press Oh."

I pressed otherwise. She spoke in a whisper, tawny and seductive. Doyle always knew what he was doing. "To leave a message (gasp), speak after the tone." After you haven't spoken to someone in nearly thirty years, what kind of message would she suggest? The breeze from the direction of the river smelled a little like Lysol. I'd never noticed that until then. It was time to leave.

"Doyle. It's me. Del. Don't pay the ransom. I've escaped."

I left him two numbers and after a week and a half, Doyle had not called back.

Doublewide McBride was endowed with one of those distinguished founding father type profiles like George Washington's or Barbra Streisand's that look great on coins. Now he had been given the opportunity that attracts the kind of attention that eventually can get people engraved. Thanks to me, he would soon audition for a career as a caddy on the Seniors tour. As a dress rehearsal for the Big Show, I had decided to enter the Florida Club Professionals' State Championship (AARP Division) up in Tallahassee. Don't laugh. Sure, you could dress most of them up like Santa Claus and they could collect year-round for the Salvation Army. But I'd played with some of those characters. You'd go around wondering, "Won't he ever stop farting?" Then, after eighteen holes, he'll have shot 66 and you'll owe him his next five mortage payments. Cold-blooded, too. Steal the butter off a blind man's cornbread. Like they say back in the oil patch—they wouldn't take the time to piss on you if your brains were on fire.

Outside my ersatz adobe, brown stucco condo, Doublewide was packing our stuff into my maroon Olds Cutlass. Wham! He kept slamming the trunk. He was pumped.

Upstairs in the condo, I decided to try to reach Easy Tradin' Doyle again and perhaps gather some last minute inspiration. Surprisingly, I got through. Yeah. It was Doyle, all right, although he'd picked up what sounded an awful lot like a New England accent and I rationalized that was why he didn't sound very glad to hear from me.

"Congratulations on that recorded telephone lady," I said, trying to warm him up. "She must be something."

"Oh. You mean Coco. She weighs in at about three-fifty." No elaboration. This Doyle I was talking to did not seem as loquacious as the old one. Furthermore, he did not seem impressed with the details of my career since being abandoned by the PGA tour.

"Yeah. Just the other day, some economist on CNN was saying how the backswings of people seventy and over was the biggest challenge facing America today," he said. Then came a sound that reminded me of gears grinding. The noise was coming somewhere from Doyle's insides.

Great salespeople don't have time to be cynical. Sarcasm would ruin your attitude and after that, you couldn't sell Senate pages at the YMCA. That's what Doyle had stressed. Maybe all of this Internet stuff must have gone to his head.

"Well, shit, Doyle. Teaching's the most honored profession there is."

Doyle made that awful coughing noise that sounded like the gears grinding on those used Dodges he'd loan me on weekends. Now he got to the point. "What you're doing doesn't matter. What you're not doing is all that counts."

"I don't get it."

"Then I'll outline it. I was sellin' lots around Slow Leak Lake up there in Oregon and I'd sit all my buyers around the TV on Sundays and watch you play. 'See that kid? That's my son-in-law and he's gonna win the U.S. Open someday soon.' Then you'd knock in another birdie and I'd close the sale."

"Not son-in-law, Doyle. Ex-stepson."

"Ex-stepson sounds too trashy. Anyway, you got some bad ink and then you took to the hills. You wimped out and quit. What an embarrassment. I had to leave the state." Then he made those strange sounds again. Hiss. Croak.

"Doyle, I'm not making excuses. But back in that day and

time, when a public figure got in trouble because of something involving a chick in a moving car—well, you just couldn't overcome it."

"Didn't seem to slow Ted Kennedy down much."

I'd forgotten that lesson. Never cross swords with Doyle. He would slice your gizzard out. Time to change the subject. "Sounds like you've got a little cough there," I said.

"What I've got is a tumor the size of a billiard ball in both lungs. I'm coughing up black gunk you could insulate your roof with. If I was a younger man, I'd can the stuff and sell it," he came back.

Athletes in their prime learn early to speak only in cliches and it was amazing how quickly those instincts can return. "Well, medical science has made all kinds of advances and . . ."

"That's crap. Medical science hasn't made any advances since they invented Pepto-Bismol. In fact, they're stuck in reverse."

If ever somebody had wanted to change the subject, it was me, talking to Doyle. "Look," I said. "The reason I'm calling is to tell you that I'm still going to win that U.S. Open for you. OK? It's the Seniors version. But Nicklaus is in it. And Gary Player. And all kinds of people you've heard of. And it's on national TV. Not network, granted, but ESPN. But I've got half a plan in place and I'm going to win that fucker."

"Does that half a plan include a means to finance the project?"

I hadn't anticipated that particular question. "Well, there's this rich old lady down here and—,"

"Do this." All of a sudden, Doyle sounded interested. "When you hit on her for the money, don't look her in the eye. Look her square in the nose. People can't tell the difference. And then, sit back, relax, and don't do anything but lie like Lyndon."

Click.

Outside, Doublewide was blowing the horn. Motivation. What a weird sensation for a person my age. Load 'em, boys. We're goin' to Tallahassee.

4

America's modern anesthetic, otherwise known as driving on the Interstate, had kicked in nicely. Only ninety minutes into the all-day run from Caloosahatchee Pines up to Tallahassee and my gums were already numb and there was no sensation whatsoever from the waist down. This would be, I hoped, the first of an endless series of road jaunts with my caddy and valued staff aide. Despite that macho, soldier of fortune exterior that he relentlessly presented to everyone he encountered, it was clear that Doublewide McBride, at the core, remained a little kid. I didn't realize how much of a kid until he started to play the alphabet game.

"I'm stuck on Q," he announced.

"Well, there's one, right there, on that New Jersey license plate."

"License plates don't count. Not the way I play the game, at least. Goddammit. Where are all those fuckin' Quaker State billboards when you need one?"

Yes. The man with the three hundred–page resume had finally found the career of his lifetime. I had convinced him of that. Rehearsing for my upcoming fund-raising mission with Mrs. Ridge, I looked Doublewide straight in that ten-gallon nose of his and promised, "There is no life like the life of the touring caddy. When you're walking along the fairway inside those yellow ski boat ropes, you're on center stage. Everybody else is on the outside looking in and they're looking at *you*."

OK. The omission of several raw facts did not constitute lying, or at least lying on the scale that I had planned for the presentation with Mrs. Ridge. But in this Seniors tour endeavor, now that it had taken on the aspect of redemption, both for Doyle and for me, had the proportions of a crusade and a man like Doublewide now ranked as an essential ingredient. He could be trusted, to a certain extent. Caddy memories from the previous tour experience were not pleasing memories. To avoid too much detail for the squeamish, here was what Caddy Doublewide brought to the table. He bathed. He gargled. He did not have algae growing in his hair, he did not incessantly carp about what a pain in the ass his probation officer happened to be and he was sober at sunrise. On the golf tour, these were qualities that you came to respect in a man.

What Doublewide had not yet been apprised of was certain drawbacks that he would encounter with his new profession. Such as compensation. Caddies customarily worked on commission (10 percent of the golfer's gross) and an expense account that, according to the budget that I would present to Mrs. Ridge, might have been extravagantly described as modest.

And unfortunately for the tour caddies, they were required to learn to live with some unwritten realities dealing with the fashion in which they were—uh—let's use the word "perceived"—in the minds of the individuals who staged these golf tournaments. Fortunately, I never had to define that part of the bargain to Doublewide. He would comprehend it at once as we drove into the parking lot at the Whistling Springs Resort (these modern developments are no longer known as country clubs) in Tallahassee. A large hospitality tent had been erected near the putting green, and outside the tent, a banner was hung. It read: WELCOME FLORIDA CLUB PROS, TOURNAMENT GUESTS, AND VISITORS FROM THE STATE CONVENTION OF THE AMALGAMATED BROTHERHOOD OF BAKERY AND CONFECTION WORKERS. NO CADDIES ALLOWED.

Doublewide took it like an adult should. "But," he wondered. "Where can I go to get a cold beer?"

"At the caddies' trailer."

"Where's that?"

"Find a map of the golf course. Then locate the point that's farthest from the first tee, but still on the course. That's where you'll find the caddies' trailer. And look at the bright side. The caddies have a union and this trailer business was their big bargaining coup. Until last year, they used to make 'em park the trailer somewhere outside the fence and across the highway."

"Where do I change clothes?"

"In the car."

Doublewide just shrugged and wandered off, looking for the trailer. He was being a damn good sport about this. That's why I'd wanted him to be a part of what he had already started calling Team Del. At times like this, it was always good to remember what we all learned in Little League, that the letter "I" does not appear in the word team.

Saturday morning. Seventy-one of the mutually afflicted had assembled for tee time at Whistling Springs Resort. Seventy-one of the haunted. Seventy-one of the eternally damned. Each contestant in the field of the Florida Professional AARP Golf Championship, sponsored by the Florida Panhandle distributors of Swanee Lite Beer, shared a link event that destroyed their lives. Somewhere in their collective pasts, the entire field went out and broke 70, an act that would supersede the first thrust of heroin into the crook of the arm when it came to self-induced manslaughter.

That maiden voyage into the sub-70s. Oh. That was so easy, so utterly orgasmic. Oh. God. Blinded by the high-beam headlights of sheer ecstasy. Let's try that again. Now these pathetic club-pro creatures, they shared an added curse. Sometime, somewhere, they won something. Medalist in the ACC tournament, maybe. A Mid-South amateur championship. Or maybe like me, an actual PGA tour event. The Cleveland Open. Picture on the front page of the sports section, perhaps even over the fold. Green jacket, here I come.

Golf has always been over-characterized as the steel wool mistress. What an understatement. To these club pros who got one or two sips from the cup, the legion of the almost-there, golf had been no mere domineering heart-breaker. No. Golf entered their souls as Her Imperial Highness, Crown Empress of Planet Bitch.

Those seventy-one hollowed-out shells of once-proud men, that legion of losers, huddled in the dawn chill of a pine-scented wilderness, and long beyond salvation, had experienced the identical nightmare, scripted by the cruel hands of that morbid temptress, impresario of exquisite tortures. Eighteenth hole. The little, downhill six-foot putt that would establish or shatter a life's dream. One stroke. Then they could feel her two invisible thumbs, pressed against the trachea. No chance to breathe. Then the putt. Nice and slow. Trickle. Trickle. Ready to drop, and suddenly kicked aside by the unseen spiked heel of Madam Golf. YOU GODDAM PAINTED SLUT!

In countless dreams, they see that putt fall into the hole. And awaken to another day where that putt rests pathetically on the rim of the cup, and another day of, "Good morning, Mrs. Jablonowski, let me spend a couple of hours with you on the practice tee, kissing that fat Altoona, Pennsylvania ass of yours while I keep one eye peeled for the constable who has come to inquire about a hot check (the constable called them leapers—what a riot) at the Wal-Mart."

My sentiment as I approached the 7:56 tee time for my threesome was, "Screw these guys. Starting today, I am severing the chain." This was to be accomplished, incidentally, without the aid of the ultimate golf course weapon, the Enola Gay. She was locked in a closet behind the pro shop back at Caloosahatchee Pines. No. I would unveil her at a more appropriate time. Besides, if I couldn't beat these guys "on the natch," then there was no point in even attempting the big tour.

My two playing partners, for this opening round of a 36-hole medal play tournament, were introduced as Red Hastings, originally from Thermal Underwear, Minnesota, and club pro at Pelican Jowl Country Club in Varicose Beach, Florida; and Boston Bragg, an African-American operating partner of a course over West Palm, an indication that he had beaten the system to a certain extent because he didn't have to suck up to too many club members back home.

Red Hastings was a six-foot-five mannequin of a man who quickly distanced himself from Boston Bragg and me. He walked along the first fairway singing to himself, softly. His song was Johnny Cash's "Folsom Prison Blues" . . . "I shot a man in Reno, just to watch him d-i-e," and then he went "yyaahhh!" just like the convicts on the soundtrack of that Johnny Cash record. Whatever punishment the Golf Mistress had inflicted upon Red Hastings, she had done it with precision.

Neither of my two playing partners showed any sign of recognition when we were introduced but on the third hole, Bragg broke the ice. "So. I understand she bit your johnson off," he said.

"Not me," I said.

"You're not the same dude that got busted in New Orleans?"

"I'm the same dude, but she didn't bite my johnson off. That part of it is urban legend."

"You sure?"

"Reasonably."

One hole later, Bragg was at it again.

"You got any kids?"

"Nope."

"Huh."

After nine holes Bragg and me were two under. Hastings, who'd switched over to some folk song about a guy who'd beaten the warden to death with "thirty-nine pounds of Blackjack County chain," was on schedule to shoot 88. Bragg was amazing. He had absolutely the sweetest left-handed swing I'd ever seen. Imagine a southpaw Gene Littler. Pure silk. Why, I finally had to ask him, hadn't he attempted the regular tour? Because, he said, he hadn't swung a golf club in his life until he was thirty-six.

"Before that," Bragg said, "I was playing baseball in the old Negro Leagues."

"Whoa," I said. "Then how come you're not a hundred years old?"

"I lot of people don't remember, but the Negro Leagues were revived in the late fifties and well into the sixties," Bragg said. "Eight teams in two divisions. Darien, Bryn

Mawr, Shaker Heights, and Grosse Pointe in the Eastern Division. Beverly Hills, La Jolla, Del Mar, and Salt Lake City in the West. Those people would show up in droves. None of them had ever seen a black person before.

"Eventually, the novelty wore off. Some guy wrote a column in the Grosse Pointe paper, the *Daily Coupe de Ville*. He said that black baseball players were like Picasso originals. Seen one, you've seen 'em all. I like to think we did our part. They talked about how TV killed boxing. But for ten years, the Negro Leagues killed polo."

Boston Bragg finished the opening round with a 69. And it was pleasing to see Del Bonnet's name at the top of the leader board with 67.

Sunday morning. The day began as inauspiciously as the one before had ended on such a promising note. The 5:50 A.M. wake-up call at the $36 a night Olde Plantation Inn where I shared accommodations with my administrative associate, arrived in the form of a malevolent domestic thunderstorm in the room next door. "BAM-BAM-BAM! Open up, Marj-EEE. Ah know yur in there!"

"Yew git the hail outta here, Coy, 'fore ah cawl thu 'churff!"

Coy, who drove something that made the entire world shake whenever he started the motor, did, in fact, ponder the wisdom of Margie's suggestion and proceeded with an orderly tactical retreat. But, while the furniture in the room jiggled with the sheer fury of his departure, something dreadful was about to take place inside my head. I had seen these before on various occasions. A one hundred thousand–megaton migraine attack, proceeded by a light show that could have been orchestrated by Admiral Yamamoto and choreographed by Robert Oppenheimer. It was impossible to describe the visual chaos and mayhem that signaled the onset of a migraine to the uninitiated. You could only close your eyes, wait for the sickening visual display to gradually abate after an hour or so, then await Act II, in which the sufferer experienced discomfort akin to a high-speed Amtrak derailment occurring at the base of one's skull.

Those dreaded events, in my case, happened at the rate of perhaps one every other year. But why now? First place in this Tallahassee tournament was the only real basis of my funding pitch to Mrs. Ridge, since I had not genuinely expected her to believe the part about the awesome potency potential of my magic golf club. At least, I had hoped that she wouldn't. Jesus. Nobody could be *that* dumb. I swallowed an entire bottle of Advil and prayed for a quick and merciful death.

Sometime during those grim morning hours, I heard the phone ring. By now, the lights in my head were dimming and the pain and nausea had started to kick in. Through the corner of one eye, I could see Doublewide place his palm over the receiver. "It's some asshole from the Associated Press," he rasped. "I'll handle this."

"Yes. Yes. That's the same Del Bonnet who used to play the PGA tour," I heard him say. "No. I am his media representative. Durwood McBride."

Durwood! I'd never heard that before. No wonder he went by Doublewide.

"Yes. This tournament is just a stepping stone. He's planning to go on the PGA Seniors tour full-time this year," he told the reporter. Shut up, Durwood!

"No. He can't come to the phone right now. He's having some kind of seizure. Don't call back." He hung up the phone.

I tried to sit up in bed. Wham! Thud! My salvation was that as tournament leader, I didn't have to tee off until 12:30. Oh well. Some Frenchman from the Buffalo Sabres played two and one half periods after he'd had his left leg chopped off and he'd finished the entire game except that near the end, he got a ten-minute misconduct for taking a cheap shot at the Islanders' goalie. So what was this little pissant headache?

Come on, Pro! For the last God-knew-how-many generations, my family tree was the strongest tree on the block. No cancer. No heart disease. No root rot. Only consistent episodes of paranoid schizophrenia, and on the golf course, that was never a bad thing. We packed our stuff into the trunk of the Olds, Doublewide, my full-phase aide, paid the $36 room tab and he headed back to Whistling Springs Resort, eager to encounter whatever enchantment the day might bring. Maybe Easy Tradin' Doyle Getzendeiner would foster a measure of appreciation for Team Del and this new attitude. Frankly, Doyle had griped the hell out of me with that little sermon of his. Maybe that was his intent. In any event, the notion of winning that Seniors Open came more clearly into focus.

At the golf course, the field of seventy-one had been pared to a field of thirty-five for the final round. Threesomes were reduced to twosomes for Sunday's play. I was paired with Mervin Carson, who was a shot behind me at 68. Mervin was a living legend among Florida club professionals. He'd been arrested for drunk driving seventeen times, including an occasion where he'd tried to order a Big Mac and fries off the highway patrolman who'd pulled him over. Among his colleagues, he was known as Swervin' Mervin. That was the wonderful thing about tournament golf, even at this level. There was a made-for-TV movie in every one of these guys.

On the first tee box, Mervin extended the hand of friendship and said, "Listen, Del. If I don't win this thing, then I hope that nobody does." Mervin needn't have said that. I felt the same way. It's the universal code of golf.

After the third hole, I was one under par and glad about the migraine. All I thought about was how badly my head hurt. They were digging a coal mine in there. Jackhammers. Pneumatic drilling devices. Every ten minutes, the miners would use dynamite. Come back from the dead, John L. Lewis. Call a strike. By the time the scabs arrived, the tournament would be over. But because of what could have been mockingly described as the discomfort, at least there was no chance to succumb to the jitters that will betray the soul of eight and a half out of ten golf tournament leaders. One could not say the same for poor Swervin' Mervin. It had taken him three full minutes to place his ball on the tee—worst case of the shakes I had ever seen. On the third hole, he had needed a three-footer to save par and practically jerked the fucker clean off the green. "Got the yips and jingles today," he explained. Then he took a good look at me and, horrified at the sight of what surely looked like two dark caverns that existed where my eyeballs used to be, hit his next tee shot about twenty feet.

Nobody in the field offered any kind of a challenge. I shot another 67 and won by eight shots. At a short ceremony, I was presented with the winner's check—$500, which was exactly $500 more than my combined tournament earnings for the previous twenty-eight years—and ten cases of Swanee Lite beer, the sight of which, given the bereaved postmigraine status of my brain and digestive organs, made me dizzy.

But not nearly so much as something I detected up there on the leader board. A name from the past, Bruno Pratt, had finished in fourth place. This was a name that evoked the same kind of response you feel when people say things like, "Look, Daddy. There's a rabid skunk in the kitchen."

Bruno Pratt Simmons was bad news. Bruno Pratt was one of those rare individuals who, when you pick up the morning paper and don't find a front page story about how Bruno had fallen off the top of the World Trade Center, then you throw the whole paper into the trash because you knew that there wasn't anything in there worth reading.

The long drive back to Caloosahatchee Pines, during which Doublewide drove and imposed a serious dent into the Swanee Lite supply, should have been a joyous occasion. A triumphant one.

Instead, all I could think about was the absolute reality that before I could win this Seniors Open for Easy Tradin' Doyle and grant myself, if not an unconditional pardon then at least a conditional parole, that somehow and some way, Bruno Pratt would be out there, lurking in the evil mist, sharpening his teeth with a rat-tail file and conjuring some evil mechanism to sabotage my plan.

$$5$$

Peculiar changes happen to people's bodies after they finally crash through the Age Fifty barrier. Chronic psychiatric problems—quicksand of the mind—begin to evaporate, ever so gradually, only to be replaced by orthopedic ones. Just the other morning, while massaging my gums with a 35-horsepower Water Pik and pondering the fact that I couldn't remember my last paranoia-driven panic attack, the power-squirter hit a tender spot behind a molar. When I flinched, something popped in my left knee, and the old pro was limping for the next forty-eight hours. And that morning, for instance, I went through what should have been a reasonably invigorating forty-five-minute workout. But my body rejected it. Exercise bike. Twenty-five minutes on the treadmill. Bench presses. Squats. Curls. I looked OK, perhaps 14 percent body fat, but I felt like I had all the flexibility of a frozen garden hose. Doublewide McBride expressed it best: "Everything that I have two of, one of them doesn't work anymore and the other one is sore all the time."

For the last week, I'd enjoyed ample free time to visit the gym. The Caloosahatchee golf course got sideswiped by Hurricane Evita, and most of the fairways rested beneath two and a half feet of water. The entire back nine smelled like a worn-out inner tube.

Tyler LaGrange, the stuffed owl who served as club president, continued to expand his role as a passive-aggressive nemesis factor in my little pro shop domain. Now Tyler, lifetime veteran of many committees, was bitching and moaning because the golf course wasn't draining as well as he'd like. I tried to explain, as patiently as possible, that I didn't design the course, and that my sphere of responsibility advanced no further than peddling Tom Watson visors and providing spiritual guidance for old ladies worried about a hitch in their backswing.

Naturally, Tyler wasn't satisfied. He muttered something about "necessary precautions." Basically, he impressed me as a discontented sort of fellow who couldn't figure out why. That could be due, in part, to the actuality that Tyler looked as physically impressive as a hard-boiled egg. And another aspect of his difficulty might have been directly attributed to a general discomfort derived from wearing these Izod shirts that he had heavily starched. That only served to enhance the impression that the man was made of gypsum wallboard.

"I know you're frustrated about the golf course, Tyler," I told him. "We all are. But there's an old saying—patience is a bitter plant, but it bears sweet fruit."

Tyler gave me this look that left no doubt that he simply regarded me as some kind of pothole that needed filling. He just stared at me for a moment, trying to fashion some snotty response. But Tyler couldn't think of one, and so he left without another word. Our relationship now stood about one or two degrees this side of full-scale hostile. But, as Eddie Fisher used to say, when the chef is in heat, stay out of the kitchen.

The truth happens to be that I'm lucky that a Tyler LaGrange has appeared at this point in my life story. Everybody needs a Tyler every now and then. He supplies the initiative to abandon a sort of comfortable stagnation and boldly advance into the uncharted depths of the Next Phase. I swallowed, whispered a "ten-nine-eight . . ." countdown and, feeling the same kind of adrenaline surge that happened that year when I choked in the U.S. Open, dialed the phone number of Dorothy Ridge. It was time to pitch my mission.

Instead of an answering machine, Mrs. Ridge herself picked up the phone. "Yes?" she said. Not "hello" but "yes?" Right away, I felt off balance.

"Uhh—Mrs. Ridge. This is Del Bonnet, at the club."

"Yes?"

I should have written a script. Suddenly, from some distant treetop, the voice of Easy Tradin' Doyle rang out. "Don't fuck around with this woman. Get to the point!"

"Mrs. Ridge, I was hoping that we could meet in person to discuss an investment opportunity."

What came next was the uplifting sound of laughter, full-throated, genuine, gay, and unrestrained. At least I'd had the satisfaction of realizing that I'd made the woman's day, if not her entire goddam year.

"Could you be at my house at seven tonight? Is that convenient?"

Mrs. Ridge, the colonel's wife, was full of surprises.

"What do you drink, Mr. Bonnet?"

"I drink wine."

"What *kind* of wine?"

"Lately, I've been buying wine from the Isaac Newton vineyard. What goes down must come up."

Again, that laugh. Old Doyle, probably, would have issued a C-minus for the presentation. What mattered was that I scored an appointment with a cold call. Now I had about five hours to somehow transform myself into a courteous, low-key sales professional who could convince a virtual stranger to hand over more money than I'd earned probably in the last five years, total. What was there to lose? When Mrs. Ridge throws out her marvelous laugh after I finish my proposal, it simply means that I'll probably be spending the remainder of my years managing the Kiddie-Putt and wearing a squirrel costume to work every day.

The priority now became one of focus. Approach this like the final round, when you're tied for the lead. Don't get distracted. Take it one shot at a time. On short notice, the first shot involved wardrobe decisions. Don't show up wearing some outfit that appears to have been lifted from the rack of your own golf shop. What luck. My Pierre Cardin claret blazer, the one I bought about eight years ago because it wouldn't show wine stains and quit wearing because I'd put on some weight, appears to fit again. Those workouts, excruciating as they were, might have been paying off after all.

Now. A hastily contrived sales strategy. Should I take along the secret video of me socking 320-yard tee shots with my new Wonder Driver, the Enola Gay? Probably not. I tried to remember the key points from Doyle's unpublished manuscript, *How to Bullshit Your Way to the Top*. One thing Doyle always advocated was ending every pitch with the line: "Is there any sound business reason why we shouldn't move forward with this?" According to the master, that little curve ball works effectively against people who are programmed to never say "yes."

Again—from afar—I could hear Doyle's mellow baritone. "Don't over-program yourself. Get a haircut and go wash your two-year-old Jeep Cherokee. Relax and be prepared to beg. When it comes to women, if you beg long enough and hard enough, they'll eventually come around. Women are very compassionate in that regard."

The entrance to the causeway leading to the Ridge estate on Sanibel Island, where the swellest of the swells on the Florida Gulf Coast mostly reside, remained cluttered with tree branches and other crap left over from the storm. Traffic was brutal. So I didn't reach her front porch until 7:15. No reason to panic, I said. Better to arrive fashionably late than fashionably drunk. The house itself, pink granite with a second-floor veranda and rust-colored Spanish tile roof, was set back a quarter-mile from the road and hidden behind a hodgepodge of tropical foliage.

Mrs. Ridge herself met me at the door and it was only then that I realized that I'd had her mixed up with some other woman at the club. Good God. If this woman was seventy years old, then I was Fats Domino. Back in Topeka, in high school, I'd had a teacher, old Miss Parker, who, from the neck up was Jessica Tandy in *Driving Miss Daisy* and from the neck down was Marilyn Monroe in *The Seven Year Itch*. Now Mrs. Ridge, from the neck down, stood out as a lankier and more angular version of Miss Parker all over again and—from the neck up—I saw a raven-haired and substantially less haunted version of Kim Novak in *Vertigo*. Slight horizontal creases adjacent to Mrs. Ridge's mouth and eyes suggested that her remarkable body presentation might have been a marvel of nature and not the product of the modern sciences of reconstruction. Because I am a golf pro and not a poet, a more detailed description will remain forever unavailable, except to say that this was one of the healthiest looking human specimens I had ever seen.

"Call me Dottie," she said, putting a mild stress on the second syllable. "Dot-TEE," is how she said it, but I thought it more prudent if I stuck with DOTtie for the moment. She sat me down in a den with a big window and beyond that was a swimming pool, and I assumed Dottie had made ample use of that. Various photographs of the colonel appeared throughout the den, but the picture that dominated the room was a photo of Dottie apparently masquerading as a fruit salad. Dottie brought out the wine and noticed me gaping at the photograph. I presumed that she was sizing up my every gesture and probably trying to guess where I had grown up from whatever she could glean from my speech patterns.

"That," she explained, "was from my tenure as Chiquita Banana. Actually, there were eight Chiquita Bananas working at the same time. We were hired to dance and perform at conventions and do some commercials in early TV. The work was more fascinating than you'd think. That's how I came to know Colonel Ridge. I was entertaining at a fundraiser for Ike and the colonel was there. After five years as a Rockette and three as Chiquita, he was the first man I'd dated who wasn't packing heat." Then she laughed that laugh.

The wine was stupendous. The label said Pommard, estate bottled, 1961. Two swallows and I could already feel a modest buzz. Now Dottie made it evident that it was my turn to contribute to the conversation, and I presumed that meant approaching the awkward topic of money. My preamble, at least, had been rehearsed. In three hundred words or fewer, I explained that $45 million in prize money was available on next year's PGA Seniors circuit, that I was absolutely capable of collecting one-forty-fifth of that amount, and possibly twice as much, and I would split the earnings if she would back me for one year.

Then I waited for Dottie to laugh. This time she didn't,

although it was obvious that she was deeply amused. "Well, thank God," she said finally. "I was afraid you had driven here to interest me in an emu farm."

Not certain whether she was serious, I requested another glass of wine and continued what was now an unmitigated hard sell, keyed around the miracle powers of the Enola Gay. "Last month, I entered and won my first tournament in over twenty years—using conventional weapons. That happened against modest competition. That Enola Gay club will provide the edge against the people out there gunning for their cut of that forty-five million. After thorough testing, I'm certain that I'm twelve to fifteen yards longer off the tee than the biggest hitters on the Seniors tour. The golf club has a titanium shaft. That's nothing new. But the club head contains a lead ball filled with mercury. (All right. I did not tell Dottie Ridge about the kryptonite club head because she would not have believed it and I didn't think that I did, either.) No average golfer and damn few pros can even marginally control the thing. By the time any tour player catches on to the Enola Gay, I will have already won five tournaments, minimum." Goddam, that wine tasted good. Dottie uncorked another bottle so it could breathe while we finished the first one.

"There have been some stories around here . . . ," and for the first time, she seemed to hesitate, "that some years ago, during a tournament, you were involved in some kind of, uh . . ."

I finished the sentence for Dottie. "Involved in what they referred to at Three Mile Island as an 'incident.' Thanks to the passage of time, there are all kinds of versions of what happened. But the truth does happen to be that I was arrested, live, on national TV."

Here came the big laugh again. "Next to Jack Ruby, you're

the only person I've met who ever experienced that sensation," Dottie said.

"You *knew* Jack Ruby?"

"When you're Chiquita Banana, you meet all kinds of people."

Now Dottie popped the question. "Del, when you ask me to 'back' you, how much are we discussing?"

"Only two hundred thousand dollars. That would include partial funding for Mr. McBride, the groundskeeper at the club. He'll travel with me as a caddy and kind of valet," I said without blinking. Doyle would have applauded the "only." Then I quickly explained how the most speculative aspect of the venture involved the process of actually being allowed on the tour. First I would have to pass through qualifying at the infamous Q School where about three hundred guys are competing for a dozen slots. "If I have an off-week there, it's over, of course, before I even start."

Dottie stood up and poured from the next bottle. She was wearing these stretch pants like you see on the young housewives at the mall, except that Dottie's were made out of some kind of satiny fabric. The wine made a cheerful, high-pitched giggling sound as it hit the glass. I was about to launch into the part about how endorsement contracts by the basketful would arrive after I won a couple of events, but Dottie never let me begin.

"If you survive that Q School, then consider yourself 'backed.' By the way. Have you read *The Bridges of Madison County*?"

"No. That's the only Clint Eastwood book I've never read. Why?"

"Oh, just wondering."

Now buoyed by that feeling of half-crocked nirvana that sometimes appears after four quick glasses of top-shelf joy juice on an empty stomach, and euphoric over having just been bestowed with the financial miracle of the modern age, I wondered what to say next. Suddenly, the words came easily.

"Dottie, how in the hell do you manage to maintain your looks? I've seen those Miami Dolphins cheerleaders up close and, compared to you, those girls look like slum clearance."

My benefactor looked surprised, as if nobody had ever asked her that. Perhaps nobody had.

"A variety of ways, I suppose. There's no set formula. If you want to look good at seventy—which is what I will be the end of this year—you need to start working toward that when you're eighteen. In my case, I had a good start. I made up my mind early on to avoid network television altogether and also to expose myself to the American Medical Association, the American Bar Association, and the music of Neil Diamond as little as possible."

"It's that simple? Jesus, I wish somebody would have told me."

"There's a little more to it than that. I stimulated myself by taking risks. I used to take risks with relationships, but I can't begin to explain how tiresome that became. So then I started taking some financial gambles and discovered a high satisfaction quotient. And, by the way, this investment in the Seniors golf tour is by far the biggest longshot I've bet on."

"What made you decide to do it?"

"Because you're making an active attempt to reinvent yourself at a point in life when most people refuse to try."

Here, I thought it prudent not to explain that this grand reinvention adventure was the product of necessity, not choice. "You probably don't find all of that wisdom among the beauty tips in *Cosmopolitan*," I said.

"No. What they advocate is rubbing Preparation H beneath your eyes every night because it tightens up the little baggy areas, and I've discovered that it works. But what works best for me is yoga." Dottie leaned forward and touched her left ankle with her right elbow. Then Dottie inhaled, exhaled, and touched the back of her head with her left heel.

"Something else I'd recommend is to throw away the bathroom scales," she said. "There's only one way to monitor yourself, and that's to take off all of your clothes, stand in front of a full-length mirror, and bounce up and down. The mirror cannot lie. It's the ultimate motivating device."

As if this evening had not taken on enough unpredictable aspects already, Dottie then took me by the hand and walked back into a master bedroom the size of half a city block, a room that featured, yes, a floor-to-ceiling, eight-foot-by-ten-foot mirror. Then we bounced, taking turns at first and then together. Perhaps it was the quality of Dottie's wine, but whatever the reason, the mirror exhibition seemed an entirely natural manner in which to get better acquainted.

The mirror test had clearly served Dottie well. Her perfectly contoured ass actually seemed to grin at me and say, "Hey, Pops. Ain't you glad you drove out here instead of watching *Monday Night Football*?" In a sudden and spontaneous reaction, a particular portion of my body jumped up and stood at attention at a jaunty 45-degree angle. "What do you call that thing?" Dottie demanded.

"What thing?"

"You know what thing. All you guys have a pet name for it."

"Well, I don't. But I used to be married to somebody who called it Big Luther."

"That's absolutely inspired. You've probably missed putts that weren't that long. And that's what we'll call that magic golf club of yours from now on, too. Big Luther is a turn on. Enola Gay definitely is not."

As previously mentioned, I'm a golf pro and not a poet. I am also not a romance novelist—"Renaldo's trembling hands explored the tantalizing moisture of Millicent's loins, and then he thrust the proud avenger home"—therefore I cannot adequately articulate what took place for the next few hours. But thanks to Dottie's yoga techniques, Big Luther scored his first double hat trick since 1968.

Then Dottie bade me *adieu*. "I think," she said, "that for the time being, we ought to limit our association to a financial and physical basis. Perhaps later, a friendship can develop."

On the drive back across the causeway, I groped through the console of the Jeep. Finally, I located my Neil Diamond cassette and tossed it out the window.

6

A stylishly anorexic teenage ingenue stood in the parking lot of the Ramada Inn smoking a Marlboro and watching some of the Q School hopefuls check in. The girl had about sixteen rings stapled into her ears, four more plugged into both nostrils, and no telling how many others pierced into God knows where else. From a short distance she looked like a bucketful of paper clips.

"Who," this metallic mistress asked me, "*are* you guys?" I was wondering the same thing myself.

"Mid-Florida regional convention," I told her.

"Regional convention of what?" she said.

"Alcoholics Anonymous."

"You're full of crap. I've done that Betty Ford routine, and these guys ain't alkies. They've all got suntans." Doublewide McBride, whose obligations now seemingly also entailed the role of the golfer's bodyguard, interceded on my behalf. "Take a hike, you low-budget whore," he said.

"Cram it, dickhead," America's future replied.

Thus began the week that would determine whether I spent my remaining years functioning as a swan or just another duck. Already, my agenda had become surprisingly hectic. A producer from *60 Minutes* called that morning and said that Ed Bradley wanted to interview me. He was actually doing a segment on the novelty of the Q School, and I was selected as an example of a guy who had cratered on the regular PGA tour and now, years later, was attempting to resurrect my golf career.

"Actually, Ed is in that part of the world anyway," the producer said. "He's working on a story about some woman who claims she's Amelia Earhart."

"No shit?"

"Yeah. She's about a hundred years old and says she planned the whole disappearance thing in advance. Landed on some island and escaped in a private submarine. Said she was just tired of the rat race."

"That'll be a tough act to follow."

"I'm sure you'll do your best," the producer said.

Doublewide had a seizure when I told him about the program. "No way. No way in hell I'm going to allow that interview," he shrieked. "You can't afford any distractions this week, and haven't you ever watched that program? They'll make you look like a fool. Particular that Ed Bradley guy. He'll hit you with the old bait-and-switch routine every time . . . start the interview with the Mr. Nice Guy routine and then slap on some hidden video where they show you fondling a child."

After about ten minutes worth of intense discussion, Doublewide was partially mollified by the argument that I had absolutely nothing to lose by talking to Ed Bradley. "Well, at least insist that they blur your face and use a fake voice. After you finish the interview, you'll *think* it went OK, but after they cut and edit and rearrange the thing, they'll fuck you like a tied-up goat."

Ever since securing my successful partnership with Dottie Ridge, Doublewide had become pathologically driven to grasp control of the entire Team Del concept. Doublewide insisted that he and he alone would act as my agent to gather endorsement possibilities. We pointed out that people with some kind of track record were conventionally retained for that chore.

"Track record? I had some agents in my army unit in Vietnam. I know what they're like. Oily buncha scam artists, every one of 'em. Steal the butter off a blind man's cornbread. Remember what happened to that Tampa Bucs halfback, Gonorrhea 'Look At That Sonuvabitch Run' Buchanan? Had the world by the balls. And then he got *two* agents, each one of 'em carving fifteen percent off the top, and they picked him dry. Then the IRS got on his ass, and now the poor bastard's living in a forty-dollar-a-month storage bin over in Bradenton!"

Dottie Ridge seemed to appreciate Doublewide's protective nature but suggested that I get him on some kind of pills.

We filmed the *60 Minutes* interview on the first tee at Tarpon Valley where this six-day, 108-hole Q School ordeal was to begin the next day. Exactly three hundred candidates for the Seniors tour would be shooting for seventeen available slots. Actually, that was sixteen because I was an absolute cinch to get in. Of that three hundred, almost a third were delusional nonprofessionals who had been seduced by the mirage of grandeur that they associated with a road show. Tarpon Valley is only about fifteen miles up the Gulf highway from Caloosahatchee Pines. I didn't bother with any test runs at Tarpon Valley. All of these Florida courses played the same.

Ed Bradley seemed almost sympathetic. He didn't even bring up the New Orleans episode. Bradley seemed intrigued by this Don Quixote pilgrimage of half-baked Arnies, half of whom I suspected had been deported from their households by their spouses because they'd reached that point in life when they farted through their ears. I didn't say that to Ed Bradley.

"Quite an amazing assembly of entries here," Bradley read off a cue card set up behind the camera. "To name a few . . . there's a rabbi from Camden, New Jersey; a former Branch Davidian from Waco; and Dr. Ambrose Crain, the distinguished surgeon who recently performed the world's first successful prostate transplant—why would people like this trade their previous existence for a life on the golf tour?"

"In the case of the guy from Waco, I think I can understand," I said.

"Well, other than him."

"In my case, the Seniors tour offers me the unique opportunity to take care of some unfinished business involving what a couple of sportswriters described as unfulfilled potential," I said, telling Bradley the truth. In fact, that's the first time I'd even admitted that to myself. *60 Minutes* really brings out the candor in people. "As for all of these other fellas, they have one thing in common. They all want to sleep with Shirley McLaine. Well, two things, actually. They like challenges. After they bomb here, they'll go and try to climb Mount Everest, freeze their feet off and write a book. At least, they'll have something to tell their grandkids. And the nice thing is that they won't have to wait twenty years to tell 'em, because they've already *got* grandkids."

"And what about you, Del? What happens if you *don't* qualify for the tour?" said Bradley, suddenly looking grim. All of these *60 Minute* features arrive at a crisis point.

"In my case, the 'if' factor has been eliminated from the equation. There is absolutely *no way* that I won't qualify."

All of that was said for effect. The bigger the horse's ass, the better the chance of appearing in a Coors Lite commercial. But after round one, I wished I'd kept my mouth shut. No matter how thoroughly prepared you think you are, the element of the unknown lurks behind every puddle and every palm tree. At 7:10 A.M. on the first tee, I learned that my threesome included a certain Carlos O'Bannon from Santa Fe. He was dressed up like the Cisco Kid, complete with ostrich-skin cowboy boots with golf spikes on the bottoms. I liked Carlos at first—until he lit his cigar. The stench was overpowering. Odious and toxic chemical substances less foul than that cigar have been banned by the Geneva Convention.

And damned if Carlos didn't position himself directly downwind from wherever I was standing so that the Christ-almighty-awful smoke was constantly blowing straight into my face. Conditions and situations like this constitute the ones that the professional, if he is indeed that, will ignore and overcome. Mind over matter. If you don't mind, it doesn't matter.

The real pro can overcome anything. Hangovers. Sandstorms. Smallpox. Locusts. But a cigar that spews nerve gas and causes disorientation, nausea, hallucinations, and an overpowering urge to defecate? By the fourth hole, a strangling queasiness took hold of my equilibrium, much worse even than the time I blew my beets on the roller coaster at Atlantic City. On the fifth hole, my driver, now officially ordained as Big Luther, belted a shot 340 yards in a disastrous arc that came to earth in a bunker that guarded the 14th green. Triple bogey and I was riding a fast freight to skid row.

There would be no salvation, no pathway to recovery, and almost four tortuous hours later my doomsday round of 79 was complete. That number looked even more pathetic when it was posted on the big scoreboard. After the first round, I was six shots behind the Branch Davidian, eight shots behind the Rabbi and worst of all, exactly ten shots behind that prick Chunkie Simmons who was the only person I was afraid I might not beat before this thing got started.

Doublewide McBride became philosophical on the ride back to the motel. "I guess," he opined, "that when Dottie Ridge reads that score in the paper, she'll assume you were out all night with Honey Bee."

"Who's Honey Bee?"

"She's my domination goddess. Want her 1-900 number?"

"Let's wait until Sunday. As for what Dottie Ridge will assume . . . I guess she'll assume that she just saved herself two hundred grand," I said.

By the dawn's early light, I found myself positioned 266th in the pack of 300 entries. Good old Doublewide. In the van heading back to the course for Round Two, he played tapes of the theme song from *Rocky* and *Chariots of Fire*. That only served to compound my misery.

Round Two was better, as it would have had to be since the polluting presence of Carlos O'Bannon was placed in a new threesome. Big Luther, if not out of control, was often erratic. I missed five fairways and wound up with a 71.

Back at the Ramada Inn, Doublewide dragged me into the lounge. "Have a couple of pops. Unwind. Couldn't hurt at this point." He was probably right. My tee time for the third round was past noon. Those couple of pops had graduated into an even dozen by the time the entertainment came out, a Joan Baez clone named Coco something or other. She led off with "The Night They Drove Ol' Dixie Down."

"An' all the people were singin' . . . and they went 'ya na na na na na na . . . ya na na na . . . ya na na na na . . .' "

I turned to Doublewide. "You know, if all they did was

sit around and go 'ya na na na na na na . . . ya na na na . . . ya na na na na . . .' then no wonder they lost the goddam war."

Doublewide's eyes narrowed into a couple of mean little slits and then he said, "You've just hit on the whole problem. For the last two days, you've been tip-toeing around that golf course with your finger up your ass, going, 'ya na na na na na.' It's like you're afraid to win." Even though that diatribe was largely induced by the theology of Reverend Tanqueray, Doublewide was right.

That next afternoon, I stormed the golf course like the Fighting Irish taking the field after Knute Rockne made his speech about the Gipper. Naturally, I should have known better. All of that fire-in-the-belly rah-rah becomes counterproductive in a hurry when you're standing over a downhill six-foot putt. The ball trickled to the hole and then, in what appeared to be super slow motion, curled around the entire circumference of the cup and then came to a rest on the edge. The dimples on that miserable little golf ball actually appeared to mouth the words, "Screw you, Mr. Has Been." This is why the majority of the world's greatest golfers spend their golden years in the madhouse, wearing diapers and making ugly faces out of modeling clay.

After four holes, I remained at even par and needed a fifteen-footer for a birdie on the fifth, a par three with one of those greens that is set in the center of a big pond, a standard feature in modern golf course architecture. The task at hand appeared clearly defined. If that thing didn't drop in for a birdie, it'd be time to piss on the fire, call in the dogs and head for the house because Team Del would have established zero momentum, and the leaders of the event would be so far ahead that their taillights would have disappeared over the horizon.

The green seemed absolutely flat. But just before it was time to stroke the thing, Doublewide, who probably knows more about the life of Parson Weems than he does about the game of golf, muttered something strange.

"This putt," he whispered, "is going to break toward Disney World."

"Say what?"

Doublewide made a gesture; east northeast. "After the flood at Caloosahatchee, when the course finally started to drain, I noticed that all the water poured off toward Disney World," said Doublewide, again pointing off in the general direction of Orlando. "I suspect that this course is just like that one and the putts should roll that way, too." Doublewide was explaining all of this sotto voce, so that the other two players in the threesome, twin brothers from Great Falls, wouldn't overhear this highly classified data.

Well, why not? Remember the immortal teachings of Janis Joplin: Freedom's just another word for nothing left to lose. Whatever the fuck that's supposed to mean. With my readjusted line, the ball rolled up toward Tampa, took a quick right turn in the direction of the Magic Kingdom at the very last instant, and this time, the defiant little bastard plunked in.

The putts continued to plunk every other hole and when another one went "plunk" on 18, my shot total rested at 66, which, in turn, meant that I had leap-frogged over about 120 of these turkeys. With three rounds still left to play, the outlook had become entirely less hopeless. Even more gratifying than my 66 was the flat 80 that stood posted on the scoreboard next to the name of Bruno Pratt, who happened to be paired with Carlos O'Bannon of Santa Fe on this bright Thursday.

Since the 66 stood up as the best round of the day, they dragged me into the press tent. The dramatic turnaround, I said, was largely due to the encouragement of Janis Joplin, Joan Baez, and the Daughters of the Confederacy.

Doublewide was revved. Back at the Ramada, he was changing into his white shoes, meaning that he would shortly be embarking on an expedition in search of whatever enchantment the night might bring. The white shoes also meant that he would be of absolutely no use for the remainder of the week. I stayed in the room at the Ramada Inn, reading *The Bridges of Madison County*, richly confident that the conclusion of the story would include a satisfying scene where this photographer guy gets his nuts shot off by a liquored-up farmer.

The anxiety of Q School disappeared for good during the fourth round. All of the rest would be anti-climactic. Disney World continued to draw those 15-footers home to birdland and, with Big Luther finally starting to hold up his end of the bargain, Team Del shot a 63. Doublewide McBride moved rather gingerly around the golf course. He said he'd befriended some hot shot basketball announcer the night before—couldn't remember his name—and they'd wound up in some twenty four-hour whoopie parlor that actually honored Doublewide's Texaco card. They had a whale of a time.

Had it not been for that hideous and now forgotten opening round of 79 and also for the fact that three of my putts on Sunday missed Orlando entirely and got mysteriously hijacked to Havana, I would have broken the record for the lowest score in the history of the Seniors Q School.

Also, there was encouraging initial contact from some guy claiming to represent Grecian Formula shampoo. "That's not the one where the guy in the commercial washes just one side of his head, is it?" I said. "That's where I draw the line."

"Oh, fuck no!" the shampoo rep said. "That's Denorex. We're the ones who get the gray out."

The only downside to the completion of the qualifying tournament was that Bruno Pratt, the sleaze, staged a nice comeback and wound up with one of the remaining "coveted" exemptions for the upcoming tour. That and the disappointing outcome of *The Bridges of Madison County*. I would have written that one differently.

Over in the press tent, Team Del glistened in the spotlight, uttering all of the correct platitudes. I thanked Doublewide. I thanked Dottie Ridge. I thanked all my friends and supporters back at Caloosahatchee Pines and stopped just short of saying, "Thank God for Big Luther."

The golf writers, and it's amazing how many of them are females these days—females with hair the color of Jell-O vanilla pudding—started firing a bunch of questions about my personal life. Here, I followed some long-ago advice from Easy Tradin' Doyle about how to deal with the media. Just pretend like you're under oath in a court of law, and then tell every possible lie that passes through your head.

Finally, one of the women said, "Now that you've conquered the Q School, what are you doing to do next?"

I thought for a second and said, "I'm going to Disney World!"

7

The immediate consequence of being voted Most Valuable Player in the Super Bowl involved a likeness of the Chosen One appearing upon a Wheaties box. Players on teams that won the World Series got invited to meet the president in the Rose Garden. Some little Camp Fire girl won a gold medal at the Olympics with some hip-hop bounce on the balance beam and they slapped her picture on the cover of the Gideon Bible. Prevail in the ballroom dancing competition at the State Fair of Missouri and you landed on David Letterman. Register the best score at the PGA Seniors Q School and your name appeared in a wire service account of that historic occasion. Approximately half of the newspapers in the continental United States—well, perhaps a third—published the wire service account in stories that ran as long as two sentences at the bottom of page eighteen in the sports section.

Yet . . . from that modest notoriety, I received mail, phone calls, faxes, and E-mail from individuals—total strangers, each and every one, throughout every corner of the country offering congratulations on this monumental accomplishment. These folks represented investment and estate planners, tax consultation agencies, and managed health plans. Others introduced themselves as sports motivation therapists, weight-loss counselors, and advocates of tobacco industry executives seeking financial support in their hour of crisis. I even got a letter from Ed McMahon, claiming he could make me rich if I'd simply subscribe to *Better Homes and Gardens*.

Someone named Claude Millsap called from Chicago to discuss the soybean market, which, he said, would sky-rocket because that year's crop had turned to shit—"Ugandan root rot"—and that people like me could cash in because the impending worldwide MSG shortage was threatening to kill billions.

"Everybody loves a winner," philosophized Doublewide McBride. "Imagine what would happen if you got your name in the paper because you went to the hospital to get a hernia fixed, and they sawed off both your legs by mistake. Man, you'd have the world at your doorstep."

Once I had time to absorb the reality that my secure and predictable, albeit quaint, sort of nonexistence as the golf pro at Caloosahatchee Pines would shortly incur an up-heaval, a feeling of bewilderment had set in, and it was un-comfortable. Change, like prescription pain relievers, should be patronized in moderation. The notion of joining this en-tourage of 4-iron mercenaries and sand wedge vagabonds meant severing all ties with familiarity. Cloistered down there on the Gulf Coast, with its year-round climate-controlled environment and its serenely mature populous that moved through each day in tune with the peaceful rhythms of their pacemakers, blissfully sheltered from the Promise Keepers, we got a *Father Knows Best*, strangely turmoil-free, almost staged version of Americana where a person could drive his wheelchair along what passed for life in the fast lane. You saw all these new, baby blue '98 Cad-illacs, freshly adorned with Reagan-Bush bumper stickers. People with consistent values. There was a certain charm to that, and I wondered now if I really wanted to abandon it. My malaise hung on like a fungus for about a week.

These concerns were articulated in mild and passing fashion, via telephone, to Dottie Ridge. "Quit acting like such a pussy," was her rapid response. Most women don't use that word. Not around me, at least. Dottie was out in Las Vegas, getting elected to the board of directors of Alliance Gaming. From there, Dottie was to fly to North Carolina, where she owns half of a two-car racing team, Crescent Wrench Inc., on the NASCAR Winston Cup circuit. She promised to bring me back a Valvoline windbreaker.

Dottie's intrigue with the NASCAR industry happened to be based around what she called "the eternal river of sponsorship dollars." Her two drivers, Blowtorch Barnes and a rookie, Tommie Napolean "TNT" Trumaine, ranked as big potatoes. Compared to them, a Seniors golfer became a brussels sprout.

Placed aside from Dottie's priority ventures, her sponsorship of my efforts on the golf tour simply acted as a hobby, and she was about as financially preoccupied with my deal as John D. Rockefeller was concerned over the value of his collection of antique chess sets. And that alleviated most of the pressure. If I missed the cut at the Sominex Classic, Team Del wouldn't hear a cheep out of Dottie Ridge because she would be standing in the pit at the Firecracker 400, watching Blowtorch and TNT run laps at 220 mph.

Dottie's succinct admonition to quit wheedling and start behaving like a full-fledged adult born to swing Big Luther restored my enthusiasm for the coming adventure. Meanwhile, Tyler LaGrange, president of Caloosahatchee Pines, grew more dictatorial with each passing half hour. Now he functioned as chairman of a one-person search committee to locate my replacement. Plenty of worthy candidates remained at large. Yet I was reluctant to recommend any, despairing at the prospect of positioning an acquaintance beneath Tyler's diabolic thumb.

Tyler failed to understand that Doublewide the groundskeeper and master of mulch loomed as the person more difficult to replace. With Doublewide joining me at the Seniors mardi gras, the elysian acreage of Caloosahatchee Pines stood destined to assume the landscape identity of a gravel pit. With his habit of pacing around with hands folded behind his back and wearing an ever-present anguished and bug-eyed look that suggested he was about to pass a kidney stone, Tyler seemed all too Stalin-esque. Plus, the constipated little scum bucket vetoed club funding for a gala "Farewell Del" going away party. So, while Tyler preened and huffed and glanced at his wristwatch three times a minute, the prospect of life in the motel and on the highway suddenly had regained its appeal.

"The only aspect of this Seniors tour that seems so peculiar is that everybody expects that this is a ticket to riches and I can't envision that." I made that remark to Jarrell Saledo, a typical member of Caloosahatchee Pines—typical in the aspect that his only genuine cross to bear in life was a chronic slice that kept his score everlastingly locked in triple figures. Now Jarrell and I were going through the motions of the final installment of what must have been four dozen tutorial sessions designed at ridding him of that slice. In all my years as a teaching pro, Jarrell and his slice stood as my single and one outstanding failure. We'd tried everything. Grip. Stance. Different golf clubs. That poor sap in *The Sun Also Rises* will get a hard-on before Jarrell hits a drive that lands in the fairway.

"What's your problem with a ticket to riches?" wondered Jarrell, a wiry little character who maintained the sort of benignly misplaced predatory look of the coyote in the road-runner cartoons. I suspected that the source of that slice might have been too much caffeine.

"There's no hang-up about getting rich," I said. "But common sense and self-awareness tell me that it can't happen. Not at this stage of my life. I read this article about people who were dead broke, eating their own crap for breakfast, until they passed forty. Then they got an idea, or maybe they just got off their ass. Anyway, they cashed in after forty. Colonel Sanders is the only person on that list who I can remember.

"But my point here is that I've never seen anything written about people who scored big after fifty. By then, most people find a way to become content with whatever it is they have. At least, that's the way it seems in my case." I was trying to get Jarrell to aim about thirty yards left of where he really wanted to hit the ball. The pro suggested that only as a final resort.

"Aw, shit. I'm the same way," Jarrell said. "Twenty years ago, I was consumed by the money thing. But now, I'm happy with my simple pleasures. I got my little house and my dog and my fishing pole."

That was right. Also, Jarrell had his 80-foot sailboat and his horse that won the Preakness and his private game preserve in Costa Rica that was stocked with exotic bird life and Swedish prostitutes, and now he was telling me all about how he envied my independence. Jarrell demanded that I swear and sign a blood oath not to sacrifice that and, as he put it, "Fall prey to the wealthy widow syndrome, like old Pete."

"I don't believe I know old Pete," I said.

"No. And you never will, either, because he changed his name to old Jesse and moved to Saskatchewan," Jarrell said. "And he didn't marry her, he just moved in. But Pete learned the hard way that behind every wealthy widow there are some mean-ass stepkids. Always putting brown recluse spiders in his sock drawer and strychnine in his Cream o' Wheat. They never could kak him, but they came goddam close."

Jarrell sighed. "Good old Pete. He'll be cussing those Kennedy kids until the day he finally croaks." Here, Jarrell paid seventy dollars for a one hour golf lesson, and yet he imparted all of the wisdom. Once again, the teacher became the pupil.

Officially, only three days remained on my contract at Caloosahatchee Pines; three weeks before the first tournament on the Seniors tour out at Palm Springs. An infinity of departure loomed large and ugly on my "things to do today" list. For instance, the battle perimeters were forming for a blue ribbon pissing match with Jerry Collucio, design architect for the golf club formerly known as the Enola Gay. Now a hot dispute festered over our registering the trade name "Big Luther." Mrs. Ridge, who eschewed the services of lawyers, mandated that I and/or Doublewide extinguish the range fire. But DW, now officially anointed as administrative director of Team Del, tended to become passionately absorbed with nonessential matters while more pressing priorities remained unattended.

The selection of the vehicle that would transport us from tournament to tournament had become a fixation. Doublewide perused consumer reports that dated back twenty years before he selected a Swedish-built RV, something called the Challenger, based on the results of some off-road endurance race on the Baja peninsula. "Doublewide, there ain't no golf tournaments *on* the Baja peninsula," I said. "And look what happened to the Challenger in that race. Caught on fire twice and then fell apart in ten thousand pieces."

Doublewide gave me a cold look, the left eye impatient,

the right one condescending. "Did you read what the driver said? Did you read his dying words? 'Substantial leg room.' That says it all. I think we need to come to an understanding here. You concentrate on trying to make birdies and leave the engineering to me."

So once the transportation issue achieved denouement, Doublewide now obsessed on strategic arrangements of the Farewell Del social occasion. Finally he announced the event would happen on the night after Christmas at Billy Crossdresser's house in Immokalee. "Ah, Jesus," I said. "If we're gonna do anything like that at all, why not do something kinda upscale, at Longboat Key or someplace? Before you know it, we're going to be living coast-to-coast in the El Cheapo Inns, and I want to have some memories of what civilization used to look like."

DW, now offended, said, "You sink a few putts at that lousy Q School, and all of a sudden you're prancing around like Joey Steinfeld." Dottie Ridge, who agreed to act as my date, could not conceal her glee. Here, finally, came the right occasion for her to wear a leather jacket bearing the blue Loew's Home Improvement Warehouse logo. Loew's had just signed on as a secondary sponsor of one of her race cars.

We drove to Immokalee (with me at the wheel) in Dottie's new Pontiac that was equipped with a carburetor the size of Connecticut. Dottie, I suspected, was fast becoming more attracted to horsepower than Big Luther. It's difficult to imagine that a person of such ordinarily sophisticated enthusiasms would go out and boink some stock car jockey. But then, how did one explain Julia Roberts and Lyle Lovett? Was I jealous? Probably, but who wouldn't be? Dottie could have walked into any nightclub in Monte Carlo, introduced herself as Gina Lollobrigida, and drunk free champagne until sunrise.

Our half-hour excursion over to Immokalee could have

been a romantic occasion. Unfortunately, the methane swamp gas indigenous to the area obscured the stars and blotted away the moonlight. Finally, we hit the heart of downtown and found a big banner draped across what used to be Main Street but was now known as Che Guevara Boulevard. The banner read: GOOD LUCK, DOUBLEWIDE . . . WE'LL MISS YOU!

We followed DW's hand-drawn map out to the home of the host. The inner city of Immokalee seemed like one of those countless off-the-beaten-path American hamlets; created by God for the sole purpose of becoming immediately forsaken. But Crossdresser's place lay three miles beyond the town. Good-bye, Immokalee. Hello, we were not sure what.

Bright lights, abundant glass, and many acute angles, the house appeared to be designed from the same I. M. Pei blueprints as some yuppie Unitarian church in Marin County. Crossdresser himself greeted us in the foyer. He wore a gray suit, probably cashmere and specifically tailored to make people like me feel like the product of inbred sharecropper stock for even wondering how much it cost. The man himself appeared to be on sabbatical from his regular duties as captain of the U.S. entry in the Americas Cup competition. Dottie Ridge, sadly, seemed to admire the cut of his jib. Crossdresser's physique brought to mind some of those off-duty trapeze artists who spent their winters in Sarasota, although he was about two feet taller.

All I could do was shake my head and say, "You're not at all the person that Doublewide had described."

"So who did you expect? Jay Silverheels?" responded the host. "Too-shay," I countered. Within thirty seconds, he confided in Dottie that he happened to be a recent product of the Wharton MBA program. Prior to that, I naturally calculated that Billy had done undergraduate work at Princeton, majoring in self assurance. He apologized for the absence of Mrs. Crossdresser, explaining that Ashley had flown out to spend the weekend with her parents back in Grosse Pointe. Crossdresser came across initially as somebody way too cocky for the holiday season, but the quality of his sherry soon provided a warmer impression. "We're all brainwashed by what passes for American history," he explained. "Take that parable of how some jugbutt Dutchman conned the primitive red man out of Manhattan Island," he was saying. "What you never hear about is how the Indians immediately loaned the twenty-four dollars back at eighteen percent, compounded semiannually.

"After one hundred years, the Indians went back to foreclose on the island, and all they found was block after block of publishing houses, and they said, 'Fuck this. They can keep it.' They taught us that at Wharton."

In the next room, Doublewide, fortified by a couple of gallons of gin fizzes, bounced on the sofa with a quartet of cheerleaders from Immokalee High. He must have been older than the four of them combined.

Dottie expressed curiosity as to why Crossdresser, equipped with an advantaged education, would return to the primeval swampland. "For the same reason MENSA moved its national headquarters from New York to Fort Worth, Texas," he said. "The rent was cheap. And . . . the idea is not to settle where the money is, but where it is going to be. At Wharton, they have the good manners not to teach that, although it is occasionally implied."

The Greater Immokalee area? Accessible only by those boats with pontoons and big propellers on the back? Billy Crossdresser must have been a person of immense vision. I just kept my yap shut, this being a party in Doublewide's honor and all, but Crossdresser has read my mind.

"This area is endowed with a natural resource, the water moccasin, that provides hormones that are amazingly useful in the manufacture of certain cosmetics, hair care products in particular. As for the leftovers, let me put it this way. Soon the frozen food section of every grocery store on the continent will be inundated with a new label . . . Mrs. Bjornsen's Icelandic Halibut Stiks. The lovely aspect of this is that the water moccasin now ranks with the mosquito and the cockroach as the only species on the face of the planet not registered as endangered. Water moccasins reproduce themselves at a rate higher even than investment bankers."

By then, the suave Seminole was pouring port. I was tranquilized, Dottie appeared somewhat dazed, and Doublewide and the cheerleaders were drunker than Sam Houston. I called them cheerleaders; Doublewide simply introduced the girls as "class officers." They were dancing to a scratchy 45—"Hot Rod Lincoln."

Dottie and I excused ourselves at midnight. Dottie drove the Pontiac back to Sanibel Island. The lingering light of a full moon, filtered and distorted by the methane gas, formed odd and undulating patterns upon the windshield, a sort of impressionistic belly dancer. Dottie talked of Crossdresser in terms that included "unique" and "clever."

"Yes, and so marvelously poised," I said. "Particularly for a cannibal."

Dottie laughed that inimitable laugh. "Men your age—you're almost attractive when you're a little bit threatened."

"Threatened, my aching ass. I'm just afraid that if Doublewide passes out back there, nobody will ever see him again. And when that happens, remind me to lay off the Icelandic fish sticks."

8

Look at this lunch menu:

*Banana soft tacos with Grand Marnier glaze and papaya
and strawberry salsa.*

Venison chili in tortilla cups with mango corn relish.

Grilled cactus-pear sea bass with griddled shallot croutons.

Oven roasted pheasant and pumpkin-molasses puree.

Nouveau Southwest U.S.—Southeast Asia cuisine. From
El Paso to East LA, that's all anybody eats anymore. I was
sitting amid genteel company in the dining room of the Va-
mos a Cama Resort and Riding Club in Palm Springs, California. According to a small pewter plaque on the wall just
behind my head, this table had been perpetually preserved
for the late Sterling Hayden. Team Del, now on its fourth
week on the Seniors tour, just completed a morning round
at the pro-am, prior to the Zimmerman Pharmaceutical
Acute Chest Pain Seniors Desert Classic. The seniors racket
has really been catching on. Somebody said that Fred Couples has dyed his gray in hopes of jumping the gun on our
tour. This is a $1 million tournament so all the swells are

on hand. My group in the pro-am included a general in the Air Force, a captain of industry, and a private investor. Team Del has posted three top ten finishes in three tournaments. Dottie Ridge has been pleased. This scheme to win the Seniors Open might not be that far-fetched. The only thing that's held me back so far is stage fright. I can play with the best of these guys. That's encouraging but we're still a light year or so away from the high tier competition, in terms of public recognition. The big boys are the ones who get the famous former film stars like Chuck Heston and Buck Owens, who co-starred in *Hee-Haw: The Movie,* in their amateur groups.

They talk a lot of theatrical stuff out here in Palm Springs. People at this very table were arguing the merits of the various works of Tennessee Williams. This was scarcely past noon, for God's sake. Finally, I am asked to join the discussion. Since someone this morning asked me if I might not be Stewart Granger, I felt tanned and confident.

I stared into my spicy pumpkin chowder with crispy crayfish, seeking divine wisdom. Finally, the golfer speaks.

"Tennessee Williams? Shit. I always thought he was overrated. I mean, other than '16 Tons,' what the hell did he ever sing?"

Now it's their turn to stare at their plates. Ansel Woodbridge, whom you remember as the guy who played the marshal on *Herb Reznick: Frontier Chiropractor* seemed to be discerning the meaning of life from within his warm squab salad with dried cherry-sorghum dressing and sweet potato confetti. And Pony Frost, who used to clip Mr. Spock's ear hair before marrying some Czech producer, just poked rather grimly at her jalapeño-smoked shrimp with plantain and broccoli-pickled eggplant stir fry.

They managed to exclude me from additional conversation until near the end of the dessert course, when the table chit-chat somehow meandered its way around to the topic of golf. Now they were interested in the status of my new career—no chance to embarrass myself here.

"Well, this will only be my fourth tournament. So far, it's been Santa Fe, then Tucson. Phoenix was last week."

"Santa Fe! Didn't you just simply adore it!" gushed Miss Frost.

"Adore it? What's to adore? All I saw was a bunch of rump wranglers dressed up like the Cisco Kid."

I looked into the faces of my seven table companions. Nothing but furrowed brows. I believed that the appropriate moment to bid these good people adieu had clearly arrived. I decided to forgo the banana tequila sorbet with cinnamon tortilla crisp dessert and excuse myself, before inflicting any additional harm to the Team Del mystique. Besides, Team Del needed some work out there on the practice tee. I had decided to open my stance slightly on the suggestion of Dolly Cartwright, greatest golf teacher in history, in my estimation. I never met Dolly, but her instructional book, *Successful Swingers*, is the only one I'd ever endorse. I'd never said this before, but I'd always wished that I was a woman. When it came to matters pertaining to golf, that is.

Women just swing the club more effectively because they aren't burdened with the male instinct to try to atomize the fuckin' ball every time they swing the club. Women are easier to teach and even at the professional level, they just swing the club more efficiently. Also, they putt better, they hold their temper better, and they just concentrate better, because when they're on the golf course, they think about the next shot, rather than men, who are more inclined to think about how much they're not getting lately. Women didn't have to worry about that, I suppose, because they could get laid any time they wanted to.

Another point that Dolly stressed over and over in *Successful Swingers* was the value of practice. "The only way to improve is through practice and you'll never get better if you don't." That was what she preached.

Doublewide McBride was already on the premises after I'd negotiated my tactical retreat to the practice tees. He'd gotten a new look. One of those triangular mustache-goatee arrangements that was introduced to the young men of this country by those scuzzy-looking Russian hockey players. They look bad enough on the young guys. On anybody over thirty-five, you automatically spot 'em as a child molester. Or a caddy. Speaking of which, Doublewide carried some hot news from the caddy trailer, where he'd just enjoyed a hot dog that came with, since were in Palm Springs, almond soup, fruit dried polenta with ancho-honey dressing, and watermelon pico de gallo.

"It's official," he exclaimed. "Tiger Woods has fired Fluff." Doublewide looked distraught, a little pale. Fluff was this guy who looked like Captain Kangaroo—and because of his appearance and the person he worked for, he had become the world's first-ever celebrity caddy. The pro should experience some concern when the caddy earns more endorsement money than the golfer.

"Well, you know the old adage about the two top endangered species—dogs that chase cars and pros who putt for pars," I told Doublewide. "Now there's a third entry to the list—caddies who think they're stars."

"Everybody out at the trailer's pretty down about this," he said. "None of us is secure anymore. You know damn good and well that this is going to kick off some kind of backgammon effect."

"You mean domino effect?"

"Backgammon effect. Domino effect. Parchesi effect. We're all screwed."

"At least, you don't have anything to worry, unless—"

"Unless what?"

"Unless you let something happen to Big Luther. I noticed you left the bag unattended this morning while you went over to ogle the girls by the pool. If anything happens to Big Luther, I'll be taking a job going door-to-door, trying to get people to let me stencil their address out on the curb. As for you, you'll be on your own."

"Oh," said the caddy, seemingly eager to change the subject. "You mentioned the golf bag. I found a death threat in it today."

"A what?"

"This letter. It was addressed to you but I opened it anyway. That's part of my job. It was these letters cut out of a magazine, like you used to see on *Hawaii 5-0*. Said something like, 'Forget the Ides of March. We'll blow up your worthless ass by Groundhog's Day.' Something like that."

"Jesus. Lemmee see it."

"Don't have it anymore. I autographed it and gave it to this old lady. She must have been damn near one hundred, but you shouldda seen her calves. Besides. More good PR for Team Del. Every little bit counts."

The mysterious note, I hopefully decided, was the product of Doublewide's happy and active fantasy world. How many grown men do you know who have an imaginary friend named Gator Bait? At least the thing was addressed to me and not to Big Luther. That part was comforting. And if Doublewide was seen keenly into the public relations aspect of our golfing partnership, I had to remind him that there's nothing like an opening round of 66 to spread around plenty of good will.

Our 6:50 A.M tee time, earliest in the history of the Seniors tour, was a benefit. The organizers of these tournaments stick the closet cases like me and my playing partners, P. J. (Petroleum Jelly) Sampson and Stinky Beavers—his Christian name is Marvin—out there at sunrise so that we'll be off the course when the big names are just teeing off. Team Del prefers it that way. At that time of morning, it's practically impossible to get too keyed up. It's also a personal theory that you can hit the ball farther before the galleries begin to assemble. With all those people walking around the golf course and gasping like they do because of the exercise they're not used to, the air gets heavier as the day grows longer.

Big Luther did not miss a fairway, which is vital on these desert courses because if you get too far out in the rough, you'll have a tarantula crawling up your pants leg in no time. It is generally believed that people move to the desert because of their health. And that's true. Because if they go back where they came from, they'd get lynched. Take the state of Arizona. It is populated entirely of people who were chased out of someplace reputable. Arizona leads the nation, and we're not just talking per capita, in people who have been indicted, disbarred, de-certified, tarred-and-feathered, or otherwise personally disgraced. The only reason they're not in Palm Springs is that they're afraid to dress in a manner that calls attention to themselves. People just like me, which is why I felt so spiritually at ease among the rocks and dust and nearby mountains of a shade of brown that reminded me of the suits that preachers used to wear back in Topeka when I was a kid.

One-hundred and forty-four guys teed off after I did in

the opening round of the Zimmerman Pharmaceutical Acute Chest Pain Classic. Two of them would equal my score of 66, nobody bettered it. That was enough to gain Team Del entry into the press tent to explain my round. They sat me down beneath a banner that contained the sponsor's corporate motto: YOU'RE NOT HAVING A HEART ATTACK . . . IT'S ONLY GAS.

If anybody had asked me, which they didn't, the biggest change in competitive golf since I left the regular tour twenty-five years ago, I would have answered that it was the makeup and demeanor of the people who occupy the press tent. In the old days, the golf media consisted entirely of fat men, drunk by noon on the free beer they used to set out in wash tubs, and bragging about the blow job they had pretended to have gotten the night before. Now the scene was half female, at least. Everybody is sipping Evian water, feet on the table, reading *Wired* magazine. The mood within the tent, which was not a tent but a temporary building made out of aluminum, was one of overpowering detachment. Here I'd shot a 66 and nobody was on the phone screaming, "Stop the presses!" Nobody cared that I had driven the 14th green, which was 410 yards from the tee, and that was fine with me because I wanted to keep the magical powers of Big Luther under wraps as long as possible. The press corps had exactly one question for Team Del. "What do you think of your chances of winning?"

"I think they're pretty damn good," I said.

That quote appeared in the paper the following day. "Look at this," I yelled at Doublewide. "They've got me saying, 'I think my chances are pretty (expletive) good!' Can you believe that??"

"At least they spelled your name right. That's all that counts."

"No they didn't. They call me Del Barnett."

After two 67s, Team Del remained tied for the lead. They were spelling our name right, finally, but nobody regarded us as a serious threat to win the tournament. And with good reason. As we drove away from the golf course in the Team Del victory transport and contemplated the potential consequences of what might take place in the final round, I was beginning to feel a certain constriction in the region of my bronchial passages, a condition known in various golfing circles as "choking."

Doublewide didn't help much. "It'll take a 65, at least, to win and to do that, we'll need to birdie four of the first five holes because down the stretch, you'll probably be getting a bad case of the yips down the stretch." I liked that a lot. "We" make the birdies while "I" get the yips. And all of these caddies wonder why they're getting canned all of the time. The decision to spend Saturday night as far away as possible from Doublewide and anybody and anything associated with that golf tournament was not a difficult one. I was longing for real food and headed to the only franchise restaurant in all of Palm Springs, a Denny's, and ordered the patty melt. The meal arrived with shiitake mushrooms with peach-smoked poblana sauce and cabbage-peanut compote. After a double helping of serrano chili ice cream, topped with Thai red curry sauce, I was primed for Sunday's round.

First off the tee on Thursday, last off the tee on Sunday. Still, no one seemed to pay the slightest attention to poor old Team Del—until I approached the tee box at Hole 1 and was confronted by a pleasant man who identified himself as a production assistant with ESPN, which was carrying this final round. He wanted to attach a cordless microphone to my golf bag. "If (and he stressed the word 'if') you're still in contention by the 17th hole, we'll switch on the mike.

That way, the viewers back home can tune into any interchange you might have with your caddy and get a better feel for the, you know, the *tension* of what's happening out there," he said.

All I could do was shrug and make a fast mental note not to explain the cordless mike routine to Doublewide, given his flair for uncalled-for theatrics. It was time to start. Big Luther hooked his tee shot, but the ball struck a rock and bounced back onto the fairway. Doublewide rolled his eyes. Choke city? Could be. They say that brand new fathers come through best under pressure on the regular tour these days. Because they all have to attend these childbirth classes, where they pick up on breathing exercises that enable them to relax. You won't see that technique employed much on the Seniors tour, though.

My caddy's game plan to birdie four of the first five holes would have been good one—the only problem being that you actually have to sink the birdie and Team Del didn't do that. After five, I was even for the round and lucky not to be five over, since last night's patty melt had started these triple back-flips. The old familiar voice, Cyber Man, is communicating with me, via the modern miracle of audio-hallucination. "Having a heart attack, big guy? Is this the big one? Doublewide says you fellas need ink. Well, this is one great way to get some. The ESPN cameras are on now. Just keel over into that pond beside the next green." Then the voice of Easy Tradin' Doyle takes over. The voice of reason. "Remember where you're at," he says. "You're not having a heart attack. It's just gas."

Gas! Of course! Just before striking my approach to Number 6, I passed wind. You could hear it halfway around the golf course. I pointed at Doublewide, to alert the gallery to the source of the indiscretion, and then dropped an eight iron a couple of feet from the pin. Suddenly momentum was on the side of Team Del. We collected another birdie at 10 and another at 12. I didn't have the balls to check the leader board, but figured that Team Del was definitely on the scent. Our playing partner, some lefty from New Zealand who was built like a tapeworm, had made a quintuple bogey after I'd gassed him back on the 6th fairway. So he was out of it. As for those directly ahead of us, the disappointed "oohhs" from the gallery far outnumbered the cheers that you hear when somebody sinks a putt. So that was an excellent sign.

Finally, on the 17th tee, a par 3, I dared a peek at the leader board and sure enough, Team Del was 14 under for the tournament, one shot in the lead. At the same time, that associate producer from ESPN was positioned off beside the tee and had given me the high sign, indicating that the cordless mike had just been turned on. I decided to give those viewers back home, my brand new adoring fans, their formal introduction to Team Del.

I pulled a tuft a grass from the tee box, tossed into the air to get the direction of the breeze, all the while knowing that there was no breeze, and inquire, "What do you think Doublewide? It's 191 to the pin. A hard 7-iron?"

"How the fuck should I know?" he says. "You're the one who's supposed to be the goddam pro."

Fortified by the enrichment just experienced by the viewers throughout this proud land, my hard 7-iron drifted well to the right to the green, struck a cart path and ricocheted off in the general direction of the Republic of Mexico.

"Nice shot, Dickhead," said Doublewide.

Team Del would lose five strokes to par on those final two holes, which were enough to knock us not only out of the lead but all the way off the leader board. We were not invited into the press room. I showered and dressed, all the while trying to pretend to be invisible. It didn't work. A clubhouse attendant recognized me easily enough and handed me a slip of paper that was inscribed with a telephone number and a familiar one at that. "It's from a Mrs. Ridge in Florida," he said. "She wants to speak to you right away. Sez it's urgent."

9

My Man Doublewide arrived at the motel at 6 A.M., attired in what he described as a Mexican wedding shirt and cheerfully oblivious to the reality that I was about to be dragged before the chief of the golfing seniors morality police. Because of the caddy's brief but celebrated TV outburst, me, the pro would have to absorb the punishment. The penalty would either be a suspension, a fine and/or a public caning.

"But I'm not real concerned, because if this Seniors tour thing does not work out somehow, I'm going to take a job with *Sports Illustrated*," I told the caddy and that seemed to arouse a combination of curiosity and dismay. "Hey, don't worry," I went on. "You can get work for *Sports Illustrated*, too. There was a help-wanted ad in the classifieds today— I've been reading those quite a bit lately, and *Sports Illustrated* is definitely looking for qualified people. To sell it door-to-door, that is. Along with *Better Homes and Gardens, Popular Mechanics, Newsweek*, and *Hustler*."

Doublewide grinned, although it was one of those pained "oh, crap" grins you make when you see the meter maid sticking the ticket underneath your windshield wiper and you're too late to stop her. This was my way of presenting the caddy with what the NFL refers to as the two-minute warning. All of this Holy Grail madness attached with winning the Seniors Open had forced me to think in terms of problems and solutions and lately, Doublewide was clearly not among the latter. I did not have the heart to tell him—he was a friend after all—that I was putting him on probation. Why create unnecessary worry? I'd just wait for Doublewide to screw up again and then I'd fire him. Ship his ass back to the swamp, where I think he was happier anyway.

True, the notion of a rookie on the Seniors tour firing a caddy would make me appear to be a prima donna. But I've got to win that Open for Easy Tradin' and can't afford too many distractions. Those lung tumors of his can't be getting any smaller. And my disciplinary session with one of the various tour "sheriffs" went well beyond the realm of distraction.

Hugo Duffleman, one of the top PGA guys in charge of player language, deportment, and protocol, ate my ass out but good. Hugo was an ex-rugby star and former smoke jumper from New Zealand who could create a forceful presence.

"You cocksuckers are giving this tour a shitty reputation," he told me. "Some douche bag in charge of PR at Kellogg's says they might pull the plug at Palm Springs. Jesus goddam Christ! Try that one more time, and I'll fine your miserable mother fucking ass all the way back to South Florida!"

"Relax, Hugo. This'll blow over in no time," I said.

"Yeah, but at first, I was sure that you'd staged it. Sort of like that tennis player at Wimbledon, ranked about 130th in the world, who had his wife smack the umpire, just to stir up some ink for himself," Hugo said.

"My caddy and I aren't that enterprising," I said.

"I know," he said.

But Team Del found itself on the hit list of some Quaker sponsored anti-profanity task force: Society for the Hinderence of Indecent Talk. Also, we received a smattering of hate mail from, let's see, Tennessee, Oregon, Vermont, and Illinois.

"I'm sending each of these folks a personal, handwritten letter of profound apology, along with a Team Del T-shirt. That way, maybe we can turn a negative into a positive," I said to Doublewide, the perpetrator.

"Absolutely," said Doublewide. "Who says you can't make chicken salad out of chicken shit?"

I wouldn't be seeing anything of Doublewide that week during the LA Seniors event, sponsored by the Prune Growers Association. He would take the week off, and we'd hired a temp to caddy. Both of us agreed that our several-day separation seemed well-timed. DW, in fact, would devote the next few days to an appearance on *Jeopardy*. He landed a spot on the program after showing up at a contestant search back in St. Pete. "Scored high on their written test," he said. "Got lucky, actually. They had a bunch of questions from my two best categories: Insects and Begins With J."

Now came the rare opportunity to concentrate on golf, and nothing but. Whatever Doublewide might say on his latest TV appearance became the sole concern of that emcee, Alex What's-His-Name. Despite the turmoil, I finished strong at San Diego. Big Luther continued to out-distance the field, and I tied for sixth. Two tournaments, two top-ten finishes. That tallied up to a quick 54 gees. Dottie Ridge called to express her approval. She was overseeing some tire tests at the race track in Talladega, Alabama. "Speed week in Daytona," Dottie stressed, "comes up next week." And guess who was conveniently hanging out in Talladega, too? Billy Crossdresser, naturally. He'd heaved a small chunk of his snake money into the racing venture.

Dottie—heavenly creature that she was—confounded me with her taste in men, a commodity that she seemingly enjoyed collecting. Beautiful and brilliant, why would Dottie settle for some orthodontically challenged NASCAR driver whose entire conversational repertoire consisted of deep thoughts about piston rods and gear boxes, and a slick, jive-talking, serpent-crazed Seminole, who, in my estimation, attempted to conceal his own inadequacies behind a closet full of threads that must have been worth seven figures? And this raised a more troubling question. What did that tell the world about *me*?

A voice from the great beyond broke into my angst, the voice of Easy Tradin' Doyle. "We interrupt this program with a special announcement," the voice said. "You never had a shot at that woman in the first place. Quit thinking like a loser."

So I marched onto the golf course at Alhambra Heights Country Club with an uncluttered mind, and for the second time in three weeks, my foursome registered the low net score in the pro-am. This time, my ex-senator was replaced by ex-police chief Daryl Gates, and the captain of industry was situated in my group, a cellular communications magnate who also happened to be a former player with the Harlem Globetrotters, Mockingbird Lane.

During his tenure with the Trotters, Lane's teams compiled a win-loss record of 2,348 and zero. "But this is the first damn time I ever won anything in golf," conceded Lane after our foursome, carried on the broad shoulders of Big Luther, signed in with a net 58. "We will see you at the part-TEE tonight," stressing that second syllable in "party" in the same fashion as Dot-TEE did when she introduced herself.

"Nah. Don't think so. I believe I'll rest up at the motel," I told Mockingbird. "Besides. They're showing *God Is My Co-Pilot* on the Living In the Past Channel tonight."

"If God is his motherfuckin' co-pilot, they must have some kinda stewardess," Lane said. "But if you keep livin' in a foxhole all the time, you're game's gonna go stale. Besides. Everybody at that party will be drinking mango-flavored bottled water."

Mockingbird Lane came close. The beverage of choice at the pro-am party seemed to be vodka and papaya juice. Lane spotted me and insisted that I join him with a duet of what those California girls that the Beach Boys sang about look like after they turn forty. One of them was identified as Carol DelHomme—which sounded vaguely familiar.

"Del Bonnet here, he's a famous golf pro," Lane told the two women. "My claim to fame is that I was born with three testicles."

"How enchanting," said one of the women, the one who wasn't Carol DelHomme.

"As a younger man, I turned that condition into a cash cow," Lane said. "You can win a lot of bets with a peculiarity like that. I even got inventive. Then one night in the Polo Lounge, I approached a gentleman and said, 'I'll bet you five-thousand dollars that between us, me and that bartender have five balls.' So, just after the guy accepted the bet, the bartender leaned over to me and whispered, 'Unless you've got four, you're in trouble.' So I learned my lesson and turned to pro basketball."

Mockingbird Lane soon left the party with the woman who wasn't Carol. She seemed clearly intent on finding out if Lane might not be telling the truth. That left me alone with Carol facing the task of following a tough act, and Carol looked like someone I wanted to get to know. Her left ring finger was vacant. A sixth sense that I didn't ordinarily have told me—in fact, could not underscore strongly enough—that golf would not be an ideal topic to pursue with DelHomme. If Dottie Ridge presented a quality that brought Kim Novak and *Vertigo* to mind, then Carol Del-Homme could easily have stood in for Sigourney Weaver in *The Year of Living Dangerously*. Grecian sculptured nose. Sleek. She appeared to somehow reflect a genetic linkage to aristocracy, as opposed to the high-class hooker look that tended to prevail at Palm Springs. In any case, I got the impression she was at an after-party at the LA Seniors Pro-Am only because something better had fallen through.

So I let her know right off that I'd rather have not been there, either. "Actually, I was going to stay at home tonight and watch *God Is My Co-Pilot*." Way to go, Del. Polished effort.

"Yes," said DelHomme. "With Dennis Morgan."

"Are you connected with the movie business?" Clumsier effort yet. If we were in Nashville, would you ask her if she had ever appeared on *Hee Haw*?

"I have to confess that I am," said DelHomme.

That's when it struck me.

"Of course you are," I said. "Carol DelHomme." You played the rebellious teenager on the TV series—what was it?—*Father Poltroon, Waterfront Priest*!"

"That's the one," said Carol. "Ruined my career.

"How?"

"CBS cancelled *Poltroon* after one season. Then Peggy Lipton beat me out for her role on *Mod Squad*. By then I was too old for *The Partridge Family* and too young for *Charlie's Angels*, and all of a sudden I was obsolete."

"But you say you're still involved with movies."

"I'm with property acquisition and development at Quad Tri-Star."

"Forgive my ignorance, but . . ."

"Essentially, I read treatments and say, 'No.' With some

of the more promising 'No' entries, I can recommend changes, revisions. And sometimes those get processed over to the 'yes' office. I stay out of the 'yes' phase as much as possible because that's where it gets sticky."

"So, hypothetically, of course, I have this script idea and . . ."

"First become a member of the guild. Then secure an agent. Then become proficient at condensing your treatment to fifty words or less."

"You mean fifty pages or less."

"I mean fifty words or less. I've memorized what turned out to be some of the greatest treatments in the history of the industry. *The Wizard of Oz*: 'Farm girl gang-banged by flying monkeys.' You get it."

Now I was feeling out of my league and not wanted to talk about the movie business. DelHomme's boredom quotient was running thin and Team Del did not want this one to slip away just yet. When in doubt, try candor. "It's obvious," I said to DelHomme, "that you are at least ten years older than you look. How do you accomplish that?"

"Icelandic kelp. I eat about two jars a day."

Suddenly, our conversation got chopped up by the intrusion of someone obviously connected with Carol DelHomme's business. He just sort of arrived like an unsolicited manuscript. I'd guessed the man's age at twenty-eight. Beige silk sport jacket, maroon collarless shirt. Equine features, wire-rim glasses. Plenty of gray hair, but there were not enough stress lines in his face to justify the gray, so I suspected he'd had it dyed that way. They handed that look out along Rodeo Drive as routinely as they sprinkled saltpeter into army food. Whoever "they" are.

He identified himself to me as Jan-Marc Samuelsen. Body posture indicated that Jan-Marc's status within the industry rested quite a few notches beneath Carol DelHomme's. But he had something that he wanted to sell her. Now that I was a salesman myself, I found nothing offensive about Jan-Marc, particularly after he said, "Man, I watched you on the course today. Those tee shots, man. Gave me chills. It was like cannon fire. Guided missiles. Desert Storm! Scuds!"

Jan-Marc, apparently, was associated with films involving action figures. "That's, ah, very generous," I said. "I was just discussing the film business with Ms. DelHomme, and she offered a fascinating view of it from her perspective. I am sure that you can enlighten me, too.

"Let's say I'm an out-of-work actor out here, but not entirely unknown, and I've written this dynamite script. Let's call it, say, *Teenage Milkman*. Mystery story. Great role for some up-and-comer. What do I do next and how, if possible, could you get me headed in the right direction? Are you somebody who could help me out? I guess what I'm really asking is what exactly do you do?"

"Fair questions. Second one first. Really, this is not the new Hollywood but the beginning of Hollywood's Eleventh Era. That's what we call it. The big studios are out. The independents are the salvation of the industry. Let's put it this way. The system always kills itself. Happens every twenty years. It happened in the mid-'50s, the mid-'70s and now, the late-'90s. Dead. Then things change and this time the independents will do it. Understand?"

Jan-Marc's speech pattern seemed stuck on fast forward. He had no other gear.

"Now. A connector is a producer or executive producer. We combine the financing. Bring in different partners who can 'umbrella' the project. Cut the bottom line. Make the movie so cheap, nobody can lose money, and we use our financial expertise to protect the Maker, who is you."

"Me?"

"Yeah. If you were an actor with a script. The actor-producer. Or the writer-producer. The writer/director. The writer-director-actor. Combine the top line. Piece the key jobs together in one role. This relocates the vitality of movie-making."

He had me confused. "Then, you mean, as the Maker, I might wind up playing the Teenage Milkman myself? And possibly direct?"

"In the context of the Eleventh Era, precisely," said Jan-Marc. "But . . . in terms of script, you might want to stick closer to your bailiwick. Something involving golf."

"Wait then," I said. "Why not something from back in the Eighth or Ninth Era? *Arnold Palmer Meets the Teenage Milkman*. No offense to you Hollywood people, but I've seen worse."

Jan-Marc gave Carol a quick glance that I interpreted to read: "Can you *believe* this old dork?" and excused himself. Carol's body language was difficult to interpret, making it tough to guess if she wanted me to take a hike as well. Naturally, then, Team Del stuck around.

"Have you ever been married to anybody famous?" In Hollywood, that was not such an outrageous question, not a bad one at all since it not only meant "have you ever?" but also "are you now?"

"Temporarily. To Cameron King. A character actor although he did catch a lead in a sitcom that never caught on. *My Friend Bosco*. He played an angel."

"Oh. Right. I remember that. Is he gay?"

Carol leveled this blue gaze that seemed to X-ray. "Why would you ask a question like that?"

"Well, for the last several years, when I am talking to people's ex-wives, they universally describe that . . . situation."

"No. Cameron likes to dress up. But he isn't gay. Want to know his big secret, though?"

"Tell me."

"His real name is Lonnie McNutt."

Time now to roll the dice. "Why don't we grab a six-pack and head over to the La Viega Grade Lodge? I've got a suite there. We could catch the last half of *God Is My Co-Pilot.*"

"*Sergeant York*, I think."

"Hillbilly psycho finds God. A four-star blood bath toward the end. Somebody should colorize that and rerelease it. I'll get my car and follow you over there."

(10)

Los Angeles. El Lay. The City of Angels. After any earth-quake of reasonable force, squadrons of local angels descend upon retail outlets and remove all of the merchandise in gro-cery carts before the looters can get to it.

In my cab headed toward LAX, I watched the eye move-ments of the angel who was driving the junk heap. I could see his reflection in the rearview mirror. The guy was ob-viously loaded on pig tranquilizers. He was spooky as hell. They ought to have made him wear shades. I found myself riding a cab to the airport for the simple reason that some angel had stolen the Team Del Challenger off the parking lot at the motel.

Despite that complication, in keeping with my previous history in that community, I had a better week off the golf course than on it. At the La Vieja Grande Dodge, I did *not* experience a romantic encounter with Carol DelHomme. We watched *Sergeant York*, then she left—although Carol supplied me with her home telephone number and a prom-ise to monitor my progress on the Seniors tour. When she could get time off from the movie studio, Carol said she might show up at one of the tournaments, although, ac-cording to the PGA schedule, the most glamorous stop for the next three months was Chattanooga.

My performance at Alhambra Heights, toughest of the courses on the tour so far, produced two sub-par rounds, another top ten finish, and another five-digit check. My earnings remained ahead of the goal—or "mission statement" as Doublewide McBride called it—that we had established with Dottie Ridge.

Still, my stomach acid cascaded well above flood stage when the tournament finished and not because of my final position on the leader board. No. This particular Maalox Moment was brought about because Bruno Pratt won the event. That morbid little pimp shot a 62 in the final round! What was it about that man that caused me to break out in welts?

A fundamental explanation dates back to the dark days of the New Orleans fiasco—my personal little Chappaquiddick. Bruno's name appeared in some wire service story attached to a quote about how the PGA needed "to start policing the hooligan element on the tour." Hooligan element. That really boiled my balls. Here this sawed-off son of a bitch at the very bottom of the earnings chart was appointing himself as arbiter of golf's moral universe. "So who died and made him the Pope?" That comment was attributed to me in *Golf Digest*, illustrating, if nothing else, my lack of imagination and maturity at the time.

Bruno's sanctimonious little popoff stood out as a major factor, but not the only one, in all this lingering animosity. Bruno was the product of considerable old money, so he was totally insulated from the real world and could concentrate on golf and nothing but golf since grade school, probably. He came from a family of prosperous undertakers in Detroit.

Perhaps that was why Bruno always maintained this freshly embalmed look. After thirty years, the only thing about Bruno that had changed was that his teeth were capped so that when he grinned, he looked like a Baldwin grand piano. Plus, he'd dyed his hair reddish brown and had it frizzed and wore blue contacts.

And then there was that walk of his. He sort of minced his way around the golf course and whenever he sank a putt he gave out this sissy-ass wave to the gallery. That happened a lot because Bruno knocked in his share of putts. I'll credit him with that. But if I hadn't known better, I'd have almost sworn that he moonlighted with the dance ensemble in *Rent*.

Sadly, the truth happened to be that Bruno couldn't control his sexual appetite for persons of the female persuasion, but only the ones who qualified as off limits. That's how Bruno operated: He would approach the wife or girlfriend or whatever of some golfer and talk about what a shame it was that "old so-and-so couldn't be faithful to a lovely creature like you. It broke my heart when I saw him out with that bruised-up old twenty-dollar hooker in Hartford." After Bruno planted that poisonous seed, he proceeded to prey on the woman's vulnerability. That was how he got them in bed. At least, that was how he got Leonique in bed and believe me, that was the last time her name will appear in this narrative.

A letter appeared in Ann Landers' column the other day from Fuming in Fargo. Fuming turned out to be some character who went to meet his new boss, only to discover that the boss was the same character who had stolen his girlfriend twenty-five years earlier. "Bury the hatchet if you want to keep your job. Put a cork in the testosterone jug. Get over it. Grow up. Etc." Typical Ann Landers response— always dubious of what she perceived as the grotesquely predictable male instinct.

Believe me, Ann. I'd have loved to have buried the hatchet when it came to Bruno Pratt, buried it about seven inches beneath his navel. Of course, Bruno wasn't my boss. Much worse. After he won the tournament at Alhambra Heights, he ranked as my superior on the Seniors money list to the tune of about 110 gees.

Doublewide McBride should remember his week in the City of Angels with mixed emotions as well after his historic showing on *Jeopardy*. Historic in the sense that Doublewide became the first contestant, ever, to get kicked off the show. I worried that his bitterness over the experience might linger.

"It happened toward the end of the taping," Doublewide told me in the defensive tone that someone might utilize in explaining how he accidentally ran over the crossing guard at a kindergarten. "I'd been ahead the whole game and even after this woman from Spokane ran the board in the Old Testament category, I was still six hundred dollars up, and then I got a shot at the Daily Double in World Geography. I bet my whole wad—nine grand. Then they showed me the question: 'What's the only country in the world that starts with 'A' that doesn't end in 'A'?' My mind went blank for a couple of seconds and then I said 'Azerbaijan.' Then Alex Trebek, he's the announcer guy, gets this phony kind of 'aw, shucks' look on his face and says, 'Oooohhhh. Too bad. It's Afghanistan.' Well, I don't say anything right then, figuring that the judges had fucked up.

"So then, during the commercial break, Trebek explains that the *Jeopardy* judges—afraid to admit their own mistake—rule that Azerbaijan is not really a country, that it's an Iranian province. So I say, 'Shit. Goddam. Somebody *could* get their ass whipped over this.'

"And Alex Trebek says, 'Well, what do you expect me to do about it?' And I say, 'I expect you to stand there and get your ass whipped, that's what.' So then he calls security. And I say, 'You don't have to get all mad about it.' But by then, it was too late and they hauled me off. I didn't even get to collect one of the runner-up prizes."

Now, for the second tournament in a row, I had to compete sans the services of Caddy McBride. He would remain in California, simmering in his own juices of turmoil while replacing the long-gone Team Del vehicular transport. I traveled away to participate in the Star-Kist Yucatán Seniors Open, the first PGA event ever held outside the United States. They scheduled the thing in mid-February, hooking into the little two-week window down there that isn't hurricane season.

Doublewide remained his conventionally hysterical self as he recited a checklist of the risk factors involved with this journey. "Chances are, you'll never arrive. If the airliner doesn't collide with some little private plane over LA, then it will fall apart in the air over central Mexico," he assured me.

"But if you do make it in there alive, remember these three simple rules: Don't eat anything, don't drink anything, and for Crissakes, don't screw anything. Otherwise, they'll send you home in a box."

"I took those same vows once before," I said, "when I married a Lutheran."

The cab ride to the airport alleviated all my trepidations about the discount flight on board Air Chalupa. My driver jumped fifteen curbs, and ran two school buses and a cement truck off the road, all the time muttering, "They're after me! Can't you see 'em? Look! One of 'em is standing on my hood!"

So—compared with the cab ride—the flight from LA down to Mérida on the Yucatán peninsula turned out to be an exercise in serenity, and on that one occasion when the cabin filled with smoke, the passengers all laughed and began singing, "ninety-nine Bottles of Dos Equis on the Wall. . . ."

I was detained at customs for about two hours at the airport at Mérida (after they x-rayed me, they x-rayed all my golf balls), but the tournament organizers supplied me with a limo for the drive through the jungle to the resort where the tournament would be held. It was not until we drove through the streets of Mérida leading to the two-lane highway and into the jungle territory that I began to notice the frighteningly palpable signs of unrest, revolution, and anarchy in the Mexican twilight. Virtually every automobile was adorned with a Dallas Cowboys bumper sticker.

My limo driver, somehow sensing my agitation, attempted to reassure me. "Despite what you read, our country remains stable," he said. "And every afternoon, millions of my countrymen stop whatever it is they're doing to watch the American television program about your great military leader, General Hospital."

Then, as daylight disappeared, I could still detect the shadowy figures of ghostlike men trudging along the roadside, some carrying machetes, some carrying rifles, some carrying both. Strange and unsettling, these silhouettes in the darkness offered the very surreal sensation that I was traveling along Santa Monica Boulevard back in the City of Angels.

While I pondered the notion that here was the perfect and ideal location for a horror movie and attempted to craft a treatment for . . . Seniors Golfer Hacked to Pieces by Bandidos . . . a banging noise rang out from the right rear side of the limo, followed by the whomp, whomp, whomp of a blown-out tire. The driver inspected the damage, opened the trunk, and announced, "The spare tire is flat." Then he grinned. "No problem about the flat spare, though, because the jack is missing, too."

I was thinking that maybe a dozen or so years hence, after some hemp farmer locates my skeletal remains and I am identified by dental charts, somewhere Doublewide McBride will be laughing and saying, "Heh, heh. I told you so." Those are the kinds of thoughts that emerge as you gaze into the jungle night, blacker than the coal in Muhlenberg County. From the abyss that extended just beyond the roadside, a cacophony of yowls and whoops poured forth; panthers on the prowl probably, with the background accompaniment of the jackal and hyena chorale. It sounded like a Tarzan movie.

After an eternity and a half, a pickup truck, sputtering and popping, coughed its way to a stop next to that crippled dog of a limo. With the limo driver working as a translator, I loaded my carrying bag and golf clubs, then myself, into the back of the truck and amid a mushroom cloud of carbon monoxide, continued what would amount to the 10,000-peso final leg of the journey to the golf resort.

At least the restaurant remained open, barely, by the time I checked in, although it was practically empty. I dined alone. The Yucatán menu selections seemed limited. The appetizer consisted of chicken soup. The entree included baked chicken and chick peas. The dessert course proved to be the highlight of the meal, a flaming chicken jubilee, followed by coffee and a chicken liqueur. Through the miracle of flight, in less than twenty-four short hours, I'd been transported from the polo set in LA down amid the polo set in the Yucatán.

During Tuesday's practice round, I acquainted myself with a golf course that abutted two-thousand-year-old pyramids and ruins stuck in the very heart of a tropical thicket so dense and isolated that it made the swamp surrounding Immokalee look like Park Avenue. After thirty-six-holes worth of practice, I returned to the resort that was designed like a mini-pyramid. The dinner selections were identical to the ones of the night before. This time, at least, I could share conversation with a companion, my caddy for the week, a young woman, Anna Leslie Xochuatlan. Marlon Brando never had an ex-wife with cheekbones as high and pronounced as Anna Leslie's. She told me she was thirty.

We talked about her Mayan heritage. "Why the great civilization vanished supposedly remains a great cultural mystery," she said. "But the Mayans, at their pinnacle, endorsed sacrifice, and not in the context that the Judeo-Christian ethic endorses it. Any society that pitches the maidens down a well, just after the witch doctor cuts her heart out, is destined to crater, I always thought. The problem is that the wrong people got pitched down the well. Ultimately, the whole tribe died off from an overdose of self-inflicted ego.

"Now some politically correct Mayan historians are trying to claim that the sacrifices never happened. But that's crap. Hell—the well's over there behind the sixth green."

Anna Leslie had gone to Texas and become a San Antonio lawyer. "That was a complete waste of six years. If I had met one lawyer, just *one*, who wasn't a complete dumbass *and* a sexist, I might have stuck around. But those characters made those old Mayan sacrifice farts look enlightened and liberated. They might as well have come to work wearing parrot feathers and carrying daggers. Same kind of mindset. Exactly. I have seen America and the 1990s," she said, "and what I saw was the third century AD in the Mexican jungle."

So Anna Leslie decided to caddy. She also sold beach condos, mostly to what she identified as Euro trash, around Cancun and only decided to caddy that week because, "I invested in this golf course property, and I wanted to experience something a little bit different."

Anna Leslie Xochuatlan knew a lot about golf. Or at least

she knew a great deal about this 7,300-yard layout that was cut through the ruins. Stare off the tee and almost every fairway loomed as a tight dogleg, some of them practically at 90-degree angles. Precision driving would win this tournament, a 72-hole extravaganza unlike most of the 54-hole events on the Seniors tour. ESPN would televise the entire show. My TV friend from Palm Springs, the guy with the microphone, noticed my new caddy. "Hey," he said. "Looks like you swapped Larry Flynt for Pocahontas."

"Yeah," I said. "Stick that live mike in her face and call her Pocahontas and see what happens."

In Round One, we hit every fairway and finished one shot off the lead. No golf course in the world could stand up to Big Luther when he was clean and sober and performing at maximum potential.

I ate dinner alone again—chicken and dumplings with chicken pudding for dessert—and crashed early. According to the leader board, I was tied for second place with Bruce Crampton, Miller Barber, and—Bruno Pratt.

In Round Two, on the back nine, for no apparent reason and without provocation, Big Luther went totally, stark raving berserk. Missed the 10th fairway to the left. Same story on 11. Off to the right on 12. Every time, the golf ball nestled down deep in that jungle rough that was textured like steel wool. What a nightmare.

On the 16th tee, I gave Big Luther Grande a pep talk. "What the hell's wrong with you?" I said to the golf club. "Up 'til now you carried us, yeah, and I gave you all the credit. Now you're screwing us, so you've got to bear the blame. I had a 6-iron that went nuts on me in the U.S. Open one time, and you know what I did? I executed the son of a bitch. Snapped its shaft against a tree trunk. You want some of that, too? I don't t-h-i-n-k s-o-o."

The Mayan princess stared at me with some expression that seemed more sad than bewildered. "So what the fuck are you looking at?" I said. "You said you came out here to experience something different. Now you're getting your wish."

So what if I was psycho? Because I putted like a mad man on that back nine, I salvaged a 74. After the round, I apologized to Anna Leslie. "That bit where I talk to the golf club," I said. "They taught me to do that in a stress management class."

I skipped dinner and retreated back to my room and watched *NYPD Blue* in Spanish. Around midnight, the phone rang. The operator said it was a collect call from Doyle Getzendeiner. Then Doyle's voice materialized on the line, the real and unmistakable Doyle and not the usual audio-hallucination. Except that he was still making these alarming sounds every time he exhaled. Sounded like he'd swallowed a tennis ball. Then, after clearing his throat, Doyle also sounded drunk. And a little pissed off.

"Watched you on *ESPN*, and you're ignoring my Fundamental Rule of the Backswing. If you can see the clubhead with your left eye at the top of the swing, you've gone too far. Cut it back at least ten or twelve degrees." That message, though punctuated with hisses and gasps, rang through with crystal clarity.

"Appreciate it, Doyle," I said. "And go buy yourself an oxygen tent." On Saturday, based on Doyle's tip, Big Luther ceased his aberrant behavior. I tightened my swing on the short irons as well and shot a 65. Just as I finished my round, the wind kicked up substantially, causing ample havoc for everybody in the seven groups behind me. Nicklaus. Irwin. David Graham. They all blew up in the final holes, and now Team Del rested deadlocked for the lead with, naturally, Bruno Pratt.

Sunday morning came, and I got out of bed focused on two ambitions: Get a good breakfast and then go win the golf tournament. The latter proved easier than the former. The breakfast menu consisted of fried eggs and chicken or scrambled eggs and chicken or a chicken omelet. I settled for the continental breakfast, featuring fresh-squeezed chicken juice and a chicken-glazed danish.

The genuine chore that lurked on the golf course would involve my playing partner, Bruno Pratt. "Ignore the SOB. Make him invisible. Make him go away." I had not yet elevated my capacities of mental discipline to a level where that had become possible. On the first tee, Bruno turned to me and said, "What's that great joke you've been telling around here?"

"What in the hell are you talking about?"

"Well . . . whenever I mention your name, everybody just busts out laughing."

Just as I was in the process of taking Big Luther and fixing Bruno's fake teeth, Anna Leslie Xochuatlan issued a glance that said, "Rise above it."

Surprisingly, it was the other guy and not me who lost his composure. Bruno sailed his very first tee shot well into the rain forest and got down in six. Meanwhile, Team Del went birdie, par, par, birdie, par and quickly it became evident that this day would belong to me and not him.

On the back nine, Bruno decided to make it seem like he didn't give a shit. The lowlife buttfucker pulled a cell phone out of his golf bag and called some stockbroker. "What about Kodak? What about Delphi Information Systems?" like he had any clue about what he was talking about. The only time Bruno appeared even vaguely interested about what was happening on the golf course happened when he gave me a very strange look when Big Luther drove the ball to the actual edge of the green on the short par 4. Actually, the strange look appeared more directed at the golf club than at me.

That sideshow in the Yucatán carried one of the top purses for the whole Seniors tour. *Sports Illustrated* even dispatched one of its staff reporters, some guy who looked like Abraham Lincoln, down there to cover the thing. My winning check amounted to $215,000 yanqui dollars, minus a 20 percent gratuity for Anna Leslie Xochuatlan. Dottie Ridge surely would be pleased when she returned home from her stockcar race, the Delco Redneck 400 in Slow Leak, South Carolina and learned of those results.

I had anticipated that when or if I ever won one of these Seniors tournaments, the whole thing would seem kind of anticlimactic after, lo, these many years of confinement in a galaxy of tedious anonymity. Instead, my mood felt closer to unbridled elation, and I told my trusty limo driver to ice down a case of Carta Blanca to embellish that effect on the ride back to the airport in Mérida.

As we drove away from the golf course, off in the underbrush, I noticed something that unsettled me, some kind of huge Godzilla-looking creature. With an enormous fin that ran the length of its back, the thing looked like a 1957 Cadillac El Dorado. It scared the piss out of me.

The limo driver perceived my dismay. "Oh, that—that's just one of our local iguanas," the guy explained. "This whole place is infested with 'em. They've become *the* food staple around here. Pretty good eatin', actually. Tastes just like chicken."

Any type of carryover euphoria that might have resulted from having won my first tournament never really took shape. Hadn't had time to. At the airport, I was presented with a letter from the Seniors protocol man. It said that Team Del was being censured. Not because of the live microphone embarrassment, but something that had happened previously, back in one of the events played out in the desert. Apparently, somebody had filed yet another complaint against my caddy for wearing a T-shirt over his orange overalls that was inscribed: "Don't wait up for the shrimp boats, baby, 'cause I'm comin' home with the crabs." The protocol fellow reminded Team Del that we should remember the words of Paul in the book of Psalms. "Look. We're all a bunch of poor sinners. But try to tone it down a little, OK?"

I hoped the a key member of the Team Del triumvirate would adhere to those thoughts as well. So a feeling not so much as apprehension but curiosity prevailed as I rode an airport shuttle for my reunion with Doublewide McBride, man of the prodigious and majestic mood swing.

Based on the tables of predictability, I would have expected to find DW brimming with, if not resentment, then alienation over being upstaged by Jungle Woman, my exotic

Indian caddy with skin of shining sienna. Predictable, thankfully, is not a word that one could apply to McBride.

So the colleague whom I encountered in the lounge at the Surf King Motel in Pompano Beach, Florida, demonstrated a disposition of effervescence without confinement or constraint. "I have a surprise for you," was the first thing he said. Doublewide led me down a corridor and out through a rear exit of the motel, into a parking lot that overlooked the beach and the perfectly parallel Atlantic horizon beyond that.

"What do you think?"

"I think that I am speechless."

This object of Doublewide's considerable pride sparkled more brightly than the high waves that crested over the beach on a windy afternoon. When I saw it, I swallowed my Spearmint. Team Del II, the new Swedish-built Challenger, resembled perhaps an H-bomb explosion with its bright enamel of burnt orange, red, black, and other colors including various shades of green. Team Del was spelled out in magenta, I think. Then again, the Challenger might have been more aptly described as patterned after one of those madras sports jackets the old-timers wear in Palm Springs—after someone has spilled a plate of lasagna on it. All of Doublewide's circus ladies should have felt very much at home in a ride like this.

"Dottie authorized me to use her NASCAR paint guys to turn the thing out quick. She ain't seen it yet, but she will tomorrow. Somebody from *USA Today* was out here taking pictures of it. I've named the thing the Birdie-Mobile."

I didn't want to dampen Doublewide's enthusiasm for this—thing. "You know, DW, the outstanding feature of this whole, uh, presentation is that nobody, but nobody, will steal *this* one."

"Absolutely. Damn right."

We wandered back into the lounge at the Surf King. They called the lounge the Wiki-Wiki Room, and it was filling up fast. The next event on the Seniors tour, the Sun Coast Kiwanis–Crown Royal Open, was attracting a crowd. And the first wave of spring break college kids had just arrived, cramming those beaches just north of Fort Lauderdale. They came from Ohio State. Villanova. Rutgers. Purdue. Bowling Green. You name it. Most of the crowd spilling into the Wiki-Wiki Room wore their sorority sweatshirts. The Theta Tau Alpha group from UConn appeared in large numbers. Everywhere we looked there was nothing but cutoffs, sandals, and snow-white legs.

After seven days, they'd depart the beaches as battle-hardened veterans. Half of them would have engaged in a fling with some tattooed janitor freak who looked like a collie, return to school with ominous health symptoms they first heard about in junior high school, and confided the experience to absolutely nobody until they get plastered at a sorority reunion thirty years later.

The live entertainment started early. A country and western singer, Sonny Boy Santana, immediately identified himself as a talent that would quickly clear the room of both the Seniors golf entourage and the sorority kids. And that was good news because, at my age, I couldn't tolerate crowds. Sonny Boy's first number, introduced as one that "Ah wrote mahself," entitled "Her Bed of Roses Was My Crown of Thorns," came delivered in a voice so profoundly nasal that the singer not only brought tears to my eyes but blood to my ears.

Locals in Pompano Beach averaged about fifty years of age, although you couldn't find anybody who actually answered to fifty. Everybody was either twenty or eighty.

Through the side mirror, I watched a couple of the elder contingent actually keel over at the alarming sight of the Birdie-Mobile as we made our way over to Bluebeard Country Club for the Wednesday pro-am. Membership at Bluebeard predominantly consisted of a beer-and-dominoes kind of group, that was consistent with the town of Pompano Beach itself. If Boca Raton ranked as a sort of poor man's Palm Beach, then Pompano could only be described as a downscale version of Boca Raton.

That much was reflected in the makeup of my amateur group. Instead of a captain of industry, I was joined by a corporal trying to land an SBA loan. Instead of an ex-U.S. senator, I got a retired justice of the peace. A chiropractor replaced my Palm Beach plastic surgeon. And the Pompano crowd played better golf and made better company. Not only that, but if they were disappointed to draw me instead of Dave Stockton as their partner, unlike the Californians, they tried not to show it.

After a mediocre round of 73 at the pro-am, I needed to present some news that was bound to piss off Doublewide. I'd refrained from telling him until then due to DW's full-throttle joy over the paint scheme on the Explorer. Dottie Ridge told me via a pay phone chat at the Fort Lauderdale airport that she wanted me to meet a potential endorsement agent whom she'd encountered at the Copenhagen Smokeless Tobacco—Cleavage 500 that had just been run up at Biscuitville Speedway in Tennessee.

Doublewide's response seemed more one of chagrin than the panic-driven outrage that had become such a characteristic trait of his. And Doublewide picked the would-be agent out of the crowd in the lobby back at the Surf King. Amazingly, I would have figured the guy for the president of the Phi Delts at Kent State, down there checking up on his sorority girlfriend. He spotted us, or at least me, walked over, and shook hands.

"Sid Block," he said. Blue Izod shirt. Dockers slacks.

"Any relation to H and R Block?" said Doublewide.

" 'Fraid not," said Sid.

From inside the Wiki-Wiki Room, Sonny Boy Santana was already grinding out another one of his home-cooked classics—"When the Moon Goes Down On Montana, I'll Be Going Down On You." Sid Block said he was going to grab a few materials out of his car and would meet us upstairs in our suite. Since taking the checkered flag in the Yucatán tournament, I beefed up our travel budget to suite status.

On the elevator, Doublewide wore a sneer big enough to paralyze his face. "All of the successful sports agents maintain the same general appearance—kind of like Burt Reynolds. Gold chain. Toupee. Dissipated face that looks like something that was left over after the wax museum burned down. This character ain't gonna cut it. He looks like Wally Cleaver."

I said nothing but could only agree with DW. Ultimately, though, Dottie would call the deciding shot. Doublewide realized that, too, of course, and now his only recourse rested in the scheme of somehow terrorizing Sid Block and hoping that he might go away.

Sid arrived in our suite with his briefcase. First Sid tossed out a roster of some of his clients. A couple of NASCAR drivers, naturally. Chuck "Third Degree Burn" Mayes and Johnny "Cervical Fracture" Foster. A Dodgers relief pitcher from Cambodia. Then the list declined rather sharply. Second string point guard with the Cleveland Cavs. Some ex-con linebacker attempting a comeback with the Steelers.

Then Sid grinned a grad school grin and said, "Right off, I've got to tell you that of all the things that qualify for 'if you have seen one, you have seen them all,' I would think that a Seniors golf tournament would top the list."

Here I must admit that Sid quickly succeeded in even pissing *me* off. Doublewide spat into a wastebasket and snapped, "No shit, Sid? Then probably, you've never been to a rodeo. Or a Super Bowl, as far as that goes. Oh, yeah. NASCAR. Watching a bunch of turkeys turn left for about five hours. Boy, I can't tell you how much that tickles *my* ivories."

Sid backpedaled quickly. "No—no offense. I simply wanted to illustrate the difficulty of securing a major endorsement contract and . . ."

Doublewide pressed the attack. "Seen one, ya seen 'em all, huh? Lessee, how about the Miss America Pageant?

"Or the Boston Marathon?

"Or indoor soccer?

"Or the daytime TV awards show?

"Or a securities fraud trial?

"Or a ski race?

"Or a mall opening?

"Or a dance marathon?

"Or a tractor pull?

"Or a dog sled race?"

Finally, Sid managed to break in. "Please. Hear me out. I just wanted to underscore the fact that . . ."

Doublewide was fast to regain the floor.

"Or a livestock auction?

"Or Wednesday night bingo?

"Or a bass fishing tournament? Ever been to one of those?

"Or a circle jerk?

"Or a cluster fuck?

"Ever watched much water polo?

"How about field hockey?"

Finally Sid Block waved the white flag, packed up and left us alone. I've never seen Doublewide appear quite so smug. Having just drunk deeply from the cup of victory, he now prepared to drink just as deeply from a jug of Jack Black resting nearby on the countertop.

I went back downstairs, back into the melancholy dimness of the Wiki-Wiki Room, just in time to hear Sonny Boy Santana begin to sing, "An original sentimental ballad dedicated to all the shut-ins. 'M-o-o-o-o-n Over Cowtown.' "

A decent-sized gallery, one of the larger ones on the golf course, stood along the first fairway to watch the 9:10 threesome tee off. Tony Jacklin. Bob Charles, the lefty. And me. Former U.S. Open champion. Former British Open champion. Reigning Yucatán Open champion.

Actually, I was beginning to develop a modest following that came to watch those bazooka blasts, courtesy of Big Luther, who had been restored to his previous identity since the Mexico excursion.

"Drive for show; putt for dough." That was the oldest cliche in golf. Happily, I'd been doing both lately. I hoped that continued. My opening round produced more promising results. Big Luther belched out some beauties, the putting was adequate, and we signed a scorecard that registered a 68 that looked solid on the leader board, along with J. C. Snead and Jim Colbert.

That night the routine, and it was becoming more of a routine all the time, would include grilled swordfish, three glasses of chablis, an hour's worth of *ER* and then bed. That routine, however, got knocked off-stride by the unexpected appearance of Sid Block back at the Surf King. Sid gave us that same, "But hear me out" look, and then he told us about an impending endorsement deal. "Major product introduction campaign," he continued, and just as Doublewide was reaching for a steak knife on a nearby buffet table, Sid was wise enough to add, "The manufacturer was impressed with that photo of your van that ran in *USA Today*. Our potential sponsor wants to show the van as part of a TV commercial."

"Not a van, goddamm it. That's an elongated sport utility vehicle," DW countered, but he looked puffed up and pleased that his Birdie-Mobile had received some attention. So Sid followed us back to the suite. "Compensation remains negotiable but here's the scenario. Well wait. Let's backtrack. Are either of you familiar with the manifestations of clinical psychiatric depression? Statistics show that either of you, or someone close to you, is afflicted—"

"Depression?" said Doublewide. "I used to be married to somebody who didn't actually have it. But she was a carrier."

"I don't think you really understand the nature of the condition," Sid came back. "But it strongly affects the demographics involved in Seniors golf telecasts and now, for the first time, an over-the-counter antidepressant medication is about to appear on the market, and before we go any further, just read this script for a television commercial. Both of you would appear. Doublewide's face, all of a sudden, took on that pre-orgiastic look that I remember so vividly from the afternoon when he nearly OD'd on Billy Crossdresser's hard-on powder.

Sid Block handed us both a script prepared, he said, by "the best of the business, the KRH and C agency in Chicago." The script read like this:

SCENE I: (*Camera zooms in on golf pro who is attaching a garden hose to the exhaust pipe of the Birdie-Mobile.*

Camera zooms in with a CLOSE-UP of the face of the caddy, who seems confused.)

CADDY: Gee, Del. What's up?

GOLFER: Search me, Doublewide. But I just can't shake the blues. Insomnia. No appetite. No sex drive. So I think I'll just *do myself in.*

CADDY: I used to know that feeling. But ever since I tried *Zombie*, I'm my old self again! You should try some, too. (*Camera zooms in for CLOSE-UP of caddy holding bottle of pills.*)

SCENE II: (*Golfer makes putt to win tournament. Camera focuses on adoring middle-aged women, applauding in the gallery. Camera zooms in on caddy.*)

CADDY: Great putt, Del!

GOLFER: Yes. And thanks to *Zombie*, I feel alive again! (*Camera zooms in to CLOSE-UP of pill bottle in golfer's hand.*)

I read the thing twice and then a third time, dumbstruck. Finally, I was able to speak.

GOLFER: What is this? Some kind of fucking joke? No. Wait. I get it. Bruno Pratt wrote this and then sent you over here, right?

AGENT (*looking concerned*): Bruno Pratt? What are you talking about? Are you deaf? KRH and C put this together. This is a half-billion dollar campaign.

CADDY (*also looking concerned*): Jesus Jones, Del. Slow down. This deal looks like a keeper to me. Didn't you read that part about the adoring women standing in the background and clapping their asses off? In real life, they'll think I saved your life and every place we stop on the tour, I couldn't beat 'em all off with a rake!

GOLFER: That's easy for you to say. You ain't the

one they've got sucking on the gas pipe. (*Facing AGENT*) Just go back and tell the fellas at KRH and C they can take their garden hose and poke it up their ass.

AGENT (*looking exasperated*): You need to realize that KRH and C won't be offering you any second chances. In case you don't know it, your national identity profile didn't justify your being included in a campaign of this size to begin with . . .

GOLFER (*to agent*): Listen, popdick. You don't realize it, but I established an identity profile as a real life nut case thirty years ago, and I'm not about to reestablish that profile on some shit heel pill commercial. And if they're so goddam slick back at the agency, then how come they didn't figure out that the exhaust gimmick would work better with one of those NASCAR fuckheads?

AGENT (*packing his briefcase*): I can't believe this shit. No wait. I can, too. You're like every other over-the-hill, Hick City client I've tried to fish out of the Nobody Barrel. Always a stage hand but never a star. (*Agent gives golfer a "so long, sucker," look and stomps out of the suite.*)

CADDY (*to golfer*): Know what you just did? You might as well have taken a suitcase with a million in cash inside, carried it over to the drawbridge and dumped it in the canal! (*Camera zooms in to CLOSE-UP of caddy as he opens a sample packet of Zombie pills, swallows the entire supply and washes the pills down with three big pulls of his jug of Jack Black. Camera then shows a CLOSE-UP of caddy as his eyes roll back into his head.*)

(12)

Lee Trevino missed the Pompano Beach tournament with a bad back. He dropped out the day before the thing started because of what was diagnosed as a herniated, or bulging disk. A long time ago, I had suffered from the same thing, except that when it forced me out of the Milwaukee Open, a typo in the newspaper said I was sidelined with a "bulging dick." That's the kind of bullshit that happens to the Del Bonnets of the golf world and never to the Lee Trevinos.

Anyway, in Trevino's absence, a new shark seemed to have arrived in the already treacherously overpopulated aquarium of Seniors golf. In the final round of the Crown Royal Classic, I found myself paired with, or rather against, the previously anonymous Jonny Mitt.

At the start of the day, I was four shots off the lead. Four shots with 18 holes to play. That was what I called my Breeze Zone. While the leader board pressure grabbed the players at the top around the neck, I coasted along in the shadows, poised to grab a big check, if not the winner's trophy. Now this Jonny Mitt character arrived out of nowhere with his barrage of Sunday birdies and suddenly the spotlight rested on him instead of Big Luther and me, where it belonged. Prior to that, the only thing I knew about Jonny Mitt was that this complete Nobody, as in Nobody with a capital "N," had gotten into the tournament as a provisional qualifier for a slot that had become available when Lee Trevino dropped out with a sore back.

Mitt defied everything that was traditional and fundamental about the touring golf professional. True—you would see the occasional unorthodox specimen on the Seniors circuit. Jonny Mitt transcended all of those. First, at about five-foot-four, he was built like a tombstone. Or a bantamweight sumo wrestler. Second, Mitt is left-handed. And third, his custom-designed swing went contrary to anything you'd see illustrated in golf's instructional texts. The motion was flat, herky-jerky, almost frantic, reminding me of the time my mother beat a rat to death on the back porch with a mop.

Every ball he hit went off in a sweeping, low-trajectory hook. His approach shots, even the short irons, came screaming into the greens with this crop-duster-on-fire-and-out-of-control-crash-landing effect. Once the ball hit the ground, you'd think it would roll forever but, instead, the thing screeched to an unnatural half stop three feet from the pin. Hole after hole, he did that, all the time, oblivious to all the people and the TV cameras and crap that can fog the most disciplined of minds out there, particularly on Sunday, when everybody could smell the money.

Every law of physics and kinetics would insist that what Jonny Mitt did with a golf club was cosmically and universally impossible. He also sported this relentless what-the-fuck-have-I-got-to-lose look in his eyes that suggests that the laws of physics and kinetics weren't the only laws he'd broken. Thunderstorm gray eyes. Not the eyes of a killer, necessarily. More like the fearless and determined eyes of a guy who holds up a liquor store with a water pistol.

Somehow, you couldn't help but like Jonny Mitt.

On the 17th hole, Mitt pulled yet another peculiar stunt. The view of the fairway from the tee created a kind of mirage. A sharp dogleg was obscured by a row of palm trees, and a long, white sand trap glared back in the sun beyond that, so it appeared that there was no fairway at all. Mitt launched his left-handed drive off toward a lagoon along an adjoining fairway. Then his ball assumed that odd flight pattern, sailed in behind the palms, and landed in perfect position—although you couldn't see that from the tee. By then, Mitt was tied for the lead with George Archer.

After another flawless approach, Jonny Mitt missed a birdie putt of the one-meter variety, just the ones he'd been popping in all afternoon. Did he choke? No way, not with that wicked little glimmer still in his eyes. I got the impression he yanked the putt on purpose.

Same trip on Number 18, with this treacherous little green about the size of a Ping Pong table. Mitt lay this 6-iron about three and a half on the low side of the pin, absolutely perfectly, and then left his putt about a foot short. Afterward, at the table where he was signing his scorecard, Mitt pretty much confirmed my suspicions.

He cocked his head toward the press tent, where Archer, the winner, was now addressing the laptop and minicam society. "I'm just not up to talking to those fuckers yet," Mitt said, the first words he had uttered all afternoon.

"Those reporters? Hell, they're harmless," I said. Actually, from my experience, they were about as harmless as stomach cancer. I was just trying to make conversation with Jonny Mitt.

"Well, I'm just not ready yet. I haven't got my story straight."

I started to ask Mitt what he meant by that, but all of a sudden, it became obvious. When we'd teed off, the PA announcer identified Mitt as being from Council Bluffs, Iowa. But when Mitt spoke that sentence . . . "I haven't got my story straight" . . . his accent sounded to me, an expert on matters like this, as being Massachusetts-Portuguese, with that carnival worker twang. New Bedford, I'd guess, tempered somewhat by a tell-tale silent "R"—"those fuck-uhs"—favored by itinerant evangelists from central Georgia. Now I would quickly confess that I was not exactly certain what people sounded like in Council Bluffs, but would have hazarded a wager that they didn't talk like *that*.

Thus, deductive reasoning led me to conclude that perhaps Jonny Mitt brought elements from his past that he wished to conceal. That possibility loomed as refreshing. Not that I wish any unfavorable reflections on Jonny Mitt. But now that the Seniors tour seemed to slowly but gradually be assembling some contestants from the realm of the unknown, this could only mean that the shadowy and perhaps dubious background would become an expanding element on our tour.

The whole truth about Jonny's background was something that I would not learn until weeks after this, our "getting to know you" encounter. Mitt, a man of daring as well as someone gifted with rare, albeit unconventional people skills, turned to golf as a livelihood via the hustle route, traveling from village to village, vanishing as quickly as he would arrive. Mitt's plan worked like this: He would ingratiate himself with the local Neds, utilizing a broad inventory of ethnic jokes. Mitt had come to realize that anybody who laughed at that kind of material loomed as someone easily duped in various facets of life. Jonny would then arrange the bet and orchestrate the match in a fashion that enabled him to lose, and lose big, intentionally, on the final hole. He mastered a technique in which he could spin a putt around the circumference of the cup twice—and have the ball hop out.

Phase II of the plan took place at the inevitable card game that followed the golf. Mitt toured the land with a partner who was equipped with rigged decks, an infrared contact lens, and a reflector ring. He also carried a straight razor in his cowboy boot, just in case. Utilization of those devices, along with secret hand signals, enabled Mitt and his traveling companion to win back the golf course losses, sometimes in triplicate. Mostly, the action had been limited to municipal courses, where the size of the stakes, both on the links and in the card room, would be large enough to sustain a living (about a grand a day), but not enough money to attract a lynch mob. Somewhere, though, Team Jonny would overstep its limits. Mitt never told me exactly how, where, or when his operation would eventually cease. All I knew was that at a certain angle, Jonny's face looked kind of lopsided, like he had been in a bad wreck.

But Jonny got lucky. He received a transmission from above. "Hey, Jonny," said the transmission. "If you can train your putts to spin out of the cup, you can also teach 'em to spin right back in." So he'd gone and spun about three dozen of them into the hole during the Seniors Q School and now the tour became endowed with a new and interesting member to its extended family. The emergence of a person like my new friend, Jonny Mitt, who looked like somebody who just stumbled in there from a hog farm, served as a refreshing element.

We retired to a dark and smoky portion of the clubhouse, each equipped with a complimentary jug of Crown Royal, to further our acquaintanceship. Frankly, I'd not really qualified as a full-fledged, card-carrying alkie. The people who run the lucrative dry-out programs would probably dispute that statement.

But I never developed any kind of tolerance for the stuff and gave up the distilled variety, except on rare occasions, after crossing over to the downhill side of the age of forty. That's when I turned health conscious, learned that two to four glasses of the house red does wonders for the heart, lungs, spleen, pancreas, prostate, thyroid, and patella, and I've adhered to the program, with damn few lapses, ever since.

Now Jonny Mitt, evidently, fell into a different category. The day that Jonny's name appears in the obits, they'll have to list Crown Royal among the survivors. He took his straight on the rocks, with damn few rocks. The first glass Jonny absorbed with a measured enthusiasm, like a man encountering an old and cherished friend he hadn't seen for, oh, about eighteen hours. The second glass slid down with the quiet zeal of somebody partaking of life's only reasonable amenity. The third he splashed away with the fervor of a man on the threshold of consummating a relationship with a cheerleader. The fourth glass disappeared with a passion that transcended spiritual rebirth. And on the fifth one, Jonny really began to guzzle the stuff.

And goddamn if I didn't hit the bull's-eye on New Bedford, Massachusetts, although Jonny Mitt was hasty to disassociate himself from what he termed "that fishing boat scum" that had made his hometown noteworthy in the 1980s. "My old man sold life insurance," Mitt insisted.

Life insurance never made its way onto Jonny's horizons, though, as, in the course of about two minutes, he presented a compressed narrative that described thirty years worth of unconnected occupations.

Highway striper in Illinois. Chicken sexer in Arkansas.

Prison guard in Kentucky. Then, after the obvious omission of other career postings, the interesting one: union organizer of the Southwest region of the International Amalgamation of Bakery Workers.

"No job for a pansy," Jonny Mitt insisted over Glass Number 6, the Crown Royal by now casting a warm and benevolent glow throughout what appeared to be his ample reservoir of self-esteem.

"I was busy trying to sign up workers at this tortilla factory in Española. That's this town, the low rider capital of North America, just up the highway from Santa Fe. Low premium on human life out there. The organizer in there before me, they unzipped his belly with a moon-shaped linoleum knife, and he exited the city limits holding his guts in with both hands. So I knew that the management people at the factory had been sizing me up for a shallow grave. And one night they sprung a booby trap."

"How?"

"I'd gone back to this motel where I'd been living, the kind with the little half-ass kitchen and all, and what happened was—the factory people had sneaked in there and unscrewed all the light bulbs, and then they took this five-foot rattlesnake, chopped its rattles off, and stuck him in a sock drawer. And sure enough, the son of a bitch popped me. The whole thing was my fault. Shit. That stunt's older than Barbra Streisand. I shouldda seen it coming."

Jonny Mitt showed off his left hand. Half of his ring finger was missing, the result, he claimed, of his bout with the snake. "Fucked up the nerves in my whole left hand—that's why I hit the golf ball like I do, with all that control. All the strength and all the control comes from the right hand."

By now, my own aspect of reality seemed a trifle hazy, thanks to the Crown, but Jonny Mitt's explanation of his prowess with a set of golf clubs amounted to the most pre-posterously absurd tale I'd ever encountered. It was like one of Dottie Ridge's NASCAR boys finally winning at Daytona with an experiment to run on two flat tires. I felt thrilled and honored to be on the same golf tour with this man.

"Ya know," I said. "Ya know (the Crown was kicking in nicely now), if I were you, Jonny, I think I might keep that story to myself for a while."

Jonny nodded a slow nod. Then he said, "How come?"

"Well, because," I said.

Jonny seemed satisfied with my response at first. Then he leaned forward, apparently desiring a more detailed explanation.

"Ya know, if you tell that to some reporter, then the next thing ya know, it turns up in this magazine for kids, the one we used to all read, ya know-aw what the fuck did they call it? Ya know. *Boy's Life*."

"Not familiar with it."

"Well, anyway. The story winds up in some fuckin' magazine. And the next thing you know, some kid . . . some junior golfer goes out and gets bitten by a snake, on purpose, ya know, and the next thing ya know, his old lady's suing your balls off. Happens all the time."

That struck a reasonable chord with Jonny Mitt. "I've been through the lawsuit ringer," he conceded. "Supposed to have been an uncontested divorce. Don't know which was worse. The uncontested divorce or the snake episode."

With Shakespearean eloquence, Mitt recalled the collapse of his marriage with Gloria, a twenty-four-year union that, like most, involved volumes of bitter and hurtful words, but no busted teeth. Then one night Gloria told Jonny Mitt about the grocery store game.

"She said that for about two or three years, every time she went to the store, just out of boredom, she started playing this little fantasy game where she could sleep with any man she chose in the whole store. But it had to be the first one she chose—if she saw somebody she liked better later on, then that was just tough shit. She had to stick with the first guy.

"Well, that whole business took me by complete surprise. I mean, we'd had our ups and downs and all, but Jesus. So I started hanging out at the store, trying to visualize which ones might be Gloria's fantasy guys. Figured it out pretty quick—this Puerto Rican kid, sacking the groceries."

Jonny Mitt started flexing his messed up left hand. "So finally, I told Gloria, 'Maybe your little pretty boy won't look so cute after I take a two-by-four to his goddam ass.'

"And she said, 'Chill out, Jonny. It's a silly fantasy game.' And then she said, 'Besides. Usually, it's not even him.' So then I said, 'Oh yeah! Well I can play that game just as easy as you can.' So I'd go off to the grocery store for a couple of hours and come home with a bag of radishes. That's when *Gloria* got jealous and, then she said, 'Don't think for a nanosecond that you're getting anybody looking back at you, you little corn-fed ape. So fuck you, Jonny. I'm going to expand this into the Wal-Mart game.'

"And the next thing I know, I'm in there in divorce court, getting slaughtered by Gloria—Imperial Empress from the Planet Bitch!"

Within one hour, maybe even less, the Jonny Mitt in this clubhouse was anything but the same Jonny Mitt with that screwball-deadly golf swing on the course. Those blue-steel eyes had turned to marshmallows. Maybe it was the Crown Royal. Probably it was the long-gone Empress Gloria.

"Uh . . ." I said. I tried to swing the conversation back on a more comfortable track. "Uh . . . Jonny Mitt. That's your real name?"

"Fuck, yeah. Why wouldn't it be?"

Oh, Jesus. Now I've yanked his chain. Look at those eyes now. Back to the mean chill that became so evident on the golf course, with a certain, "It ain't nothin' to me to whip a man's ass" ingredient tossed in as well.

"Well," I said. "Most of the players on the tour have fake names. You rarely see tour golfers with last names that have more than six letters. That's so their names fit better in newspaper headlines and on the leader board. Ernie Els, for chrissakes. You think that's his real name? Check out Tom Kite's birth certificate. Alexander Merriweather Screwdriver. I swear to God."

This Crown Royal. Not bad in the clutch. I ask Jonny Mitt about his reluctance to talk to the newspaper guys. "It worries you that they might write something about you being on the Seniors tour only because you're trying to escape from the Gloria nightmare?"

"How the fuck would they know about that, unless I tell them?"

"Good question."

By now, I was staring at my reflection in the picture window of the clubhouse and humming the melody to a distant refrain—Glen Campbell's "By the Time I Get To Phoenix." That was when I knew I was genuinely plastered. I hadn't hummed in eight years.

"Something's always troubled me about that song," said Mitt.

"Look. I didn't mean to kick off the whole Gloria thing again. Let's forget Gloria." Now I was getting contentious.

"That ain't *it*," said Jonny. "Listen to the song. By the time he gets to Phoenix, she's waking up. Well, obviously, she's back in LA or San Berdoo. Anyway, according to the song, by the time she gets to work, he's in Albuquerque. Well, given the traffic and all, it's gonna take her a while to get to work. So how's he traveling, to get from Phoenix to Albuquerque in that length of time? *Then*—by the time she goes to lunch, he's in Joplin, or some goddam place. Either he's riding in the world's fastest car or—flying in the world's slowest plane. That's the more likely option. Glen Campbell's had it with this chick, see, and now he's long gone, flying his single Cessna into a stiff head wind."

"Maybe Glen's just out of his mind with sorrow after getting his balls mashed in the grocery store game," I said.

"Or maybe Glen's freaked out because he had a wreck while some bitch was strapping some skull on him and got laughed off the golf tour," Jonny Mitt said. Jonny tipped his quart of Crown Royal into his glass, then mine, and then his bottle was empty.

Over the next five days, that sickeningly divine taste of Crown Royal seeped from beneath my tongue, a ceaseless reminder of my strange day with Jonny Mitt.

$$\textbf{(13)}$$

If any of the assembled media had bothered to solicit Team Del's Golf Tip of the Day—and none of them did—it would have been this: Avoid embarking upon a competitive round while suffering from a red wine hangover. What a misery-filled, eighteen-hole odyssey of despair this day became, as I attempted intricate shot-making efforts on a demanding uphill-downhill layout while what seemed like a full-scale Harley-Davidson pep rally echoed and resounded between my ears. I considered actually writing a book about Friday's experience and calling it *The Wrath of Grapes*.

Fortunately for Team Del, the majority of the competition was working against a similar impairment. The field established a Seniors tour record for the highest score ever to lead an opening round—73. One reason for all of the disgraceful scores could be blamed on the tour schedule maker. We'd been playing on all of these beach and desert resort courses where the terrain was perfectly horizontal and suddenly, for no apparent reason, they shipped us off into the unfamiliar strangeness of the hill country where all of the fairways seemed so . . . well . . . vertical. That situation, sadly, did not constitute the real foundation of the dilemma.

See, this week's event was something known as the Barn-yard Bordeaux Seniors Classic sponsored by the Arkansas wine industry, held at the Kissin' Cousins Golf Ranch near Eureka Springs. They brought the tour in to promote the notion that top-quality marijuana isn't the only product that grows wild up here in the Ozarks. So the tournament organizers had been kind enough to stage this big wine tasting party the night before the tournament began. Everybody came and everybody partook. The major provider of the party supplies was the local Isaac Newton Vineyard, with its proud advertising slogan of "What Goes Down Must Come Up." Doctors specializing in stomach transplants should endorse their product, particularly the merlot.

I felt sorry for all of the nice people who paid to watch what happened on the golf course the next day. They should have demanded their money back, except for the ones with a macabre sense of humor. Imagine the scenario of a hundred old men trying to play this most unforgiving of all games, while suffering from a collective case of the dry heaves. Never in the history of this tour had the seniors looked so abject, refugees from the realm of the undead, lacing their Gatorade with Geritol. One of the women volunteer score keepers watched one threesome stagger through and said, "Jeez. It smells like sulphur around here."

Prior to this unhappy occasion, we had largely remained faithful to the Team Del Wellness Campaign, so we simply were not accustomed to such attacks on our central nervous systems. Team Del does not traffic in excuses, but that amplified the grave nature of our morning-after "condition." I survived the round on automatic pilot, which meant putting Big Luther in total command. What Team Del conventionally did, and this is hardly classified information because a lot of pros did it, too, was to select a tiny little target, like a rock or a divot, way the hell out there on the fairway, where you want to hit the golf ball, and then form some imaginary cross-hairs and aim for that particular spot. You seldom hit it, but the idea, naturally, is to come reasonably close.

After the wine debacle, Team Del was not only unable to pinpoint the distant target, we could barely see the damn fairway. So we turned to Big Luther to save our ass and that's what he did. On two occasions, he scared us by steering tee shots out across a lake and then allowing a stiff crosswind to blow the ball back onto the edge of the fairway. Risky business. I wouldn't recommend it. But it worked, and at last, I awoke, wobbling toward the 18th green and needing only to two-putt from a reasonable distance to finish with a 75. Under the circumstances, I rated this as, if the not our best, then certainly our most courageous round of the tour so far. No triple bogeys and we hadn't thrown up or been required to have anything amputated. Team Del chalked this one up as a building block toward the ultimate mission, which was still winning the Seniors Open. A demonstration of character, thrust against the smirking face of adversity. That's the idea! Whenever Team Del posted a horseshit round, we would file it away as a learning experience.

As we'd trudged across the battle-torn back nine, I had peered through a self-imposed greenish mist and noticed that Team Del had attracted a gallery. A gallery of one, but still, a gallery. Doublewide kept wandering over and talking to the guy. It was not until I'd steadied my right hand with my left and signed the scorecard that I recognized our Lone Fan. It was Billy Crossdresser, the Seminole, the man who looked so perpetually refreshed. Why in the hell was Billy wandering around up here in the Ozarks, instead of back in the swamp where he belonged?

Well, he was traveling through the region for business

purposes, Crossdresser explained, and decided to stop by and check out our act. "The entire city of Immokalee has sort of adopted you guys and we're happy to see that you've enjoyed some success," Crossdresser said.

City? The old Del might have fashioned a politely sarcastic response to Crossdresser's designation of the place where he lived. About four hundred tarantula-eating degenerates with a bunch of rusted hot water heaters in their front yards. They call their high school football team the Fighting Paint Sniffers. "You think that's a city?" The new Del merely grinned and nodded. The Seminole invited us to dinner that night. Doublewide declined, since he had tickets to the passion play that people flock in to watch. All of the caddies had received freebies. This area maintains a very Jesus-driven economy, as evidenced by a mountainside statue of the man that's about the size of the Empire State Building. I agreed to meet Crossdresser. On that occasion when I'd first met him, back in his swell house on the outskirts of the 'Glades, I couldn't genuinely contend that I'd disliked the cocky bastard. No, not disliked necessarily, but he'd made me uneasy, a feeling generated by the suspicion that Dottie Ridge had somehow seemed attracted to him. Silly me. Why would a woman like Dottie Ridge fall for a rich Indian when she could have a Seniors golfer?

That night, Crossdresser and I arrived simultaneously at the critically acclaimed Aunt Sukie's Smokehouse, famous for its twenty-six varieties of cheese grits—me in the Team Del Victory Wagon and him in a 'Vette the color of French's mustard, bearing a bumper sticker that read, "Custer Wore Arrow Shirts." I was rather surprised that he didn't sport one of those little pony tails, but guessed he didn't want to overplay that Native American angle. In fact, Crossdresser wore an immaculately tailored wool suit that probably cost as much as his car. Boy, did he stand out from the rest of the crowd in that restaurant. Most of the patrons wore Xtra-large jogging suits that still fit snugly among an assembly of full-figured persons of both genders. Doublewide McBride could land work modeling swimsuit attire in this part of the world. I complimented Crossdresser on the quality of his wardrobe presentation. He grinned. "That's the first thing you're taught at the Harvard Business School," he declared. "Dress British and think Yiddish!"

Harvard, was it? That night back in Florida, I clearly remembered Crossdresser having said that he'd gone to Oxford. "Here's what they taught us at Will Rogers State," I said. "Never buy a house from a one-legged gypsy."

"Where in the *hell* is Will Rogers State?"

"Not far from here, actually."

"Were you in their MBA program?"

"I don't believe they had one," I answered seriously. "My degree is in Picnic and Rest Area Management."

The waitress, who'd identified herself as Eugenia, stopped to take our order. She was dressed up like an extra on *Little House on the Prairie*. All of the waitresses were. Crossdresser wanted trout, but asked a lot of questions. Where did they catch the trout? When did they catch it? Can you sprinkle a little fresh dill on it? And how about chopping a couple of hard boiled eggs on the cheese grits?

As previously stated, my first impression of Billy Crossdresser—and like most people, I maintained hair-trigger first impressions—was that I just didn't much care for the guy. Now I formed a second impression. On my personalized Asshole Richter scale, Billy scored a 4.5. But then I consistently rated a 4.2. It had been scientifically determined that almost everybody falls somewhere in that 4-point range if you can get 'em drunk enough, the outstanding exception being Bruno Pratt, the perfect 10.

Then Billy, who wore one of those wristwatches that had a black dial with a bunch of little numbers on it like some instrument in a B-52 cockpit, rifled me with a bunch of questions about golf and, in particular, why I hit my drives longer than anybody on the course. I changed the subject. Not because golf was an off-limits topic. I was still sort of queasy from that day's hungover round and didn't want to think about it.

"Explain, if you don't mind, what kind of business you're doing in Arkansas."

"Arkansas and other places," Crossdresser began. He talked loudly because the people at the next table were making a big racket. They were heading over to Branson, Missouri the next day, having traveled all the way from Hobbs, New Mexico just to hear Jimmy Dean sing "Big John" in person.

"I'm assembling some venture capital for the project of my life and a lot of other people's lives," Crossdresser went on. "It's a full-phase, self-contained retirement community, patterned after the Sun City concept—but for Native Americans only. I'm calling it *Habitat*."

"Where are you going to put Habitat?"

"Right outside Immokalee."

"God a-mighty. I'm not trying to sound rude, but how can you stick a retirement community in the middle of a fuckin' swamp? I've seen bugs around there the size of black angus steers. Not to mention the snakes." All of this knowing that Crossdresser would come back with the perfect solution and, of course, he did.

His mouth formed into an upwardly semicircular configuration that the average schmuck calls a smile. It was not a smile, but rather a signal that slick characters like Cross-dresser send out that says, "I've got you by the balls."

"Stilts," Crossdresser said, very much in the same tone as the guy said "plastics" in *The Graduate*. "Homes on stilts. Shops on stilts. A hospital on stilts. Several churches. And, yes, even a continuing-education community college. All on stilts! Plus—and consider the beautiful aesthetic of this—you have the security of a gated community without the cloistered effect that provides the profound psychological impression of being a captive! Think of it!"

And I thought of it. A town full of Indians living on stilts. They could sit on the front porch and drop water balloons on the meter readers. No burglar bars, either. All they have to do is grease the stilts. "I suppose that a golf course on stilts might be out of the question," I said. "But tennis courts. A bowling alley. The world's first casino on stilts . . ." Coming on too smug now. Time for a legitimate question.

"Billy, how can you limit a place like Habitat to Native Americans? Ain't that against the law? Reverse discrimination or something?"

"OK. All the potential Habitat shareholder—that's what we call them—needs to do is sign a form that certifies that they have some Native American ancestry. We don't check. Mayor Daley, in Chicago, used to make the same speech every St. Patrick's Day. 'There are two kinds of people! The Irish and those who wished they were!' I think it's the same with Native Americans. And you would be surprised how many Americans actually do have some Native American blood."

"No, I wouldn't be surprised," I answered truthfully. "I grew up in Kansas, down in sub-Lutheran country, where they've got a shit-load of semi–Native Americans. You can't tell it so much in the daylight, but at night, with neon signs reflecting off their faces, that's when it becomes so apparent. And let me tell you something else. You want to meet a Native American? You're talkin' to one!"

"What tribe?"

"Omaha. In fact, my great-uncle, Chester Moose, was voted Indian of the Year in Kentucky twice in a row. He was a well-known disc jockey in some town over there," said the golf pro, wondering whether Crossdresser thought he was being put on. Probably not. He didn't regard me as clever enough.

"Then," said Crossdresser, advancing smoothly, "I'll look forward to seeing you on our Habitat shareholder roster. As you suggested, there's no golf course in our immediate plans. Perhaps you could run for sheriff. By the way, and I don't think I'm violating any confidences here—I think that Miz Dot might be planning to become a major Habitat investor."

Miz Dot! He made Dottie Ridge sound like some old granny back on the plantation. Who does this moon-worshiping motherfucker think he is? Fortunately, Eugenia arrived with the food before I could register any sign of displeasure. It became clear that Crossdresser had been probing for one of my hot buttons and he would not succeed.

No dill on the trout, but Crossdresser did not complain. Rather, his mouth once again formed into that pseudo smile of his. "Tell me about you and Miz Dot. Any matrimonial plans there?" Next, he'll probably ask if her tits are real.

"That's not been discussed."

The fact was that it *had* been initially discussed, although not anytime recently and that had been troubling. The employer-employee aspect of our arrangement generated a negative impact on the nicer part of the relationship. No doubt about that. Male bosses are supposed to marry their secretaries. Not vice versa.

"What Dottie and I have is an agreement where she assists me in attaining my, uh, goals on this Seniors tour."

"What goals?"

"To win the United States Seniors Open, specifically. That's the mutual goal of each player on the tour. The U.S. Open is the only tournament that matters. Win it and you win whatever immortality Seniors golf can bestow on an individual, not to mention ancillary benefits, in the form of corporate representation agreements." As the words came out, the pro wondered where he'd picked up that kind of bullshit. "Of course, there are about twenty-five lesser events and if you're any good at all, you can knock down close to seven figures. Team Del, to date, is on schedule."

"What about the Open?" Crossdresser countered. "Does Team Del actually believe it can win that?"

"Yep. If it can overcome one particular obstacle." Hell. Why not tell him the truth? "There's this character, sum-bitch named Bruno Pratt, who's sort of my personal Moby Dick. Well. Not sort of. He is—he's a one-man Moby Dick. I was thinking about him a little while ago. I think about him all the time. I could give up golf and buy the whole fuckin' Habitat with pocket change simply by collecting the reward money from the various places Bruno Pratt has escaped from."

Crossdresser offered his full and complete attention. He wanted to know more about this man.

"A little-known feature about Bruno is that he's the only golfer in the PGA with a glass eye. He claims he got wounded out in Vietnam, which is a total goddam lie. He's so disgusting, the Viet Cong wouldn't even allow him in their country. Bruno cornered the market on slime. When he was a little kid, some other little kid accidently poked Bruno's eye out with a spoon. That was his nickname when he was growing up. Spooner. And one could suppose that pissed Bruno off, which was why he turned out to be such a fuckin' prick. But I know a few other folks with glass eyes, and they're perfectly normal. Damn good people, in fact."

"How is it," Crossdresser asked, seeming very intent, "that you know all this about Bruno Pratt? About the eye and all, I mean."

"Now. Now we arrive at the heart of the polemic (you're required to use that word in a complete sentence in order to graduate from Will Rogers State). There was a woman— Colleen Bateman—girlfriend of mine, ex-fiancé maybe even. She had a body like a little rubber monkey, and she told me the story about Bruno's eye. Begging the question: How did *Colleen* know that? Eventually, the truth came out, like it always does. Bruno himself told her the story and she felt sorry for him . . . 'poor little Spooner,' . . . and wound up giving him a blow job!"

"Amazing." That was Billy Crossdresser's assessment.

The next day, Team Del shot a 69. At the eighteenth (or The Last, as all the TV announcers were calling it now . . . how hokey was that?), we mis-hit a putt and it actually bounced across the green and right into the cup. Team Del wouldn't win the Barnyard Bordeaux Seniors event, and didn't particularly want to, because first place also received a year's supply of Arkansas wine. We were nicely positioned for another top ten finish, gathering confidence and momentum for the push toward the U.S. Open. But a faint residue of concern lingered about the dinner session with Billy

Crossdresser, the kind of man who can't take a leak without having some kind of ulterior motive.

He'd wanted to find something out, and I hoped I hadn't given it to him.

14

At the helm of the Team Del Challenger van, Doublewide McBride explained why Ocala ranked as one of the best known cities in America. "Ocala turns up as answers in the *New York Times* crossword at least three times a week," Doublewide said. "Five letter clue—city in Florida. It's always Ocala. Never Miami. Never Tampa. Wanna know why? Because the puzzle-maker needs that o-a-a vowel combination. They could accomplish the same thing with Omaha, but 'city in Nebraska' is too easy."

I had Ocala on my mind, too, but for a different reason. That morning's mission, which had been accomplished, involved lying in the rear of the Explorer and completing one thousand sit-ups during a fifty-minute stretch of highway between Gainesville and Ocala.

From outside the tinted glass, I could see people gawking at the Team Del-mobile, with its obscene paint scheme that looked like the aftermath of a butane gas explosion at a fruit stand. They peered at us from that annual parade of invading minivans that happened in Florida every spring . . . vans sporting the license tags of New Jersey, the Irritated Colon Syndrome State; Kentucky, the Misery Loves Company State; Texas, the String 'Em Up by the Balls State; Indiana, the Mucus State; Illinois, the Seventy-seven Years Before Eligible

For Parole State; Vermont, the Slow Leak State; Michigan, the Root Canal State; Delaware, the Ennui State; Wisconsin, the Sodium State; Louisiana, the Show Us Your Tits State; New York, the Go Fuck Yourself State. And so on.

Soon, the sit-up ordeal became more appealing than watching the license plates sail past. I hit the magic one thousand just as we whipped past a sign that said Ocala was still twelve miles ahead.

"Not bad for an old fart," I thought. And then I also thought, "That's exactly the kind of thinking that Courtney Braeswood might point out as self-defeating, had I chosen to take on her services."

Courtney Braeswood was a shrink. A psychologist, actually, as opposed to a psychiatrist. Most people think that a shrink is a shrink, which is a serious misapprehension. Doublewide, the babbling encyclopedia, had pontificated on that topic earlier in the morning. "Psychiatrists deal with the genuine coo-coos," he said. "One minute they think they're Jesus Christ, the next they think they're Ted Kennedy. Psychologists—they make their money off people who don't sleep very well because they're temporarily fucked up."

Or, in the case of Dr. Braeswood, people like me, who were fucked up but knew it, or, in her estimation, *not* fucked up but ought to be. Dr. Braeswood latched onto me in a motel parking lot in Tallahassee after I had registered yet another top ten finish, that time at the Gold Bond Medicated Powder Golf Classic. She told me she'd been watching me. She told me I should have won the thing. She said that body language over the final nine holes told the whole story.

My stride, brisk and confident through the first six holes, had become tentative. She said that at the end, I kind of shuffled down the 18th fairway, getting in touch with my inner Woody Allen, because some destructive voice from the murky cerebral depths kept whispering that I didn't *deserve* to win, a voice that was all-too commonly heard by men of my age, but a voice that could be shut out, muted, and silenced forever after about $50,000 worth of counseling.

Our discussion became contentious. "As for the tentative nature of my stride, to put it candidly, Dr. Braeswood, I was suffering this afternoon from a medical condition that is commonly known as jock itch. You know the old saying, Dr. Braeswood? 'When the going gets tough, the tough get going'? Well, I don't care how tough a person might be.

"When your balls are smokin', it's hard to concentrate. But, hey! You know what? Rather than curse the darkness, I decided to light a candle. I did something proactive. Right after my round, I went and purchased a can of the outstanding product manufactured by the benevolent sponsor of this event, Gold Bond medicated powder, and now I'm a new man. And it only cost $2.79.

"Now, Dr. Braeswood, I'm not the kind of person who jumps to conclusions. You can't tell a book by its cover, I always say, but you don't appear to be the kind of person who's ever suffered the agony of jock itch. So you probably don't know what I'm talking about. And lemmee take this one step further. You know what I kept telling myself all during that back nine? I said, 'God, awmighty. This rash burns like hell. But at least I don't have hemorrhoids.' I think that's a healthy attitude."

Dr. Braeswood, who wore earrings that looked like the chandeliers at Harrah's Casino in Shreveport, earrings that suggested she might have had a few rats of her own in the basement of her psyche, refused to let go. That jock itch fable, she insisted, stood out as an obvious symptom of a person stumbling through life "controlled by delusional rationalization."

"Check out my crimson crotch, and I'll show you delusional rationalization." I didn't say that but probably should have. What I did say was, "Dr. Braeswood, none of that matters. I didn't win the tournament because Hale Irwin shot 64-64, and there's nothing I can do about that. That's the peculiar nature of the game. You have no control over what the other guy does, and that's why golf can be so frustrating." I explained that as patiently as I knew how.

So Dr. Braeswood gave up and walked away, rather stiffly, I thought. Talk about body language. Hers seemed to announce, "Listen, you smart ass. After you miss the cut at seven straight tournaments, you'll come slinking back to me, sometime around the Fourth of July, and you'll be begging for answers. But I ain't gonna be able to provide you any, and you wanna know why, you hopeless, shriveled up, old monkey turd? Because I am through wasting my time ministering to terminal do-dahs like you. So I'm gonna blow off this sports motivation gig and open a line of cosmetics."

Don't get me wrong. I wasn't trying to trivialize what Dr. Braeswood did, or tried to do, although, if I were to avail myself of her services, I'd bet it wouldn't be fifteen minutes before she got around to the topic of how often I jerk off.

Actually, I'd be curious about her interpretation of the fact that my mother didn't quit breast feeding me until I was four years old (I went literally from breast milk to cold beer) and, with my fifty-fourth birthday coming up, I was having a sexual relationship with a woman, the former Miss Chiquita Banana, who, biologically, was old enough to be my mother. Or this latest troublesome deviation from the norm, where I had become convinced that Del Bonnet and a golf club named Big Luther were the same person. Wouldn't Dr. Braeswood have a field day with that material?

Whether or not that fascinating (at least I thought it was fascinating) pattern of events contributed to the fact that earnings were about double our original projections to that date on the Seniors tour remained. I was sure that Dr. Braeswood could have supplied an opinion. The point was, if it was working, why fuck with it?

I considered Dottie Ridge's NASCAR boys. They finally got a decent finish—around 14th at Rockingham—and then they practically gave that Ford Taurus a hysterectomy, and what do you know? The very next week, they ran 43rd and last at Bristol. Dottie didn't say anything to Moonie Van Sickel, the crew chief. She was too smart to get very involved in the operational side of the motor stuff. But I privately knew that she was hot about the changes. *Hot!*

Now there I was sixth on the PGA Seniors money list and here came this gruesome little hillbilly with mean looking teeth, Jacob Thornhill, representing something called Digi-Com Industries, trying to peddle this imaging device that identified the flaws in my swing.

Creeps like that scared the crap out of me. So did Dr. Braeswood, frankly. In fact, she was even more dangerous. What she didn't realize was that playing a high stakes round of golf in one of those PGA events can be like sitting in solitary confinement. You had way too much time to think, to contemplate.

I mean, you're out there a couple of shots out of the lead, standing in the rough with your ball half buried in peat moss, and there is Billy Casper up on the green, wearing his tomato-colored knickers, scratching his big butt and taking his usual eternity to line up a nine-inch putt. Two minutes. Three minutes. The time trudged by like January in North Dakota.

What Dr. Braeswood would have recommended called for visualizing my next shot, visualizing the calm, smooth swing and visualizing the golf ball, a perfect white dot against the azure sky, and then visualizing the ball thumping unto the green, taking a couple of cute little hops and then nestling into the cup.

Out there on that all-too-real golf course, what I visualized was this giganitic bird, circling above the green and then letting go with about two gallons of bird crap that landed right on Billy Casper's head. That was what I visualized and that was what kept me sane.

So the routine continued that week in Orlando at the Goldman Sachs Shootout, one of the biggest stops of the Seniors season and the last leg on the Florida aspect of the tour. Golf constituted a huge growth industry in Florida, the sportsman's utopia. Golf, in fact, surpassed the quest of foreign tourists as the favorite outdoor diversion among the natives—although that was still big. A few days earlier, one of the sports sections ran a feature about a hunter who bagged a seventeen-point Brit at a rest stop along the Interstate, and still another sportsman who reeled in a world record three hundred-pound Dutchman, right off a pier in Key Biscayne, using blood bait.

But nothing outweighed golf anymore, particularly at that Orlando extravaganza. Celebrities out the ass. Big prize money. Major distractions, although Big Luther and I got better at adapting to those with every tournament. Orlando, though, presented broader challenges.

On Tuesday night, I had to show up at a huge awards banquet, which was a fund raiser for the Florida Sportswriters Association, underwritten by the grapefruit people. I'm one of five nominees for one of the minor prizes, the Swede Magnusen Award that they gave to the Florida comeback sports personality of the year. Swede Nelson was this sportswriter who choked to death one night after he'd swallowed a swizzle stick.

I had been told in advance that I would be an also-ran. The winner of that year's Swede Magnusen Award was Corey Coletta, a trainer whose horses won several major stakes races at Gulfstream just weeks after he'd been released from a three-year stretch for securities fraud. So I wouldn't have to prepare an acceptance speech and hats off to Corey.

The fact that I was nominated is a major PR lick for Team Del, though. Even Dottie Ridge had flown up to attend, as my date, yet—although she usually avoided us at the tournaments, with things proceeding so nicely and all. Actually, the awards thing was a convenient one-night stopover for Dottie. She was en route to South Carolina to visit her racing team, for whom things were *not* proceeding so nicely, to see what they could fuck up next. The week before at Atlanta, they ran out of gas a full two laps short of the finish. What a bunch of yahoos. I was no longer jealous of the NASCAR boys.

Dottie was her usual knockout self at the banquet, showing up in a lilac gown. Unfortunately, Doublewide McBride also came along, completing the Team Del troika. It was Dottie who insisted on having him come. Doublewide, I must say, offered a distinguished profile in his rented formal ensemble, complete with little pearl studs on his pleated white shirt. He appeared, if not senatorial, then at least like a leading candidate for the presidency of the Orlando New Car Dealers Association.

Doublewide's appearance was not a matter of concern. His eventual mental condition was my chief worry. I knew that Doublewide was still hoarding some of the sample supplies of Zombie, those new over-the-counter pills that were supposed to chase the blues away. In Doublewide's case, the Zombie produces a side effect that enabled him to behave in a fashion reminiscent of a young, actress, Linda Blair, in a motion picture entitled *The Exorcist*. If Doublewide popped a fistful of Zombies and later on took two or three slugs of 151 rum, well, we'd have a genuine crisis on our hands.

This awards thing was set up in one of those new Orlando hotels, the Jungle Book Regency, where heavy stress seemed to have been placed on structural overstatement, an architectural showcase that had been designed to out-Vegas Las Vegas and make Dallas and Houston appear sedate. In terms of interior vastness, Carlsbad Caverns rated a distant second.

After a ten-minute stroll through the lobby, a valley of life-sized jade giraffes and sequined elephants with genuine ivory tusks, we were directed inside the Katmandu Room, which would serve as the banquet hall. That room, the size of a dirigible hangar, contained a colossal display of sculptural objects, allegedly gathered from the East, both Middle and Far. The entire interior design display might best have been viewed through 3-D glasses and the wife of a man whose name tag identified him as the mayor of Cummings, Georgia, defined the setting as "gaw-shay."

The Katmandu Room was jammed with recognizable faces—recognizable if you watched enough sports on TV. Steve Spurrier. Jim Leyland. Penny Hardaway. Dan Marino. Greg Norman. And Doublewide McBride of fleeting *ESPN* fame, who didn't give a crap who was there as he thundered like Secretariat across the rich green carpet toward the open bar. Now it was time to get nervous.

All day, I'd encouraged Doublewide to stay back at the motel and work on the chapter outline for the proposal for his autobiography that he was having ghostwritten—now with the working title of *Siphoning Tractor Gas and Rolling*

Queers: One Man's Story of Modern Survival. Of course, Dottie Ridge wouldn't hear of leaving the noble caddy behind, but if she'd known about the Zombie pills, Dottie might not have been so altruistic.

Naturally, my most dire fears soon took form there in the Katmandu Room. Doublewide's face slowly took on the look of something from a *Star Trek* episode—nothing monstrous, a good guy from another galaxy, but different enough to appear conspicuously peculiar for a man attending a sports banquet in Orlando.

While obviously attempting to stand perfectly erect, Doublewide was actually tilting at a leftward angle, about 15 degrees, and that, too, was noticeable. If he'd only displayed the good manners to topple over—the common human decency to just pass out. But no. Doublewide seemed intent on making conversation with the other celebrities in his midst.

Finally, I slid across the room, near one of the sixty-foot long bars where Doublewide was stationed. "Say, Hoss. Let's head into the john," I offered. "Looks like you could stand to blow your beets. I know I could."

Doublewide wouldn't budge. I snatched him by the elbow. "Then let's wander back over to the bar. Get a little dry sherry." Doublewide remained locked in place, like granite, gazing at Senator Carter, chairman of the Finance Committee. Yes, a man frequently mentioned as a possible presidential candidate, standing not ten feet away, chatting with Ted Turner and Jane Fonda.

"Who *is* that fucker? This is driving me nuts. One way to find out." Doublewide lurched—swaying and stumbling like a man trying to maintain his balance during an earthquake—over to where Senator Carter was standing. "I know you," he began. "I *know* I know you from somewhere."

Then an expression of benign recognition crossed Doublewide's countenance. "Of *course*," he boomed. "I got it now. You're that little sawed off sonuvabitch who runs that C and C Wrecking Yard on the highway up by Haines City. You probably don't remember me, but I bought an oil filter off you a while back, and now I believe my whole damn car's blown up. They told me to take it back down there and have you pay for it."

Senator Carter appeared appropriately stunned. "Pay for what?" he said.

"Pay for the damn motor, that's what," Doublewide countered. It was easy to hear throughout most of the room, even though the place was the size of Madison Square Garden.

"Who told you that?"

Then it dawned on the senator that this, indeed, was no joke. By then, approximately two hundred people among the star-spangled gathering had become keenly interested witnesses.

"They told me that up in Haines City, by God. They said that, by God, if he don't pay, then whip his goddam ass. You run a pretty damn shitty business anyway, I always thought."

At this point, let me say something on behalf of the Jungle Book Regency Hotel. The response time displayed by their security people must have been unsurpassed. At the exact instant that the look of profound dismay appeared on Senator Carter's face, two goons with walkie talkies snatched Doublewide—one on the left arm, one on the right—elevated his feet eight inches off the floor and transported my caddy in the direction of an exit.

"You evidently don't know who I am," I heard Doublewide scream as he disappeared through the doorway.

During the awards banquet, three chairs were reserved at

the place settings adorned with red, white, and blue "Team Del" logos. But only two of the chairs were occupied. Half-back Gonorrhea Buchanan, another nominee for the comeback man of the year award, sat at our table and kept issuing dirty looks at Dottie and me. Also at the table was Don Shula, who avoided eye contact entirely.

Dottie didn't utter a damn word; didn't have to, in fact, since this was one of those circumstances where male and female companions could communicate telepathically. She beamed out the same transmission—over, and over and over. "Goddamn you. You knew this was going to happen. This could have been prevented. Why didn't you warn me?"

I tried to respond via the same wavelength: "It could have been worse, Dottie. You should have seen what happened when he OD'd on Billy Crossdresser's sexual enhancement drug from the swampland." That message never got through. Dottie was jamming my signal.

After the ordeal ended, Dottie claimed she had a headache and went directly back to her hotel. Alone, of course. Back at the official Team Del headquarters, the Donald Duck Red Roof Inn, I found Doublewide, still in his tux, face up and asleep on the floor, snoring so loudly that the room shook. The trucker in the next room was kicking the wall and threatening to call the cops. I stuffed a wash rag into Doublewide's mouth, wishing urgently, but, of course, in vain that I had done the same thing three hours earlier.

15

Happily for Team Del, Doublewide's remarkable performance met with scant repercussions. There had been a small notation of the indiscretion in the public print. A reporter for the Orlando newspaper noted that the senator had been "accosted by a drunk Republican." Nothing more and Dottie Ridge no longer felt obligated to yank the funding plug on Team Del. Now I merely sought a reasonably quiet evening to concentrate on the day job, which was playing in these golf tournaments.

The plan, as usual, entailed early retirement in the motel room with a made-for-TV movie, *Bobo's Advocate*, then peaceful slumber. Funny thing. Ever since that woman in California, Carol DelHomme, told me that she used to be married to the actor Chandler King, every time I'd turned on the TV, who popped up but Chandler King? Here's Chandler King playing a scoutmaster on *The Brady Bunch*, there's Chandler King playing a crooked police detective on *Mannix*. Now, in *Bobo's Advocate*, he was portraying a shithead. Actually, he was supposed to be a DA prosecuting Bobo, a partially retarded washing machine repairman wrongfully accused of strangling a socialite. Bobo's lawyer is a Latino actress who looked to be all of fourteen.

She went to Chandler King, who comes across as a sexist

at best, hoping to get the charges reduced to manslaughter. He said, "In your dreams, Cupcake. In your dreams."

In the courtroom, Chandler King demonstrated a big time strut when Bobo sat there sucking his thumb, and figured he was about to fry. Of course, the little Cupcake eventually shreds Chandler's case. In the end, we saw several closeups of Chandler, looking less arrogant and a little concerned that Bobo might walk. Another closeup and we saw another expression, one that implied respect. I pictured Chandler King staring into a mirror, trying out several expressions before getting the exact nuance—arrogant but respectful. I had to admit he was a pretty damn good actor. Hard to believe what Carol had told me . . . that when she found out that Chandler's favorite song was "A Boy Named Sue," she'd ditched the fucker.

Then, talk about coincidence, the phone rang. It was Carol DelHomme, calling from California. I guessed that she might be a little bit loaded, though she was not slurring. "I've been thinking about you," she said. "Is it all right if I think about you?"

"As long as you don't dream about me. That's when it can get, well, you know. Personal."

"Uh-huh. I was thinking maybe we could do something together one of these days, but I think that you told me that you were already involved—involved with some, ah, some old woman, I think you said. Yes. That was it. You said that you'd been screwing some rich old woman."

"I didn't say that and you know it."

"Then you're saying you're not?"

"I'm saying there is no reason why we can't—do something together."

"Maybe that's not a good idea. I've known you for what? Fifteen minutes. Right now, the studio is developing a project, a true story. The Mavis Wilcox story. You might know about that one. Mavis met this guy on the Internet. They really hit it off and so he flies all the way to North Carolina and shows up on her front porch. He was about six-foot-three, so naturally, Mavis let him move in. Then he starts telling about how he's an undercover agent, hiding from these Arab terrorists and can he borrow about twelve grand? So Mavis writes him the check and you can guess what happens next. She comes home from work and he's long gone—and what's also missing is all of Mavis's shoes, cosmetics, and underwear. She's been in a coma ever since. So I got to thinking about you and realized, 'Goddamn. I don't know that sumbitch from Hopalong Cassidy.' So what do you think?"

"I think that we ought to get together and do something."

Carol hung up, but the phone call seemed to rejuvenate my spirits.

And, as a pleasing although anticlimactic footnote to that conversation, I won the fucking Goldman Sachs Shootout, along with the first place check for two hundred grand, in what I would modestly describe as the single most outstanding demonstration of golfing talent in my entire goddam career and probably anybody else's as well.

First lemmee say that the golf course where they staged this tournament, Anagustura Lakes, could be meaner than Cherokee Sharp. Cherokee was a former female acquaintance of mine from the 1970s, the decade where whatever sex you got didn't count because it was so easy, who slashed my tires one night for no particular reason. Furthermore, I believed that she unsuccessfully poisoned my cocker spaniel, Lucinda. This substance that looked like buttermilk came squirting out of Lucinda's ass for about a week, but she finally got well.

So, hopefully, that might have provided an illustration of the hardships that were scripted into the landscape by the fiendishly sadistic people who blueprinted Anagustura Lakes.

Something you saw at a lot of those country clubs was that each of the eighteen holes had its own name, identified by signs on the tee boxes—Cherry Blossom or Robin's Nest and crap like that. Well, at Anagustura Lakes, the sign on the first tee read "Betty Ford Hotline." They called No. 2 "Castration Creek." No. 3 was "Sugar in Your Gas Tank." Et cetera. I particularly liked what they called No. 8— "You'll Regret The Day You Were Born, You Stupid Mother Fucker."

The final five holes were known collectively as simply "Death Row." Here's why. Four of the holes were long par 4's, with fairways that sloped sharply to the left. Unless you could place your drive along a six-yard shelf, it'd trickle down into a lake. No. 18 included the added feature of a row of palm trees arranged diagonally along the front of the green like the teeth of a comb. There was one other hole along Death Row (those holes were subtitled "Lethal Injection, Firing Squad, Electric Chair, Gas Chamber, and Hanged By The Neck Until Dead"), No. 16, the only par 3, only about 135 yards, but the green was a dome-shaped nightmare surrounded by bunkers large enough and deep enough to hide Castro's entire army. Another alarming facet: Doublewide correctly determined that putts on Florida golf courses predominantly break toward Disney World. That wouldn't work here, obviously, because we were in Disney World.

During the opening round, I was once again paired with the human volleyball and patron saint of Crown Royal, Jonny Mitt. That left-handed hook of his proved ill-suited to the demonic contours on Anagustura Lakes. Instead of finding water, most of Jonny's drives wound up in the palmetto wilderness that lined the opposite side of the fairway. Jonny Mitt.

He was such a fearless little bastard. On practically every hole, he'd stomp off into the rain forest underbrush that came up to his chin. But Jonny'd hack it somehow, salvaging bogeys where he should have made 8s.

Mitt's prospects brightened when he ran down a long birdie putt on No. 10, "The Quadruple Bypass," according to the sign at the tee box. But No. 11, "Getting Caught In Bed with Your Mother-In-Law," was where Jonny finally did register his 8, and it finished him for the tournament. As we trudged off the green, he looked at me and said, "I think I need to clarify something."

"Clarify what?"

"That situation I told you about the other night. That grocery store game—that's not what actually led to Gloria and me splittin' up."

"No shit?"

"Naw. Something happened a year earlier. I told Gloria that maybe she should try one of those liposuction treatments. So she did. It was a disaster. She lost the inches, all right, but with her clothes off, all you saw was loose skin with these huge dimples all over her. She looked like a giant fuckin' sponge. Things were never the same after that."

Ordinarily, if it had been some sorry prick like Bruno Pratt telling me that story, between the 11th green and the 12th tee of the big jackpot tournament, I would have figured that he was attempting to jangle my concentration. But this— this was just Jonny being Jonny. And the way Big Luther was striking the ball that day, I didn't have to concentrate. Team Del, at that point, was an effortless 3 under.

"Jonny," I said. "Do you have any naked pictures of Gloria—before and after the liposuction? I'd like to see those, if you have any."

Mitt nodded. Affirmative. "I've got several 'befores' in my golf bag. The afters—" he hestitated. "I remember that we took some Polaroids. I think I might have a few afters in a shoebox back at the motel."

Team Del finished the first of three rounds at 2 under, tied with Terry Dill for the lead. Most of the scores throughout the field were atrocious—a tribute to the difficult layout at Anagustura Lakes.

They invited me into the press tent to describe my round, a brief stay since the media didn't figure that my luck would hold much longer in a tournament like that. "I only had one bad hole, the twelfth." I told the reporters truthfully. "I got a little horny just before my tee shot."

Round 2 had me scheduled for a 6:50 A.M. start—the first group off the tee. "Listen, we're going to win this thing," Doublewide said, "so keep your mind on your business. You weren't thinking about golf yesterday. You were thinking about pussy."

"Well, so was Ken Venturi when he won the U.S. Open in 1964. You can tell from the old newsreels. He was literally drenched with sweat after he finished. Anyway—it don't matter *what* I think about out there. Everything is up to Big Luther. It's completely out of my hands," I said.

"It's out of Big Luther's hands, too," Doublewide reported. "I called the Psychic Friends Network 1-900 number last night, and it's in the bag. This is a done deal."

"I thought it was settled, that you'd lay off the Zombie for a while."

Doublewide groped for words that would adequately articulate his impatience with me. "You're so smugly judgmental all the time. That perpetual skepticism really grinds people down." I had heard those identical words in the next room, on *Bay Watch*, the night before and realized where Doublewide had picked up the lines.

I decided to accommodate him. "You just made history," I said. "That's the biggest league-sanctioned crock of horse-shit anybody ever produced."

"Now you're getting defensive," he said. "But just hear me out. This psychic I talked to, I asked her if she has uncommon gifts. 'An unlimited supply,' she said. And she said that she doesn't throw out winning lottery numbers or any of that hocus-pocus. She just sticks to the basics—fuckin' and suckin' and personal finances. So right off, I test her. 'What size shoes do I wear?' I say. That tactic is called crystal ball busting, I happen to know. And she gives it to me straight. I asked her what size shoes I wear, and she laid it on me straight and told me that a planetary configuration obscured her vision and that it didn't matter anyway because she didn't deal with inconsequential bullshit like that."

"Besides. She gets all her info from five packs of cards. I could hear her slapping them down . . . nine of diamonds, jack of hearts, four of hearts, eight of clubs. 'This is *nice, very* favorable.' What it meant was that I have, or used to have, an association with somebody whose name begins with J, S, or D—as in Del—and that person will inherit an enormous sum of money, and soon, and that I'll get a cut."

"Inherit? You're shit out of luck."

"Inherit. Win a golf tournament. What's the difference? The woman is a psychic. She isn't God."

After Round 2, I was ready to take on Doublewide in a spirited debate. Maybe she *was* God. Big Luther, always good, kicked his genius onto lofty plateaus previously unseen until that day. Also, I found one area where Anagustura

Lakes offered some compassion. The greens, if you could manage to hit enough of them in regulation, seemed textured like cashmere.

While Team Del, off the first tee at sunrise, was putting the finishing touches on a 66, the wind began to kick up. While I relaxed on the practice green, I could hear loud "a-a-w-w-w!" sounds rumbling in from the galleries watching another of the gaudiest names in Seniors golf conk another one into the drink.

By day's end, I owned a five-shot lead with eighteen holes to play. One marginal source of concern came from the identity of one of the players in the cluster tied for second. Jack Nicklaus. A person with my professional background, with my overall stature and standing in the game, should honestly have pondered the ramifications of that.

On the trip back to the motel, I told Doublewide, "Don't call the Psychic Friends again tonight. She might change her mind."

Since I was the sole leader heading into the final round, that naturally meant I'd be the last player off the tee, at 12:10. We arrived at the golf course around nine, with time to kill, and, for once, the minutes seemed to drag past like wounded animals. Yesterday's capricious winds had returned, although that wasn't such a bad feature—it would have been tougher for somebody deep in the pack to mount a charge.

Big Luther, though, after a routine session on the practice tee, did not seem quite up to yesterday's Herculean standards. "I think he's got a bit of an upset stomach," I reported to Doublewide. "But he'll be OK."

Jack Nicklaus, in the threesome immediately in front of me, was about to blast off. I could hear them announcing Nicklaus on the PA system . . . "from Columbus, Ohio . . .

four time champion of the U.S. Open . . . five time Masters champion . . . ," ad nauseam. Huge applause.

At last it was my turn. Was I nervous? Not especially. Was I going to choke? We'd soon find out. The PA guy identified me in terms less grandiose than Jack Nicklaus. "From Caloosahatchee Pines, Florida . . . winner of the Chichen Itza Sun-Kist Tuna Seniors Classic . . ."

I would like to say that I received a smattering of applause. But there was no applause. That was perfectly understandable, however, because my threesome *had* no gallery. Everybody—maybe five thousand people—was marching along and following the group ahead, the Jack Nicklaus group.

The five-shot lead held up for four holes. But on No. 5, labeled "99 Years In Sing-Sing" by the sign on the tee, Team Del got dealt its first test of faith. Big Luther belched his customary mortar shot, slightly to the right side of the fairway. The golf ball took a peculiar hop and skipped at a right angle into the nasty rough. Doublewide went pale. "What the hell happened?" he gasped.

What happened was that the ball hit a beer can, tossed into the fairway by somebody in the gallery following Nicklaus. Everybody knew about Arnie's Army. Now I was going to have to cope with Big Jack's special forces, up there laying a minefield. In that cruel Anagustura Lakes rough, my lie could not have been more demanding, down in five inches of thick grass. "Here's where you find out what you've got inside," Doublewide whispered. "Balls of brass or guts of wet Kleenex."

My approach hit the middle of the green and rolled off the back. My little chip shot wasn't all that great, rolling about twelve feet past the hole. But I made the putt, and then I could feel my brass balls knocking together as I walked to the next tee.

That sensation of relief disappeared in a hurry. Up on the next hole, the most difficult one on the entire front 9, the gallery cut loose with a huge cheer. That meant only one thing. Nicklaus had made a birdie, something he tends to do in combinations once he gets started.

For the next hour, Jack's big following continued to cheer while I was gritting my teeth, knocking in a series of 4-footers just to rescue par. On the 13th hole, the one they called "Certified Letter from the IRS," calamity sank its ugly fangs into my vulnerable fetlocks. This time the 4-footer didn't drop.

What did matter, though? Jack Nicklaus was demolishing the golf course. Seven birdies in eight holes! As I stood on the 14th tee, awaiting the shot that would lead down that finishing stretch that they called Death Row, with an ABC camera there to beam the event nationwide, Doublewide offered encouragement. "So Jack blew your ass to hell and back. Nobody really cares," he said. "Besides. The only people who watch golf on TV must be loaded on marijuana. That's damn sure the only way I could ever watch it."

It must have appeared that I was loaded on marijuana the way I played 14. Big Luther's drive landed in the right rough. It wasn't his fault—I lined him up that way. Sheer carelessness. My approach shot was OK, winding up on the short fringe about fifteen feet to the left of the green. Six more inches and it would have toppled down into a creek. I decided to use my sand wedge to chip the third shot, actually topped the thing and almost whiffed entirely. The ball squirted acrosss the green, struck the pin, and hopped down into the cup.

The realization that I had just recorded the strangest birdie in PGA annals generated a peculiar sense of tranquility throughout my entire body. The sensation materialized as something those people described on the Sally Jessy Rafael program, the ones who died, temporarily, and talked about that feeling of being drawn into the big light. "Well, this is it," I thought. "I'm having a stroke. It's all over, baby."

Instead of keeling over, Big Luther and I made another birdie at 15—still locked into this odd bubble of euphoria. That horrid and malicious slice of landscape, the short hole, the 16th, produced yet another birdie. The ball rolled to the lip of the cup and seemed to spin around and around, a leaf in a whirlpool, until falling into the hole. Now we were back tied with Nicklaus.

This condition of immaculately blissful nirvana became interrupted when I hit a dogshit approach to 17. I salvaged par, but my little cocoon of bliss appeared to have popped a seam, and the peaceful rapture was leaking out fast.

Big Luther rescued our ass on 18 with our best drive of the day. He must have knocked the fucker 340 yards. We lofted a 9-iron over the trees that obstructed the entry to the green. The putt we needed to win the tournament measured no more than fourteen feet. I didn't bother to try to line it up, not wanting to give myself enough time to talk myself out of sinking it. With a quick stroke, the ball rolled straight in. No fuss. No frills.

Then I was talking to some guy wearing a red jacket with an "ABC" stamped on the front pocket. He was holding a microphone. "This must be as good as it gets," he said.

"No. Poking it into Dottie Ridge is as good as it gets."

That's what the *Old* Del would have said. But the Old Del no longer existed. Not around there, at least. I sent the Old Del away. Signed him up in the Peace Corps. Shipped him off. He was serving his country now, giving golf lessons to Eskimos on the island of Kiska.

The New Del talked on television about what a great guy he'd become, smug in the special joy that's experienced exclusively by people who fashion lofty goals, and by Jesus, stick with 'em. From the winners come the platitudes. That's what Easy Tradin' Doyle also tried to teach me.

"The satisfaction does not come through winning a major tournament," said the New Del. "The satisfaction comes from the realization that I was not entirely happy with my life and made the effort to try to change it."

I wasn't through, either. "The satisfaction," I said, "comes when we receive a message like the one we received the other day at our Team Del E-mail address. It came from a man who said that he'd started doing deviant sex acts because Paul Harvey told him to do it on radio broadcasts, and then he was arrested at a peepshow when he tried to talk an undercover cop into giving him a hand job."

The ABC guy appeared astounded. "He thought Paul Harvey told him to do that? Was that on his regular newscast or 'The Rest of the Story' segments?"

"Actually, it was on the commercials that Paul Harvey does for Tru Value Hardware stores. Anyway, he read where Team Del qualified for the Seniors tour, overcoming what some people might call a dubious past, and that inspired him to go into therapy, and the other day, he got elected judge someplace in Texas."

"And the therapy enabled him to overcome his, uh, sexual deviancy?" said the ABC guy.

"Actually, he's still a pervert. But at least he doesn't hear Paul Harvey's voice anymore."

"That's—that's a remarkable story."

"Goddam right it is," I said. "In fact, they're making it into a made-for-TV movie . . . written, produced, and starring Robert Duvall."

From there, I slid over to the press tent to enlighten the little people from print media.

16

Somebody in the olive drab station wagon, the one with significant body damage and the "DON'T BLAME ME—I VOTED FOR GEORGE WALLACE" bumper sticker, took a leak out of the window on the rear passenger side. We'd been stuck in a massive traffic entanglement behind that car for what seemed like a week. Such was the pomp and pageantry of NASCAR big league automobile racing.

I knew why Dottie Ridge had insisted on our coming up here on what would have otherwise been a welcome and much needed weekend off from the Seniors golf grind. Dottie seemed to think that if we immersed ourselves in the cultural aspects of America's fastest growing sport . . . the only sport more Caucasian than polo . . . here at the Thank You, Jesus—Tylenol 600 in Upper Bowel, South Carolina, that Team Del might be inspired to produce newer and better marketing schemes. But at this point in our relationship, Dottie and I were entitled to some creative differences and on the whole, I would rather have taken seventy-two hours off to catch up on my laundry.

The magnitude of the crowd, I had to concede, stood out as impressive. They'd crammed more people into that station wagon up ahead than I'd seen in any gallery on the golf tour. Once inside the gate, Doublewide parked the Team

Del van on the infield and we wandered toward the garage area to try to locate Dottie.

Immediately, I was struck by the profound difference in spectator demographics between stock car racing and golf. A cloning factor had been employed in the people who come to those Seniors events. Everybody wears Ralph Lauren signature attire and all the men wear golf shoes and they walk on cart paths whenever possible because, apparently, the "klat, klat, klat" sound of the cleats on the pavement makes them feel macho. But here, inside this race track, everywhere we looked, it was nothing but Confederate flags and tobacco juice. Six billion people living inside campers and reeling on the downslope of a six-day drunk. The whole area reeked of stale beer, Lysol, and reefer. Some woman hollered out at a little girl, about age seven, who closely resembled a red-headed, seventy-five-pound basketball.

"Tammie Soooo-uuuuu! Yew git back in here right this minute, and help Granddaddy find his teeth!"

Doublewide looked misty-eyed. "I gotta say. I'm impressed. People look down their noses at the trailer trash, but, by God, their family values are still intact," is what I thought he said, although it was damn near impossible to hear him or anything else over the incredible racket of the race cars turning a few practice laps.

I always deferred to Doublewide when it came to matters of social engineering, but what impressed the crap out of *me* was the merchandising skill of these stock car people. They were light years ahead of the golf promoters, who, you'd think, would know better. A line of vendors' booths stretched for about a mile. Mark Martin T-shirts. Rusty Wallace beer mugs. Jeff Gordon gimmee caps. Jimmy Spencer cigarette lighters. Doublewide bought a Dale Earnhart action figure for $26. Pull a string and the little fucker would sing, "The Wabash Cannonball."

"Look at *all* the *bread* this crap's pulling in," Doublewide exclaimed. "Tiger Woods' old man would have a wet dream."

Big time security guarded the gate of the garage area, laid out along the main straightaway. State cops who might have been off-duty offensive linemen from the Washington Redskins carried billy clubs that looked like something Babe Ruth would have used to whack Number 714. The cast of extras from *Cool Hand Luke*. Mirrored shades. Twenty-six-inch collars.

"Wonder what it's like in this county to be Mexican with a burned out headlight," Doublewide said.

"Keep your voice down," I told him.

Inside the magic gate, the people-watching took a dramatic turn for the better. This was clearly a Dottie Ridge milieu—a cascade of humanity that largely consisted of guys who looked like TV game show hosts, wearing a "Guest of the Manufacturer" credential, accompanied by top-shelf Park Avenue whores. Jeremy Mayfield strutted around in his blue, flame-retardant Mobil One driver's suit, while all the pussy eyed him like he was some kind of Aztec god. Ginger Spice drifted among the throng. Ginger was there to sing, "The Star Spangled Banner." Doublewide had begun to salivate.

"Bend over, Baby, and I'll drive you to Tuscaloosa," he said.

The spectacle served as a clear reminder that America was the greatest country in the universe. Then and there I changed my mind about NASCAR. About a dozen mechanics hovered around each of the race cars. They tinkered with all kinds of crap. People have been shot off to the moon riding in contraptions that hadn't received as much attention to detail as these 800-horsepower neutron bombs cleverly disguised as Fords and Chevrolets.

We located Dottie's team—the purple and gold Number 72 car sponsored by Gallo Hearty Burgundy (Preparation H had cancelled a deal because of the car's non-performance)—at the very end of the garage set-up. They were positioned there in conjunction with the team's shitty status in the Winston Cup point standings. The car, driven by Blowtorch Barnes, had met with some new calamity on the final practice lap. Moonie Van Sickel, the crew chief, lay on his back with his head stuck beneath the car.

"S-h-e-e-i-i-t," said Moonie. "That bearing's done burned plumb through the casing."

"Wut?" said Blowtorch. His face was the color of roast beef.

"You got ears, ain'tcha? I said the fuckin' bearing's done burned plumb through the casing."

Blowtorch wore the expression of a man who had come home to find his front porch stolen. "Well," he said after lengthy consideration. "Fix the fucker."

Dottie Ridge stood outside the garage, oblivious to the human drama that took place within. Compared to the Rent-a-Slut brigade that the spark plug executives had flown in for the event, Dottie radiated a Cleopatra-like quality. Very regal. She stood and talked to a writer from *Cosmopolitan* who was there to write a story—"Chrome On The Range," subtitled "Ball Joints and Drive Shafts: 10 New Ways To Torque Your Love Motor"—about the only woman car owner in NASCAR. The woman from the magazine looked like the character Og Ogleby who appeared in a W. C. Fields movie.

"So why would a woman of your obvious sophistication be attracted to an activity that seems so . . . ah . . . rustic," Cosmo Butch wanted to know. And I thought the *Golf* writers asked dumb-shit questions.

"What attracted me to NASCAR competition was that the

people involved are the *only* category of successful men I've met in *any* professional category whose dicks are bigger than their egos," Dottie said.

Jesus. Just because she used to be Chiquita Banana, Dottie thought that she could get away with anything. Dottie saw me and waved.

"Isn't it true that many women experience orgasms at the sound of these racing engines?" said the *Cosmo* woman.

"Oh, yes," said Dottie. "Absolutely."

Conspicuous by his presence, right there next to Dottie, was Billy Crossdresser. When Dottie responded to the question about the noise, Crossdresser patted her on the shoulder and gave this wise and knowing nod, like Marcus Welby, M.D., after he'd correctly diagnosed a case of whooping cough. He wore white slacks and a teal silk shirt, attire more appropriate for a regatta than some Dixie-fried car race. The earl of the swamplands did not appear overwhelmed with joy when I approached the scene.

"Hello, Billy," I said. "Where's your wife?"

"I sent her off to Tuscany for a couple of months. She wants to learn to sculpt." Then he gave me his thin and artificial little "everything is under control" grin.

"Tuscany, huh? I would have thought she'd be more into Native American art. Pottery and beads and shit like that." There's nothing like the evil adrenaline produced by jealous instincts to bring out the hyena in a person.

Crossdresser ignored that. "Hey," he said. "Look's like you've put on some weight."

"Prosperity doesn't come without a price," I shot back. Chalk up another one for the good guys. You gotta get up awful early in the morning to put one over on Team Del.

Meanwhile, the woman from *Cosmo* asked Dottie about the exotic use of valve stems.

"Just rub a little STP on the thing and you're good for the whole day," said Dottie.

Mercifully, race time had approached. The pit crew shoved the Gallo car onto the racetrack. Tension oozed beyond the flood stage level. Blowtorch Barnes experienced a transformation of demeanor, from melancholy to out and out angst. He took on the posture of a man who had been issued the request: "Would the defendant please rise?" Barnes' wife, who I later learned was a former runner-up in the Miss Jailbait USA competition and answered to the nickname of "Buckets," gave her husband a good luck kiss and said, "Now don't you go out there and get your ass killed, ya hear?"

I gave Ginger Spice a B-minus on her effort with "The Star-Spangled Banner." She hit the high notes with surprising authority but played a little fast and loose with the lyrics. ". . . and the rocket's red glare . . . the bombs bursting in air . . . gave proof through the night . . . that my firm little ta-tas were still there . . ."

Dottie's race team set up a little buffet behind the pit area. Country ham. Grits. Deviled hawk eggs. And an unlimited supply of Gallo Hearty Burgundy, compliments of the sponsor, a product that goes well with anything, breakfast, lunch, or dinner. Crossdresser was practically curled up in Dottie's lap. He looked so damn smug I finally had to say, "You know, Billy, it was your people who established the automobile racing tradition. Chief Sitting Bull watched Custer ride over the hill and looked over at Crazy Horse and all his other assistant chiefs and said, 'Gentlemen, start your Injuns.' And then all fuckin' hell broke loose. Right, Billy?"

Crossdresser rolled his eyes. "Sand trap humor," he said.

I turned my attention to the car race and proceeded along

the assumption that if I drained enough jugs of the Hearty Burgundy, that Crossdresser might become invisible. On the track, Blowtorch enjoyed a promising effort. After two-hundred miles, the wine car had moved up to 17th place while Buckets Barnes supplied me with some biographical tidbits regarding the race driver. I learned that he liked to play a little game that he called "pet the monkey" and that during race week, he "gets so uptight that he acts like a fuckin' RE-tard. The fact is that Torchie doesn't feel comfortable in public unless he's wearing his white hood. Sometimes, I think he'd be better off if he went back to his law practice."

No sooner did Buckets utter those words than a small mushroom materialized out by Turn 3. Poor old Blowtorch. He'd smacked the wall. "S-h-e-e-i-i-t," said Moonie Van Sickel, the crew chief, for the forty-fourth and final time of the afternoon.

Somebody from the track rescue crew radioed the pit crew. Blowtorch Barnes was basically OK but a radiator hose had ruptured and "scalded his peck-uh." Blowtorch came back to the pit in an ambulance. I'd seen healthier looking specimens delivered in a Domino's pizza wagon.

Moonie Van Sickel looked at his driver. "Are we having fun yet?" he said.

Doublewide and I decided to exit and marched about four miles, back to where the Team Del van was parked near the tunnel from the infield. After I witnessed the condition of Blowtorch Barnes and realized that any future "pet the monkey" tournaments were on indefinite hold, I felt more secure than ever in my identity as laborer in the relatively serene universe of the Seniors golf tour.

The warmth of that seeming well-being lasted about ten

minutes. When we located the Team Del van, I noticed an envelope stuck under the windshield wiper. It was addressed to "Team Homo," handwritten in red ink and inside was a note:

"I know you're kweer for that Big Loother and I know you two suck each other awf all the time. Git awf on it while you can because Big Loother is fixing to dye."

My first notion was that Doublewide had put the thing there as a joke, but then I realized that the wording was too precise and that it couldn't have been his work. I handed him the note and said, "What is *this* bullshit?"

"Godammit! You stupid fuck! I told you so! I told you this would happen!"

"Told me *what* would happen?"

"Told you not to go on that chickenshit program. That *60 Minutes*. See? Now you've attracted the lunatic fringe. Ever since you did that, I've been sleeping with a sixteen-gauge sawed-off shotgun under my pillow."

"Well," I said. "Keep it loaded." I made a mental note not to tell Big Luther about this for the time being. No point in getting *him* all bent out of shape.

Now my words to Billy Crossdresser seemed prophetic. Prosperity doesn't come without a price.

$$\textbf{(17)}$$

Tara Nova Estates, smack in the heart of what has been celebrated as the New South ever since the Andrew Jackson administration, did, in fact, represent all of the amalgamated elements that have come together to form what was truly the New Golf. The Seniors tour had at last evacuated the perpetual agenda of palm shrouded courses and we competed now on a layout surrounded entirely by the back yards of households of 50,000 square feet and upward. Red brick. Platinum blonde brick. Lilac brick. Tile rooftops. One after another after another. You could buy the entire city of Allentown, Pennsylvania for what these backyard stone fences must have cost.

I was standing on the 11th tee and realized that it was also 11 A.M. because the chimes from the various grandfather clocks inside the homes were chiming in simultaneous proclamation that Bloody Mary time was over and bourbon time had begun. For the first time since I embarked on this golf tour, it began to register how abnormal this all seemed.

The grass on the fairways didn't seem real, although, even for a golfer, I'd never paid any particular attention to grass. This stuff was more like the carpet that you sink into practically up to your ankle, the kind that undertakers installed in their funeral parlors to hush down the acoustics. The green dye was staining the soles of my golf shoes. The sand was obviously fake—way too white. Probably some kind of chemical. Most of the tees were situated atop artificial mounds. The creeks and ponds—all ersatz. Golf courses used to be designed around the natural landscape. People who built these modern courses created their own terrain.

Gun-metal gray rain clouds drifted off to the east. They were probably fake, too. And as I looked around at the golfers, we all seemed sort of battery-operated, too.

I passed these observations along to Doublewide while waiting for the group ahead to finishing putting on the par 3 11th. "So who gives a shit?" he said. "The checks are real." The childlike wisdom of this man was captivating. The difficulty, the source of this small and temporary malaise, came with the fact that Team Del had been experiencing a frustrating round, a rare occasion recently. Big Luther performed to the max—ordinarily I would be on schedule to shoot maybe a 60 at the opening round of this, the Kennesaw Mountain Buttermilk and Sour Cream Seniors Classic. Big Luther's usually reliable, albeit less celebrated companion, the hickory shafted putter whom I had recently come to refer to as the Little Corporal, was misbehaving. Horrendously so. The longest putt that I would make the entire round was a tap-in. The old guy in that poofter wig who wrote, "These are the times that try men's souls," was clearly a golfer.

In those non-team sports like tennis and boxing, when you screwed up, you didn't have time to feel sorry for yourself because two seconds later, another serve or another left hook was headed for your teeth.

Golf, on the other hand—hit a crappy shot and sometimes you had to stand around for ten minutes and fulminate about it. You felt a jillion little termites, munching away incessantly at your innards. The survivors (there had never been such a creature as a bona fide, certifiable winner in this game—God aw mighty, it killed Bobby Jones) were supposed to be immune from the termite sensation. But on certain days, you just couldn't avoid it. On 17 and again on 18, I knocked a simple wedge about two feet from the pin. What happened next reminded me of this Irish joke.

O'Leary went to confession. "Bless me, Father for I have sinned. I used profanity on the golf course."

"Tell me about it," said the priest.

"I was about to break eighty for the first time in my life, but I knocked my first three balls into the lagoon," O'Leary said.

"And that was when you used the profantity?"

"No, Father. Then I hit my ball into a deep bunker and took eleven swings to get out. On the twelfth swing, I finally knocked the ball to within an inch of the cup but by then, I was doomed to shoot ninety-five instead of breaking eighty."

"And that's when you used the profanity? I must say, it was understandable," said the priest.

"No, Father. Not yet."

"WELL, DON'T TELL ME YOU MISSED THE FUCKIN' PUTT!"

That's what happened to Team Del. On 17 and 18, I missed the fuckin' putt. What might have been a 57, which might have gotten me on a Wheaties box, became a 71 and now I was buried one-third of the way back in the pack.

As we headed back to the motel in what, until today, I had started to call the Team Del Thank-You-Jesus Victory Express, still grinding my teeth, I turned to Doublewide and said, "Take the Little Corporal out of the golf bag and leave him out on the patio tonight."

Doublewide gave me an odd look. "Why? It's supposed to rain. The Little Corporal might get all warped."

"Well, that's just too bad for the Little Corporal, isn't it? We've got to teach him a lesson."

"I think you're overreacting there. We all have bad days. If the Little Corporal sits outside, then I'll sit out there with him."

What this was all about, as we used to say back in Topeka, was this: Doublewide had been reading too many golf magazines and he has been listening too closely to the guys out there at the Seniors caddies' trailer. I was beginning to worry about what went on out there at the trailer. To have heard Doublewide tell it, at first, all they did was eat fried eggs and pimento cheese on toasted white bread and trade Pokémon cards. But lately, I'd been hearing some second-hand accounts of possible seditious behavior. This caddy that they called Joey D. who worked for, you guessed it, Bruno Pratt, had emerged as some kind of cult leader. That evoked dark images. Senior caddies, programmed by the evil Joey D., prowling the countryside on moonless nights and murdering people in their beds.

He'd already started working on Doublewide's head. Back in Orlando, Doublewide mentioned that Joey D. had posted a reprimand in the trailer concerning the issue of golfers and caddies sharing motel rooms. That went against all of Joey D.'s protocols. "Joey says," and here Doublewide appeared to select his words with tact, "that by rooming together, it makes us look like a couple of hobos."

"So what?" I'd countered.

"Ummm. Well. Joey didn't exactly use the word ho-BOs, if you know where I am coming from."

"Yeah. I know where you're coming from and I know where Joey D. is coming from, too. He's coming from his boss. Bruno. The little rat man. That's so damn typical of him. Patron saint of the small lie. Plant the seed and watch it grow."

Doublewide had merely frowned. "I don't believe that. Joey D.'s his own man."

"If you think that, you don't know Joey D. and you sure as hell don't know Bruno Pratt."

That exchange had happened three weeks earlier. Now he was defying me over the Little Corporal issue. I realized now what was happening at the caddies' trailer. Between trying to get bets down on the fifth race at Bay Meadows, they were talking mutiny and Doublewide had the look of rebellion in his eyes. Apparently, the spirit of civil disobedience had blinded him because he'd missed the turnoff to the Sweet Magnolia Discount Inn and we were now headed toward Alabama, the Halitosis State.

Doublewide was expendable. The caddies had been carving each other up behind their backs. Just last week, I'd found the resume of a caddy, Gaylord Faircloth, stuffed into my locker. In the off-season, Gaylord operated a tree service and now he was offering discount firewood as a term of potential employment. I had no need for firewood, but if a caddy could bring a discount deal on a '55 T-Bird to the table, I might be willing to listen.

Doublewide hadn't entirely realized it, but in the not-too-deep recesses of his persona, I suspected that he *wanted* to get fired, just to see his name in the bold face agate type in *USA Today*. But he wanted to hold on until I hit the inevitable back-to-back-to-back seven-over after 36-holes and hit miss-the-cut skids, the moldy ranks of the over-fifty trunk-slammers, so that he could move on to some PGA geezer with hotter dice. Reasonable prognosis on Doublewide's part, with only one significant notable flaw . . . Seniors golf was still battling calf roping for sports section space and a caddy couldn't get his name in the paper if he burned down the Pentagon.

But I rode along with the van window lowered, inhaled honeysuckle fumes, wondered what had ever become of lightning bugs, avoided comment, and allowed Doublewide to rave and flail away, a tactic that became tedious because everything that he said was tainted with the foul aroma of truth.

"You're getting obsessive about winning the U.S. Open for your old man, or whatever that Easy Tradin' Doyle character claims he is. Take your mind off the old bastard. Just chill. That Open is still six weeks off. You're peaking too early."

"So how do I avoid peaking too early? Tank a tournament or two?"

"You might consider it."

He actually appeared to believe that. The man was part moron, part maniac, traveling benignly in the wrong direction across the Dixie landscape. And he was right. I'd started to worry that I might show up at the Open, scheduled in that great American Grease Stain that we call Detroit, riding on an empty tank.

Another concern. After Team Del had won one of those Florida tournaments, I'd phoned Doyle to give him the good news and it had been like talking to a cement mixer. He'd said that the recent X rays revealed the billiard-ball-sized tumors in lungs were now softball-sized and growing by the minute.

Everybody knew all about how Babe Ruth socked the home runs that saved the life of little Johnny. What the public never heard about was how, the next day, the Babe had gone 0-for-5 and killed little Billy. My deathbed promise to Easy Tradin' Doyle had been quite the driving force for Team Del over the past six months, but suddenly I'd come to regret having made the offer.

Doublewide presented an interesting question. "What happens," he said, "if you *don't* win the Open? Since you've put all your apples in that one sack, or whatever that saying is."

"I've thought about that," I lied. "After Doyle's funeral, I was thinking that Dottie Ridge might let me move in with her for a while and I could take up finger painting."

Doublewide gave me a peculiar look, one that I couldn't read, and said, "I don't think you should come to rely so strong on Dottie." Now he'd gotten philosophical. "They say life begins at fifty, which is a big load of dog crap. My friend Chuck Heston told me that he was actually nineteen years old when he played Moses. Life is for the young." Now I was getting some vintage Doublewide. Straight from the gut.

"But," he said, "life doesn't end at fifty, whether you like it or not. Jazz saxophonists have a saying—they might be too old to cut the mustard, but they can still lick the jar."

We compromised about the punitive measures regarding the Little Corporal. He spent the night outside, but Doublewide wrapped him in a garbage bag so that he wouldn't get wet and warp. The lesson paid off. On the first hole, we rolled in a sixty-foot birdie putt and for the remainder of this tournament, there would be no catching Team Del. Saturday's round—a 65—was another one of those that just as easily could have dipped into the sub-60s. Since Big Luther was not only hitting every fairway dead-center and forty yards in advance of the rest of the field, and with the

Little Corporal suddenly cashing in from long distance on every other, there was only one person to blame for us not setting a course record at Tara Nova and that person was Doublewide.

He under-clubbed me on a par 3 (his Bushnell laser range-finder could still give him fits) and that cost me my only bogey of the round. "Better grab some more garbage bags because tonight, *you're* the one who's sleeping outside," I told him after the bogey. I hadn't meant it. But Mr. Wide had seen something in one of those insipid golf magazines, where you never saw a photograph of anybody who was not smiling, that all of the *top* touring pros treated their caddies like hog dung—beat on them like a rented mule when a tournament was not proceeding according to the master plan—because it helped the *top* pros to relax. So Doublewide recommended that I take on a more abrasive attitude toward him during moments of stress that happen during a key round.

I took the lead for good after the 15th hole. A 340-yard drive. Thanks, Luther. A 25-foot birdie putt that we hadn't even bothered to line up. Well done, Little Corporal. "This is easy," I whispered to Doublewide. "This is stealing."

After I'd scored the low round of the tournament, they interviewed me on national TV. The Slim Whitman's Greatest Hits Cable Network was covering the big event, which illustrated just how far Seniors golf had enlarged in public stature. The microphone guy asked me to comment on my round. "I went out on the golf course (as opposed to the bowling alley? I really did need to upgrade my interview technique) with the hope of playing well because I wanted to dedicate the round to my dear friend back in Immokalee, Florida. Billy Crossdresser. My caddy told me that Billy's wife is planning to file for divorce and if she does, this one could really get nasty. So I just wanted Billy to know that he was in our thoughts."

"Jesus, why did you blab all that? You're liable to embarrass him," Doublewide said later.

I gave him an honest response. "When I played as good as I played today, I couldn't think of anything else to say."

Sunday's final round turned out to be just as easy. A 64. It had been as though I was the only guy in the tournament. I won by twelve strokes, biggest margin of the season on the Seniors tour. At the awards ceremony, a regular Dixie princess, the reigning Miss Buttermilk and Sour Cream handed me the check and another glass trophy. That was an odd-looking thing, kind of bowl-shaped with a bunch of spout things sticking out of the bottom.

"What the hell's this thing," I asked, but not loudly enough to be overheard on the loudspeaker.

"It's an utt-uh," she said.

So my spirits were soaring—until I got back into the parking lot. Something bulky and not altogether appealing was stuck under the windshield wiper of the van. It was a dead crow, wrapped in butcher paper, onto which, in red crayon, somebody had printed: "Motown Is No Town To Be In." That was in obvious reference, I feared, to the upcoming site of the U.S. Seniors Open.

"What's going on?" I asked Doublewide.

"That? Aw, that's no big deal. Just some voodoo nut. Voodoo's gotten real big in this part of the country."

"Voodoo's ass. I can smell Bruno Pratt at work again."

Doublewide was plainly undisturbed. He put a new tape in as the van roared triumphantly away from the Tara Nova parking lot. Bluegrass. Old style.

"That Jaw-Juh mail trail's tearin' down the rail, rail, rail . . .
"They outta throw that engineer into the jail, jail, jail . . ."

My caddy was singing along and driving 85 by the time he hit the Interstate. It *was* a catchy little tune. I found myself tapping out the rhythm with fingernails, making a tinkle-ting-ting sound on the big glass udder that was resting on my lap and felt, suddenly, quite insane. And the sensation was overwhelmingly emancipating.

18

Luminous signs posted on the Interstate reflected the headlights of the Victory Wagon that rolled due west. According to the signs, the Victory Wagon had just passed the exit that led to the hamlet called Hefty, and the exit to Bovina lay three miles ahead. That told me that we had crossed the state line into Mississippi.

That night, the van included an extra traveler, Greg Hart, who was sharing his business strategies with Team Del. Greg Hart came to us after our four-shot win at the Savannah Fruit Cake Classic, making us back-to-back winners on the Seniors circuit. The winner's check was half what we earned at Orlando or even in Mexico, and with no Jack Nicklaus in the field, the tournament was not carried on network TV. But this latest hundred grand was better than a kick in the nuts with a frozen boot, and they also presented Team Del with a seventy-five-pound Waterford crystal fruit cake.

The competition element had served as the easiest portion of the week's work. It grieved me to say it, but serious critics of the sport might have had ground for concern about the quality of the talent pool on the Seniors tour. With all of the so-called headline attractions skipping the tournament, nobody raised a serious challenge to Big Luther.

So while we walked around and popped out easy rounds

of 68-69-69, every other player in the field scored at least one round of 74 or higher. I figured that I'd identified the source of their difficulty—overexposure to the 1990s. Too much time with the Sports Shrinks—a thriving occupation field that didn't exist back when sanity and men like Easy Tradin' Doyle Getzendeiner ruled our proud land. Jonny Mitt, who had reverted back to his hustler motif and actually won some old man's new Buick during the pro-am, might have been the only player in the pack who wasn't plugged into some line of Thought Management program. They were all cult programmed, like robots.

A classic example: Andy Spriggs, a guy who played in our threesome for the Friday round. Andy walked like he was kind of butt sprung, which was understandable because he used to ride bulls professionally. Poor bastard. I could tell that somebody thought they'd taught him self-hypnosis. So he would stand there on the tee box, doing his breathing exercise routine, and I wanted to yell out, "Fer chrissakes, Andy! Stop visualizing and just hit the fucking thing!"

Instead, Andy visualized himself into a 79. Oh well. It wasn't my problem. But then a big percentage of the oxymoron known as the modern Seniors golfer would script every shot, mentally, before swinging the club. That clogged their natural instincts.

While on the topic of clogged, Bruno Pratt left the course after the sixth hole (when he was already 3 over par) of the opening round. I was told that he turned green, doubled up into a square knot and fell over. Goddam, I was sorry that I missed that. Passed a kidney stone, they said. Nothing worse, they said. Don't look so amused—the same thing could happen to you, and soon, they said.

Fine. And if it did, then Bruno Pratt could claim every right to laugh as hard at me as I did at him. Most of the Sports

Shrinks, like Dr. Braeswood if they realized the extent of my Bruno fixation, would recommend additional therapy to banish that curse. Well, fuck them. That was crap. God put Bruno Pratt on this planet for the singular purpose of sharpening my concentration whenever I sensed that the vile little creature might have been lurking around the same golf course.

Just because Bruno's karma—ha!—seemed to have gone slumming a lot lately does not mean that I regarded him as less of a threat. He was like the psychopath serial slasher in the horror movies. Just when they'd shot him with a bazooka and dropped him from 30,000 feet into the China Sea, the fucker would bounce back more lethal than before. Guys like Bruno tended to be a lot more dangerous when you thought they were dead.

So, because Bruno was off somewhere all doped up and waiting for a piece of pea-sized gravel to pop out of the end of his pecker, winning this tournament was not as satisfying as it should have been. With nine holes to play, we were so far ahead that Team Del even attracted a fair-sized gallery. Predominantly female, which meant they were probably following Doublewide and not me.

While my playing partner Arnie (Arnold Moon of Pendleton, Oregon, not Arnold Palmer) took five minutes to find his ball in the pine tree woods beside the 16th fairway, I finally asked Doublewide about the source of his unlimited magnetism.

"Women have a sixth sense about decency and character. So if there is a quality about me that turns women on, it's simply that they appreciate my sincerity," Doublewide told me, right there in the middle of the fairway at Azalea Hills, home of the Fruit Cake classic.

"Sincerity?" I swallowed my Wrigley's Spearmint.

"Yeah. I sincerely want to sleep with every one of 'em. Remember what they taught us back in grade school. See one tit, and you wanna see 'em all." Thanks to Doublewide's candid testimony, I finished the tournament bogey-par-bogey but still won and now sit in second place on the over-all tour-money list and only about $3,000 short of Hale Irwin, who sat on top. Team Del now attracted the scrutiny of global corporate empires, Greg Hart, our companion and potential endorsement advisor, told us. And he owned the magic blueprint that would stimulate a "meteor shower" of endorsement riches.

"You're like the barracuda, swimming along Miami Beach. The tourists are in the water, and now is the time to strike." Those were Hart's exact words. This was right outside the press tent at Azalea Hills, where my performance had been pretty solid. It was possible that I'd laid it on too thick when I said, "I hope the entire nation joins me by extending its thoughts and prayers to Bruno Pratt and his urinary tract."

Doublewide McBride surprised me by actually inviting Greg Hart, a person who would stand out in any crowd with his Bela Lugosi haircut and the two red M & M's that served as his eyes, to ride with us to our next tour destination, all the way over in the Lone Star State. My bodyguard displayed evidence of maturity. One month ago, he would have attacked Greg Hart with a can of bug repellent. Now Doublewide was attracted to this stranger after announcing right away that in a previous but recent life, Greg Hart was known as Felix "The Can Opener" Baroni, freelance collection agent, working what he called "the Eastern Seaboard region."

Now he'd completed the upheaval, from collection agent to marketing engineer, and Greg Hart became a name that he selected only after exhaustive research. It was through that research that he learned that Mike, Chuck and anything ending in "y" received poor marks in the confidence realm of public perception.

"Can you imagine Mike Reagan in the White House? Chuck Clinton?" This was Greg Hart talking, now inside the Victory Wagon. "Jimmy Carter got elected by default, practically, after Ford pardoned Nixon. But look what happened in 1980. The Iran hostage crisis didn't have nothing to with it. It was the Jimmy that did him in."

"That's gripping material, Greg," I said. "But how does that help us? You want me to change my name? Rex Steed always had possibilities, I thought, but it's too late for that."

"No. You're right. Actually, Del isn't all that bad. Jason or Josh would be better. Most of the consumers who relate to the Seniors golf tour, right at seventy-eight percent, in fact, have grandchildren that are named Jason or Josh."

Greg explained this while I drank my late-night energy cocktail, that consisted of papaya juice with organic rye flakes, psyllium husk, and desiccated liver powder stirred in.

"In a perfect world—with 'perfect' as defined in sports marketing parameters, you wouldn't be a Seniors golfer. You'd be a gold medalist on the U.S. Women's Olympic team, either in gymnastics or figure skating."

"Jail bait," Doublewide interrupted from the driver's seat. Greg Hart didn't hear him.

"The problem is not your name, but certain facets of your identity," Greg Hart went on. "Persons in your age group, well, in the minds of the people who control the thought processes of the advertising industry, they're convinced that you do not sell products."

"That's not entirely true. I mean, they use June Allyson to sell that special underwear to old folks who piss in their pants all the time," I pointed out.

"I'm talking about products that are purchased by the general population."

"OK. Then what about that old guy who sold Grape Nuts cereal? What was his name? Ewell Gibbons. Remember? He said that Grape Nuts reminded him of wild hickory nuts. I even bought a box, just because of the ad. I remember the Grape Nuts, too. They stuck in my teeth."

Greg Hart refused to be one-upped. This *was* supposed to be his game, his home court. "Ewell Gibbons was *not* a typical product spokesperson. His real name was Johnny Silverstein. Before he became a naturalist, or whatever he claimed to be, Ewell Gibbons was America's leading porn star, all throughout the 1930s. Most people knew him from that—Long John Silverstein, they called him, and that's why he sold all that cereal."

Because of Greg Hart, I was becoming depressed. "So given the realities of the industry, as you describe them, then why are they fucking with us?"

Those little red eyes of his began to glow in the dark. "Because winning these tournaments *is* impressive. But *somebody* wins every week. What you have to do is accomplish something out of the ordinary that grabs media attention— something that is not connected entirely to coming in first, and while you don't realize it, you have the capacity to do that."

"I tried that one time in New Orleans, and it didn't work out so good," I said.

"I'm thinking of something that comes packaged with a more positive pirouette—a word I much prefer to the cliched 'spin.' What I have in mind is this. Who's the greatest, most recognizable American athlete of this century?"

"Muhammad Ali—and there's not even a close second.

And forgive my saying so, but I haven't seen him on too many Oldsmobile commercials lately."

"Well, ah, I wasn't thinking of Ali. I had Babe Ruth in mind. Now let's go back to the context of his times. The Babe socked all those homers, but the public took that for granted. What was it that Babe did to capture the imaginations of each and every American household and wound up on the front page of every American newspaper?"

"That time he called his shot. When he pointed to the centerfield fence."

"No. You're missing the point. Pointing at the fence—that was an *on-the-field* event." Greg seemed frustrated. "What I am talking about was the famous Little Johnny episode, when he promised the dying child in the hospital that he'd hit a home run for him. And he did, and then Little Johnny got well."

"Whoa. I think I can tell where this is going," I cut in. "I remember reading the Babe's book. First off, Little Johnny made him promise to hit *two*, and the Babe said, 'You're getting a little pushy, ain't you, kid?' But he hit the two and regretted it until the day he died because of the stacks of mail he got—anybody in the whole fucking country with a sick relative came pestering the Babe."

Greg gave me his I'm-already-two-steps-ahead-of-you smirk, that he accompanied by the act of pressing his index fingers together and gazing into space with a contemplative look in his miniature eyes, a tactic that was widely taught in Persuasive Gestures seminars.

"What if . . . (healthy pause) . . . what if you paid a visit to a hospital and . . ."

"No hospitals, Greg."

"Then you visit the guy's house. That's even better, actually. Cosmo DePaul. A man of your approximate age, in the prime of life, but he had to take early retirement as a letter carrier because of this disability. Cosmo's in Livingston, New Jersey."

"Why Cosmo?'

"Personal friend of mine. Former associate. Great human interest. So, hypothetically, you go and visit Cosmo because he's such a big fan of yours and all, and you give him your solemn vow that you'll win, say, the Claxton Fruit Cake tournament, just for him, and that, in turn, gives him the guts to go get this much-needed artificial hip replacement surgery."

"What happens next?"

"Cosmo undergoes the surgery and bingo! He's got a whole new hip joint, a new life, and better yet, a future."

"I'd figured that out already. What I mean is, what's in it for me, or, as they say nowadays, can you show me the money?"

"What happens next represents the simplest step of all. The media gets word of this through anonymous sources. You'd never tell them because you're too modest a guy. WIN ONE FOR COSMO. Coast to coast headlines. And *then*, you'll be promoting everything from farm machinery to shampoo."

"Suppose that comes off just like you say it will. Doesn't that draw me into the same trap that caused the Babe all of that grief? I'll get hammered with impossible demands. I can see it now. Ten times a day. 'OK, Pop. Del will win the U.S. Open if you promise to take your vitamins. Now. Go take your nap.' Jesus Christ, Greg. Talk about a hassle."

Greg had not anticipated that response, but he was thinking fast and said, "That's the *beauty* of this whole thing. After the money that pours in from the Cosmo affair, you won't have to play anymore. If you don't play, you don't have to go around promising to win tournaments for shut-ins."

"All right. Another question. What kind of compensation is Greg looking for?"

"It's an amount that's written in the boilerplate of deals like this. I need one hundred and twenty-five grand for a retainer, and most of that goes to expenses, and after that, I take twenty percent. Off the top. Cosmo gets the same. I have the contract with me. It's already drawn up."

"You say Cosmo gets the same? That includes another one hundred and twenty-five thousand dollars for him for the retainer, along with a 20 percent?"

"That's the industry standard. Call it a signing bonus."

For perhaps a half-hour, the Team Del Victory Wagon shot along through the Dixie darkness while a peaceful shroud of silence enveloped the interior of the vehicle. Finally it was Doublewide who spoke, as he wheeled the Victory Wagon off the Interstate near Parasite, Louisiana, and into the parking lot beneath a sign that read SODOMY BOB'S ALL-NITE TRUCK STOP AND CHOP HOUSE. "Anybody needs to take a leak, do it here, because we're not stopping again until we get to Texas."

Greg Hart got out, stretched, and walked into the truck stop. The instant he disappeared, Doublewide grabbed Greg's suitcase and briefcase from the rear of the Victory Wagon, pitched those onto the concrete, started the engine, and roared away like Mario Andretti pulling away from a pit stop.

Doublewide wore the exultant expression of a man who had just won the cabin cruiser on *The Price Is Right*. "That joint back there is notorious, even for Louisiana" he cackled. "Sodomy Bob lives in a cave. By sunrise, they'll be passing

Greg around like an Ole Miss cheerleader. After that, they'll sell him to those turkey farmers who live down in Faraday."

I couldn't fully share Doublewide's enthusiasm for what had taken place. The golf tournament aspect of the Team Del concept was functioning on a grand scale. But it was supposed to. I'd penciled that in as the easy part. But the marketing element, which was designed as the backbone of the enterprise as I had presented it to Dottie Ridge in the first place, was, it was obvious to all of us, going no place fast.

Of course, neither, in a very literal sense, was Dottie's first love, the NASCAR team. With the person I now knew and resented as being Dottie's other first love, Billy Crossdresser, calling the shots on the racing program, that's hardly a surprise. Dottie should known better, and she certainly deserved better.

The speedometer on the Team Del Victory Wagon rested at 90 as it passed the State of Texas tourist information center off to the right. It wasn't nine months before that I spent one hour on the practice green at Caloosahatchee Pines, telling Louise Marchmont, the sweetest seventy-one-year-old granola pancake you'd ever meet, to place three golf balls down in a line, a couple of inches apart, and concentrate on putting the ball in the middle—an ordinary teaching technique that helped beginning golfers make contact with the sweet spot on their putting blade. I thought I'd be doing that for the rest of my natural life.

Now, on a distant AM channel on the Victory Wagon sound system, I heard my name mentioned at the tail end of the weekend highlights report on *ESPN* radio.

Monday night, I would pick up Carol DelHomme at the D-FW Airport, and she would spend a gala, luxury week with Team Del as it tried for three-in-a-row at the Smith and Wesson Seniors Open in Grand Prairie. I was not interested in initiating a relationship with Carol DelHomme. And I would have been nothing short of amazed if Carol had not boarded another jet back to LA by noon Tuesday.

I had entered a universe of instant change and rapid upheaval. Who knew what would happen next. My life is beyond planning. Perhaps Dottie Ridge would find out that I was spending time with this California woman, and maybe that would re-ignite her interest in me.

After that, perhaps Dottie would ship Billy Crossdresser back down to Immokalee. The annual Mosquito Festival had to be coming up pretty soon, and that event would not be the same without old Billy on the scene. Those were the peculiar kinds of things a person could think about on an East Texas Interstate at four o'clock in the morning.

19

Contrary to the carefully tended and jealously guarded Texan ideal of handguns and cowshit, Dallas and the surrounding area worked relentlessly to promote a cosmetic bestowal that suggested excellent hygiene. Visitors to the area are immediately dumbstruck by the overwhelming absence of periodontal disease among the populace.

One municipal outpost on the western fringe of Dallas County—Grand Prairie, site of that week's Smith and Wesson Seniors Open—maintained a sublime defiance against the arrogant prissiness of the clean-tooth culture that surrounded the town. In an American decade so completely earmarked by the concept of brotherhood and sisterhood and universal peace and understanding, in Grand Prairie we rediscovered the long-lost "I don't start fights, by God, I finish 'em" ethic that made America great. The school colors at Grand Prairie High were camouflage and gold.

A billboard at the city limits said it all: WELCOME TO GRAND PRAIRIE: THE CITY WHERE THE TATTOOS OUTNUMBER THE TEETH AND IF YOU DON'T LIKE IT, THEN WHY DON'T YOU GO BEAT YOUR MEAT? Eighty-eight percent of the in-town census has or has had a blood relative who had served hard time. That was three percentage points lower than the number of motor vehicles with a bullet hole in the windshield.

Protective of their demographic, a citizen's committee fought strenuously to keep out the Seniors golf event, lest the promotion attract, as they expressed it, "some desirables" to the town.

Most of the trucks and what few cars one saw in Grand Prairie had those bumper stickers that proclaimed, lest any of the Seniors entourage receive the misconception that they were unresented: SEND ALL THE CORPORATE GOLF COCKSUCKERS BACK TO SANTA CLARA. That bumper sentiment seemed to slightly prevail over I ♥ MY AK-47 and VISUALIZE WORLD SHIT. We'd have thought that a place like Grand Prairie would be national headquarters for the Pit Bull Breeders Association of Southwest America. But it wasn't. Backyard and indoor pets favored most in Grand Prairie were lions and leopards, with plenty of cheetahs, ocelots, and werewolves— eternally on hand to greet the intruder.

Team Del liked it here.

Carol DelHomme was to arrive at 8:10 that night on a Delta flight from Los Angeles, which will probably be too late for us to attend the big Monday soiree for the golfers that would be hosted by the Texas Association of Goat Ranchers, with its organizational slogan, according to the letterhead on the invitation, ". . . And The Bleat Goes On."

Carol also missed out on the Grand Prairie hospitality committee's opening day festivities for the Seniors' golfer's wives. The itinerary for that was set up as follows:

—A morning VIP excursion of the Grand Prairie Palace of Wax, where a life-sized likeness of the winner of that week's golf tournament would be enshrined along with Hitler, John Wilkes Booth, Rupert Murdoch, etc.

—A visit to Texas' leading tourist attraction, the Grassy Knoll at Dealey Plaza in downtown Dallas.

—Lunch at the Zodiac Room at Neiman Marcus.

—A Grayline bus tour of gaudy castles where the over-mortgaged rich folks lived in North Dallas.

Activities like those were customary on the golf tour, outings that kept the "little wimmen" occupied while the menfolk played in the ritualistic celebrity pro-am event with the social elite. In North Texas, that group largely consists of slip-and-fall lawyers and lottery jackpot winners. What the local hospitality committees didn't comprehend (and how could they?) was that while the Seniors golfers themselves might have been arthritic, phthisic and over-the-hill in a glandular sense, a healthy, and I mean healthy, allotment of the "little wimmen" checked in at a median age of twenty-two.

As a footnote, it was also worth adding that these Seniors golfers did not meet their spouses, traveling companions, or whatever at a young adult retreat sponsored by the Fellowship of Christian Athletes. Here was a typical "for instance," supplied via the investigative resources of the McBride Detective Agency.

Bunny Pratt, aka Mrs. Bruno Pratt, first encountered her famous golfer husband in a waiting room outside the office of a distinguished Chicago-area clap doctor. On Bunny's behalf, I need to clarify that she was employed there as receptionist and not, unlike Bruno, a patient.

Unfortunately, though predictably, the wives' junket became a fiasco. The Palace of Wax trip went well enough. "O-o-o-o. Look at that gross Jimmy Hoffa. He looks s-o-o-o undead."

But the wives soon got restive at the Grassy Knoll—"B-o-o-r-r-ing." Then a food fight broke out during the lunch at the Zodiac Room at Neiman's, a result of that being that it took a week for Bunny Pratt to comb all of the vichyssoise out of her hair, and immediately after that, a quartet of "little wimmen" proceeded downstairs and were promptly busted for shoplifting in the lingerie department. Britt Clanton, the overworked PGA media director, was forced to spread out a serious display of C-notes to keep that item out of the newspapers, which he would admit to me at a later time without also explaining where and how the cash had been distributed.

The girls then eschewed the Grayline tour of homes and headed out in a block-long caravan of taxi cabs to Ma Brand's, a C&W pressure cooker dance hall on I-30 East that was favored by big ol' boys wearing ol' hats. Once inside, the out-of-town girls discovered a live band that calls itself Saved By The Governor At 11:59 and sings songs like "If You Don't Think I Love You, Ask My Wife," and they weren't seen again until Saturday morning.

By arriving a day late, Carol DelHomme didn't make the hospitality tour and consequently missed out on a lot of memories. I hoped to atone for that by arranging an empty schedule, although I was hopeful she would desire to spend ample time in Grand Prairie where they offer the freshest breathing air in all of Dallas County.

To hedge my bets regarding the enchantment potential in Grand Prairie, I booked us into the Stoneleigh Hotel where Greer Garson used to live—sedate and without ostentation— in Dallas. *Separate* but adjoining rooms, by the way. Team Del has not gotten as far as it has by taking significant details lightly, or for granted.

Even though Team Del's tour earnings now approached a half-million dollars, the plan called for sticking with the original format. That means taking it on the cheap. With success, one must avoid the large and hungry temptation to maintain the status and blow off the quo.

Two rooms at the Stoneleigh Hotel—a minor and necessary extravagance. If you didn't throw yourself a bone occasionally, you would go nuts. You go nuts, anyway, if you share a room with Doublewide McBride at the Sniper's Nest Motel in Grand Prairie.

That was where I left Doublewide, amid the usual accompaniment of new female companions. That was in the Crosshairs Lounge, which is what they call the bar at the Sniper's Nest. Merle Haggard was singing "Misery and Gin" on the jukebox and my caddy was regaling the ladies . . . "and then she hears . . . thump, thump, thump against the bedpost and Hillary says, 'Is that you, Wilt?' Haw, haw . . . titter titter . . . tee hee."

I left him there to pick up Carol at the airport, having rented a green Cadillac for the occasion. The D-FW Airport, designed by George Orwell, happened to be bigger than Manhattan Island and easily as intimidating for the first-time pilgrim. A map of the various traffic arteries looked like an MRI of the human brain.

The fucking signs were engineered to guarantee that you'd miss your exit and when I finally *did* find the Delta terminal, the closest parking spot was halfway to Paraguay. When I finally located the right gate, it was already twenty minutes past the scheduled arrival. Fortunately, the flight was a half-hour late.

My reunion with Carol came off a smidgeon awkwardly at first. I'd anticipated that, but not for the reasons that took place. We'd only spent about three hours together, and that was months ago. So, when she got off the plane, I wasn't exactly sure which one was her and she wasn't certain which one was me.

Because of the harsh, artificial effects of the lighting in the airline terminal, I may not have appeared as young as Carol perhaps remembered me. So I stood there swinging an imaginary golf club until Carol walked up and shook hands, while in the background, the security woman was saying something into her walkie-talkie about, "Code Red. Get a straitjacket to Gate 44."

Carol, traveling light, was not the same person that I remembered from our short but happy encounter in California. I'd anticipated that, too. Now that I finally recognized her, she *did* look the same.

From the perspective of Carol's left profile, the classic configuration of her nose was just like I remembered it, like on those four-thousand-year-old Greek statues where there is no nose because it has eroded away, but what the nose would look like if it was still there. You know what I mean. Her eyes were the same color as the denim jacket she wore. Designer blue jacket. When Dottie Ridge told me how much she paid for those things, I nearly shit.

What made this person, riding beside me in the rented Cadillac on the Arby's Roast Beef Highway that connected the airport to Dallas, a different Carol from that party and its aftermath in LA? That could be defined, I suppose, as a lack of effervescence. Not that the club soda had gone entirely flat. But the snap, the elan. That seemed missing.

Carol looked tired. More than tired, she looked disillusioned. That would probably derive from one of two sources. First, and most probable, Carol was thinking, "What the hell am I doing, flying to Texas, of all places, just to hook up with Grandpa Jones?" Or then I might consider the happier alternative, that Carol has diagnosed the entire spectrum of her personal life and determined that it was in shambles.

Fortunately, the root cause of Carol's unrest lay with her work situation at the motion picture studio. We arrived at the Stoneleigh Hotel, close to downtown, after a fifteen-minute ride.

"Listen, we've got two rooms—and, uh, do you wanna get something to eat?"

"No. I want to get loaded."

The Stoneleigh Hotel has a good place to accomplish that. The Lion's Den. Dark teak paneling. Quiet, dark, and discreet. Only three other people were in the bar. Old guys. Chain smoking and drinking single malt scotch. They were talking race horses. Comparing the great three-year-olds. Citation. Native Dancer. One of the old guys had seen them all run and knew what he was talking about. I recognized him. Sherwood Black. He was a sports columnist in Dallas. Syndicated. Very well known. In the realm of doctors and lawyers, he'd have been the one elected Indian chief.

Carol and I moved well away from the race horse discussion. She ordered a double Tanqueray on the rocks with no twist. I stuck with the house red. The waitress, a skinny brunette wearing a black miniskirt and a white tux shirt, brought the drinks and Carol began to talk.

I'm not going to say that Carol presented a nonstop diatribe about the personalties who controlled her work situation. She didn't. What she did present was a smooth narrative, water gently pouring over the spillway. Her plot included a few key players. Carol named a quartet of investment bankers, none of whom knows shit from wild honey.

They told the studio what movies to make. All the major studios had four more investment bankers just like Carol's guys. That was why, she said, so many high budget films featured the artistry of actors such as Bruce Willis.

And there was Matthew Macarro. He ran the studio. "Matthew sleeps under his desk every night," Carol said.

"Not on it. *Under* it. Curled up. That's what all the California computer industrialists do now, so naturally . . ."

"So that's required of everybody in the office?"

"It's implied. Situations like that come and go. The Matthew Macarros come and go. Fairly rapidly. It's Hisatoki Komaki who's got me down. Matthew is one of thirty-nine million, six hundred thousand followers of Hisatoki Komaki. And out of that thirty-nine million, none are more devout than Matthew."

I didn't say anything. From the other end of the barroom, I could see Sherwood Black staring at us—or at Carol, obviously, while she gestured to the waitress to bring over another Tanqueray.

"Spirituality, see, it starts and ends with Hisatoki Komaki. The discipline requires chanting. Powerful chanting. NAM-MYOHO-RENGE-KYO. It means, 'Absolute obedience.' Repeat the chant, over and over and over, until your balls fall off. Only then can you attain Goal Four.

"So Matthew channels tons and tons of money to Hisatoki Kamaki, no telling how much of it belongs to the studio. Or used to belong."

The cadence of Carol's speech pattern accelerated. Usually, she didn't talk quite as fast as most California people, but now she was. She knocked down half of her second drink in two swallows.

"So—with Matthew being such a heavy contributor and all—Hisatoki Kamaki actually appeared at the studio office, in person. Weirdest man I ever saw. His head is the size of a fucking *tennis ball!*"

While Carol articulated that picturesque scenario, Sherwood Black, the sports columnist, stood up and started walking. He strayed several feet from his direct route to the bathroom so that he could pass close enough to our table to pat me on the shoulder and reveal, in this raspy bass voice, "I know who you are." The way he said that made me hope to God that he didn't have me mixed up with somebody else. Sherwood Black kept on walking.

Sherwood's little salutation served to pull Carol away from the alarming topic of Hisatoki Komaki. I could practically see his evil, tennis-ball head, coated with fuzz.

"I know who you are, too," Carol announced. By now, a third glass of Tanqueray had arrived at our table.

"Compliments of Mr. Black," said the waitress. A glass of gin for her. No wine for me. Huh.

"How serious is this? How does this impact my attainment of Goal Four?"

Carol shook her head. "Well, here's where you finally catch a break. When Hisatoki Komaki was leaving the office at the studio, I heard him say to himself, under his breath, but I heard him anyway, he said, 'If there's anybody I can't stand, it's back-stabbers, chickenshits, and most of all, it's those purple motherfuckers.' That's what I heard him say."

The rest of the night worked out OK. Carol, seemingly having said what she needed to say, appeared to brighten some. And while I will not go into the detail I used to describe my first encounter with Dottie Ridge, around midnight I attained Goal V.

And around 6 A.M., I was up and headed for the golf course in Grand Prairie for one of the customary pre-tournament pro-am things. Carol DelHomme wanted to sleep all day.

They called the course at Grand Prairie Pecan Oaks. "Where'd they get that? They don't grow pecans on oak trees," wondered Doublewide, a leading authority.

"All I know is that I don't see any palm trees and pine trees. First time I haven't seen those in twenty years," I said, which was true. No trees of any type, actually, with the exception of a few brown mesquites, about five feet high, perhaps a half-dozen per hole. The fairways at Pecan Oaks had been cut long and wide. The big hitter off the tee would prevail on this golf course and, of course, that again meant Team Del.

For purposes of the pro-am, I gave Big Luther the day off. I left him asleep on the bed next to Carol DelHomme back at the Stoneleigh. The Team Del golf bag had been refitted with a special compartment that kept Big Luther completely segregated from the irons and the rest of the riffraff in there. That note that had been stuck under the windshield at the NASCAR race in South Carolina—the one that contained the death threat on Big Luther—still bothered me some.

Even though I played with a substitute driver, I one-putted twelve greens and won some cash for me and my other three pro-am partners—two celebrities and one Grand Prairie community leader. The celebrities, other than me, included Delwyn Ray Roberts, a Grand Prairie native who won a silver medal at the 1996 Atlanta summer Olympics, competing in video poker, and Purvis Montgomery, a second-string halfback for the Dallas Cowboys.

Purvis walked around the golf course with a cellular phone. "Every half hour, I'm supposed to report in to my probation officer," he explained.

The remaining player in the group, the pillar of the community, introduced himself as Buster Cherry, youth director at the Midway Park Baptist Church, right there in Grand Prairie. Buster was blessed with a damn good swing.

After the ninth hole, when our foursome had posted a composite 9-under, fortified by preacher man Buster Cherry's eagle on the 515-yard par 5 opening hole, I was tempted to borrow Purvis Montgomery's phone and call Carol back at the hotel and then decided against it.

Carol might have gotten the wrong impression, that I might be about to display my potential as a Senior Stalker.

Actually, I didn't really need to talk to Carol. I was curious to find if Big Luther was awake yet. It worried me, sort of, those two being in the room alone like that. The fact was, I didn't trust either one of them as far as I could throw a haystack.

20

The Waterford crystal collection of ours had expanded to museum proportions. First we won that big ass crystal tuna at the Star-Kist tournament down in Mexico, and don't think that fucker didn't set off some odd looks at U.S. customs.

"Never seen nothin' like that before." That's what the customs cop said. He had these thin cruel lips, and I could tell that he was the kind of person who got off on looking up would-be smugglers' asses with a flashlight.

"If it makes you so goddam nervous, then why don't you x-ray it?" I said right back.

That was the New Del talking. The Old Del, the one who shipped off to the Peace Corps, used to turn into oatmeal every time he saw a police car. That's a conditioned reflex, stemming from the silly New Orleans fiasco that the New Del had officially deleted from his memory file. The New Del didn't take any shit from cops.

"Before you start getting too cocky," the customs man said, rebounding nicely, "we've seen plenty of cases where people take items like this stupid fish, melt them down, put the liquid in little gram bottles and peddle it over in China-town, where it gets shot straight into Proud Mary."

"Who's Proud Mary?"

"In the vernacular of the drug culture, Proud Mary is the

artery they shoot junk into. Anyway, I'm going to pass you through. *This* time."

"Why?" I was in a mood to argue.

"Because you don't fit the profile of somebody trying to carry narcotics through customs."

"I don't? What's the profile?"

"Mainly, the smuggler will have little beads of sweat on his upper lip."

"Is that why so many Cubans grow mustaches?"

"Bingo," said the customs man.

Anyway, Team Del now owned the tuna, the crystal fruit cake, and a three times larger than life crystal Smith and Wesson .357 magnum. The generous Smith and Wesson people also tossed in, along with a gift assortment of their handguns and silencers that are ideal for stocking stuffers, a handsome bronze-plated sign to stick in the front yard, if I ever got one. The sign said: FUCK THE DOG—BEWARE OF THE HOMEOWNER."

Our championship at Grand Prairie gave Team Del three in a row. We nailed the trifecta, and now we were the rage of the Seniors tour. What I liked was winning each one in a different fashion. That bizarre burst of birdies at the last holes that beat Jack Nicklaus in Orlando, then that wire-to-wire walkaway in Georgia.

Grand Prairie, though. God-aw-mighty. The U.S. Marines prevailed at Guadalcanal with less effort than it took to win the Smith and Wesson Open. All three rounds, Big Luther performed erratically. He seemed distracted. The problem, I was afraid, might have been that Luther had become jealous of Carol DelHomme. He was right there in the room at the Stoneleigh Hotel while we were . . . well, you know.

"Looks like I'm going to have to have a chat with Luther after all this is over, and get a few things straightened out,"

I told Doublewide when the competition became almost unbearably brutal in the final round. Doublewide nodded. But he'd been acting funny all week as well. One might have supposed that Doublewide worried that Carol's sudden entry into the story line might throw Team Del's serendipity trip out of kilter. Big Luther and Doublewide. Jesus. They were like a couple of children.

Anyway, with Big Luther's head stuck somewhere out in cyberspace, Team Del was forced to rely on other resources. Namely, the short game. I, and I say "I" instead of "we" because Luther damn sure didn't contribute anything (although, in fairness, there have been plenty of occasions when he could say the same about me), I holed out from a sand trap twice for birdies, back-to-back on 6 and 7 and almost again on 8, the first time that'd ever happened, to me, at least.

Two birdies from bunkerville threw me into a tie with Bob Charles and Gil Morgan and the three of us fought back and forth and to and fro all day Sunday. Charles is a left-hander from New Zealand who won the British Open back when I was trying to get started on the regular tour. Morgan is a reformed optometrist from Weewoka, Oklahoma, not far from Will Rogers State where I went to college.

When it came to crunch time—"when the blood turns to piss," as my old college coach, Hoppie McBee, used to put it (I never could figure exactly what he meant by that, by the way)—Bob Charles and Gil Morgan were collectively and individually controlling the back nine holes in the fashion of a billiards hustler running the table.

Finally, on 18, the shortest par 4 on the golf course at 435 yards, Big Luther finally awoke from his snitty little trance. With a big wind at our back, Luther whipped one that bounced onto the front apron of the goddam green. I heard this guy in the gallery whisper, "Holy shit, Mildred. Did you see *thet?*" And Mildred said, "See *whut?*" These Grand Prairie galleries were wonderful all week, I need to add. Drunker than Sam Houston the whole time. Several excellent knife fights. ABC's sponsors got their money's worth that week.

So we made the easy birdie on 18, although, just as I was stroking the putt, this guy came on a loud PA system, startling the crap out of me. He said, "Would Wanda Jo Feemster please report to what's left of her truck in the public parking area?" But, like I said, the putt went down. So me, Bob Charles, and Gil Morgan finished in a dead heat. The three of us headed back to 15 for the sudden death playoff. By now, the Texas sky was turning from black into a frightening shade of dark jade, and the civil defense sirens were going nuts all over town.

Just as we were about to tee off for the playoff, this same voice boomed out on the PA: "Yore attention, please . . ." I thought they were going to tell everybody to run for cover, which none of the playoff entries—Charles, Morgan, or me—wanted because we wanted to get the thing over with and get the hell gone.

But the PA guy surprised me. He said, "Would Johnny Bob Watley please phone home? Bobbi Lynn called, and she said she can't get Lannie in from the front yard."

With the wind whipping and the thunder booming like cannons in the *1812 Overture*, and with the end of the world apparently at hand, I made a birdie putt that was longer than a whore's dream, and the sudden death was over, well, suddenly.

While a tornado tore the ass end out of every building in downtown Grand Prairie (Charlie French, the mayor, said that damage estimates might have reached five figures), I sat in a mobile home, waiting to be literally sucked into heaven and talking live on ABC. Rusty Katz, the same guy they used in Orlando, fed me the hot question: "Do you have any moms you want to wish a Happy Mothers Day out there?"

"Special moms? That's kind of a loaded question, ain't it?"

"Huh?"

"Never mind. I'd like to say happy Mother's Day to my Mom, Connie, in Topeka, on the bizarre off-chance that she might be watching this, or if anybody who knows her might be watching, tell her that I lost Doyle Getzendeiner's phone number, and I know damn good and well she's got it around the house somewhere. We've had no luck whatsoever in getting any decent corporate endorsement offers, and I know that Doyle might have some ideas as to how to get this ox out of the ditch, ya know? Mom can contact me at the usual address, www.TeamDel.com."

Rusty looked at me with this practiced half-smile the experienced TV interviewers use a lot and asked, "Well, you're here on national television. Why go through your mother? Why don't you ask Doyle directly to give you a call?"

"Now *that's* what Barbara Walters would call a damn good question, Rusty, and with people like you starting to come through the ranks at the network, Barbara's days are numbered on *20-20*. That's for damn sure. But to answer your question, Rusty, I thought you wanted me to limit my comments to all the moms out there. Doyle Getzendeiner might be a lot of things to a lot of people, but he's damn sure nobody's mother."

"Uh, let's shift gears here," Rusty said. "What a great finish to a great golf tournament. You. Gil Morgan. Bob Charles. Sudden death. It's really a shame that any one of you had to lose in a terrific competition like this one."

"I have to disagree to some extent, Rusty. I think it would have been a damn shame if I had lost. No question. But those other two. They can go screw themselves."

Rusty Katz grinned that Emmy-winning ABC grin and said, "Congratulations, and thanks for your time."

Carol DelHomme missed that production. She missed the finish of the golf tournament, too. When the sky became so threatening, Carol evacuated the course and listened to the sudden death climax on the radio of my rented Cadillac. She wore the battery down, too. Cadillac, my ass. But we were in the right town to solve that problem. The guy who gave us the jump, his tattoo read, "Eat More Possum," and he looked at me through an everclear shroud and finally said, "You're the fucker that won the golf tournament, ain'tcha?"

"Got lucky."

"Wanna buy some quaaludes?"

I was in the process of peeling off a $20 when I heard Carol yell, "Del! Get your ass back in the car."

We drove west, to Fort Worth, for a modest celebration. We were supposed to meet Jonny Mitt at some Mexican restaurant. Jonny was celebrating, too. Not only did he finish fourth in Grand Prairie and pick up his best check to date on the Seniors tour, but he and Gloria had agreed to try it again.

Carol got impatient when I mentioned the problem with Big Luther. "Look. I used to have a doll and talked to her a lot. I was three years old at the time. But this business with you and that golf club. For a man your age, that's just . . . (she groped for the right word and finally found it) . . . sick."

I liked this conversation. It demonstrated that our new found alliance was progressing quickly, into the Next Phase that inevitably arises at some point after a couple have dispensed with the physical question. That is where it always becomes absorbing. When the love birds begin to explore deeper beneath the surface and discover all of those regions in the matrix of their partner's psychiatric theme park—the selfish, the angry, the unstable, the insecure, the hangups, the kinky neuroses, the fetishes. All of that and much more, the toyland of wacky and combustible hormonal material that make people fun.

How sad that after the Next Phase, most folks agree to never speak to each other again. Of course, old Carol had already scanned a rather abridged version of my own tortured landscape in the public print and was fully apprised of the notion that I might have qualified as what the mental health professionals would term "an odd sock."

In one short and blissful week, it was reassuring to learn that Carol could claim a few impressive cracks in her own asphalt.

Briefly married to the character actor Chandler King—I knew about that, of course, but now I was learning about this other person she once "dated" who, according to Carol, was the only person to appear on-screen in *Planet of the Apes* without makeup. When she was seventeen. Every night for the previous twenty-five years, her mother slept in a full-length, white ermine coat that she turned inside out. And once, when Carol was about eleven or twelve, her father sat her down and said, "Honey, I think it's important for you to understand that for a long period of my life, before I met Mommy, that Daddy also went by the name of Clarence Henry Albright, and when you're a little bit older, I'll fill you in on some more details about that."

Carol also had an older brother name Conrad who spoke several languages, can fart the "Battle Hymn of the Republic," had never had a driver's license in his life, lived in Grand Rapids, and limped. Because his wife shot him one night.

I want to learn more, more, more. But I was afraid. Afraid that very soon, Carol would come to see this existence of mine on the Seniors tour as the glorified carnival act that it was. And she would drop me like a hot rock. Carol didn't acknowledge or appreciate the glamor that surrounded her life. Mel Gibson actually threw up in this woman's kitchen one night! She knew Dustin Hoffman and called him "Dusty"!

"So what? Everybody calls him Dusty," she said. And I was expecting her to recline in a perpetual state of gladness and cheer with some saggy old nutsack whose entire professional identity entails the everlasting quest of making putts.

Well. I'd worry about that in a couple of days. Carol told me that she enjoyed Grand Prairie, that she thought the tension in those tournaments was "break taking," and that there was something "sexual" about that crystal .357 magnum on the backseat of the Cadillac. She couldn't take her eyes off the thing—"eyin' the prize," as they say in Texas.

Furthermore, Carol insisted that she dreaded flying back to Hollywood. She had convinced herself that the studio was destined to crater. "Look at our two major summer releases—engineered through the genius of Matthew Macarro, the prick. *Ishtar II*. And a motion picture version of *Mayberry RFD*."

"That one might work."

"Not starring Howard Stern, it won't. And he's budgeted four hundred million for the big Christmas blockbuster. That's called *Jesus, Mary, and Joseph*, with Leonardo DeCaprio playing all three parts. After that, we'll all be out on the street. Living in Dumpsters. I don't want to go back."

Frankly, I didn't earnestly believe that Carol had withered into the burned-out case that she attempted to portray. "Perhaps," I said, "we could rent a small U-haul trailer, hook that onto the Team Del Victory wagon, and you could live in that." Carol shrugged.

We drove through downtown Fort Worth, which was nothing like Dallas. Or Grand Prairie. A blend of the old and the new, as the Chamber of Commerce brochures liked to point out, a cross between Dodge City and the Las Vegas strip. We met Jonny Mitt and Gloria on the north side of town, at Joe T. Herrera's restaurant. At that moment, I was experiencing the best of times—a sports section celebrity who remained totally unrecognized from coast-to-coast. Joe T. Herrera's was jammed, and Joe T. himself made a point of shaking hands, so it was evident to everybody in the restaurant that I was probably *somebody*. But nobody gave a shit.

"Fort Worth seems like a helluva town," I told Joe T., while we waited for Mitt and his wife to show up. I was trying to think of something to say.

"Ohhh. It's all right. But these real rich guys, the Trout Brothers, they own the town, and every six months or so, everybody has to offer tribute."

"What do you mean?" said Carol.

"Oh, you have to go over to one of their houses and leave a little gift on the front porch. A couple of hens. A bushel of corn, maybe. One year, I was really on my ass and didn't have nothing to give them. So I took my eleven-year-old daughter over there, and she sang 'Amazing Grace' to Mrs. Trout. I could tell that Mrs. Trout wasn't all that thrilled about it. But they didn't throw us in jail or nothing."

"This Trout family. Sounds like they're nobody to fuck with."

"Yeah," said Herrera. "They've got their own private army. Next month, they're going to invade Poland."

Finally, Mitt showed up, Gloria in tow. Naturally, Gloria

was not at *all* the way Jonny described her. Trim redhead. Pretty, mid-forties. Damn good education at someplace like Northwestern. In fact, I'd bet good money that Gloria had gone to Northwestern. I have got a rare and uncanny knack for that kind of stuff. Mitt kept shooting me this look that clearly said, "Don't tell Gloria that I told you about the grocery store game," and I suspected that Gloria could interpret the look just as clearly as I did. I attempted to picture Gloria naked, and what I saw didn't look like any giant sponge. Jonny, obviously, had been feeding me a bunch of crap.

We ate and drank for two hours, mostly talking about Carol's job. When it occurred to Carol that we were actually interested, she told some wonderful stories. The truth about Rosebud, for instance. Carol's problem was simple. She needed to get out of town more.

Furthermore, the topic of golf never came up until the end, and only then in the context of my inability to arouse any reasonable notice from the endorsement people, how the marketing experts believed that anybody over the age of fifty must automatically be encased in amber.

"Yeah. Look what happened to Eddie Weems last year," said Mitt.

"What happened to Eddie Weems?" Eddie was a mid-level Seniors tour player. Won about one tournament a year.

"Eddie came up with a great gimmick," Mitt said. "He invented this diet and lost forty or fifty pounds, eating nothing but baby food for about six months. Then he went to the Gerber people and said, 'Let's do a deal. I write the book. Do all the advertorials. This is a natural. We'll make a *mint*.' And the Gerber people, naturally told him to get bent. So he got all bummed out, quit the tour, took a job at a country club at Myrtle Beach and gained all the weight back in about a week."

"Myrtle Beach?" I said. "And then his wife starting screwing the tennis pro."

"How did you know?"

"Just guessed. I've got a rare and uncanny knack for that ind of thing."

Carol went to sleep on the ride back to the Stoneleigh Hotel in Dallas. It was raining again. Hard. I could scarcely see five feet beyond the windshield. I got melancholy. Those little fly-in sessions were never a good idea. Either the couple got tired of each other within a week, which was usually the case, *or*, like this situation, I am overcome with this hollow feeling because Carol left in the morning.

Of course, given Carol's disposition, I could probably pry her back out on the Seniors trail for another a few days again in about a month. The real reason for my despondency was Jonny Mitt's story about Eddie Weems. Eddie Weems, I thought, as the old saying went, might have defined my generation.

$$\textbf{(21)}$$

There was a special quality to the savage voice of nocturnal thunder in Mayes County. An odd and eerie sequence of echoes hammered off the Cookson Hills to the south, an unearthly crescendo that rattled the angry dead souls that traveled the Trail of Tears. Their spirits still prowled in the mists of the Oklahoma wilderness and the thunder served to call their meeting to order.

That is what the Cherokee mystics claimed and who was to argue with the premier practitioners of the arts and sciences of supernatural transactions? Mayes County, with its jagged, middle-of-nowhere landscape, presented a countenance of primeval loneliness, even in the sunshine of late spring. So when the clouds exploded at midnight, transmitting ectoplasmic presences that twisted along the treetops, the territory got spooky in a hurry.

That Cherokee thunder, rebounding back from the rocky cliffs down in Tahlequah, was what I was listening to on a Monday at midnight in May. It was like the sound of long-ago cannon fire. This was the same storm system that almost blew us sky high in Texas and now we were en route to that week's Weird Hills Seniors Open in Tulsa.

On this trip, I had agreed to serve as vehicle commander while Doublewide McBride sat in the back and rode the exercise bike. We continued to add more and more conveniences to the Victory Wagon as it grew more victorious with each passing week. Doublewide had also secured some of those license tags with a wheelchair stamped on them so he could park in the handicap zone right at the front door of the liquor store.

I saw him back there in the rearview mirror, pedaling with a fury. Doublewide's face was crimson, matching his new, offically sanctioned Team Del sweatsuit. Like that poor bastard in *The Fugitive*, chasing while being chased, my caddy seemed desperate. On this curving highway through the Sooner badlands, where Pretty Boy Floyd and Ma Barker used to hide out, Doublewide tried to lose five pounds. He had staged a reunion with his ex-wife, LouJeanne. She lived in Broken Arrow and Doublewide, who hadn't seen the woman in a decade, "wants to look the same."

"Why would LouJeanne even bother to see you?" I wanted to know. "Divorced couples. Aren't they supposed to stay eternally bitter? I thought that was required by law."

"That's (huff) bullshit (puff)," Doublewide said. "As long as you're timely with the alimony checks, they don't even change the locks."

Doublewide talked about LouJeanne in his sleep. Now, on the exercise bike, he related the whole story. When recounting the events of his past ("Everybody experiences peaks and valleys; it's the foothills and gullies that eventually do you in"), my caddy never lied. We would sometimes inject interesting perspectives in presenting His Side of the Story. Doublewide McBride was very human in that regard.

"I was nuts to get hooked up with LouJeanne to begin with. Her maiden name was Rottweiler. That shouldda been a tipoff. Anyway, me and LouJeanne opened a restaurant together in Tulsa, right there on Archer Street. My concept was perfect. It was a New York styled deli—I called it Herbie Moskowitz's—and this was gonna be one of those places where the guy behind the counter, that being me, is rude to all the customers. Those Okies, I figured, would regard that as one hell of a novelty," Doublewide informed me.

"And the concept *was* right, but I don't think I orchestrated it too well. Some woman would come into the restaurant and I'd frown and say, 'What'll you have, you goddam old pot-bellied pig? Well, don't just stand there with your thumb stuck up your ass. Make up your fuckin' mind.' Stuff like that. Well, LouJeanne tried to tell me that I was way overdoing it. And I suppose she was right. Instead of getting rich, I wound up getting the crap beat out of me."

The deli soon closed and with the onset of financial trauma, Doublewide and LouJeanne began to quarrel. "I was still convinced that we could salvage the marriage and she was, too, so we decided to see a marriage counselor. LouJeanne picked out the counselor, some woman with tits the size of your head," Doublewide said.

"We went to see the counselor together, then separately. I was sincere with the counselor—that's my policy, as you know. Anyway, I found out that this counselor was trashing me pretty bad with LouJeanne. Everything that was wrong in the relationship was caused by me. Me, me, me. One hundred percent.

"So this counselor convinces LouJeanne that I'm a psycho and an abusive one at that, a terminal asshole through and through, and right away, she filed the divorce papers."

The monologue continued. "At first, I figured that since this counselor was a woman, that she would naturally side with the woman on every aspect of our problem marriage. It wasn't until two or three years later, after I was packed up and long gone, that I was finally able to figure out the real truth. That marriage counselor," Doublewide revealed, "had the hots for me, big time. So she manipulated the so-called counseling sessions in a way that would be certain to torpedo my deal with LouJeanne and then, I, of course, would become available. Boy, did that scheme blow up in her face. After I found out all the shit that the counselor had been saying about me, I quit asking her out altogether and left the state."

With the healing process that sometimes accompanied the passage of time, Doublewide thought that LouJeanne might be ready to accept the truth about the scheming marriage counselor.

"I'm not so sure," I said.

"Well, I am," Doublewide said. "After I was out of the picture, LouJeanne hooked up with this slick promoter who ran a business that he called Dr. Hanson's Chiropractic Tax Service and Video Store and that's when she found out what it's *really* like to be married to an asshole. That deal didn't last six weeks."

So, as Doublewide sought atonement or whatever it was that he looked for, I drove the Victory Wagon and thought about Carol DelHomme. I hadn't heard from her since she flew back to Hollywood. But I had heard from Dottie Ridge that morning. And Dottie, I'm afraid, did not really sound much like Dottie.

She said she'd heard that I had a woman in town back in Grand Prairie and her tone was sort of, I'd say, wistful. At the same time, Dottie was all business. She was pleased as hell over the general progress of the Team Del thing. How could she not be? But Dottie offered some professional advice.

Dottie thought that one of the reasons we hadn't nailed

down a reasonable endorsement might have stemmed from the fact, as she expressed it, that I had, "come off like some brain-damaged Appalachian chalk-eater" in my recent post-tournament television interviews. Funny. Carol DelHomme had offered a similar assessment. Very similar.

"I'm just saying that stuff for effect. Attempting to sound a little bit different," I said to Dottie.

"Unfortunately, you come across as a little bit off your nut," Dottie said. "And you sound like somebody who is deliberately intending to antagonize the media people."

"I *am* trying to antagonize 'em, Dottie. Because they antagonize me. Ever since the American media started circulating all that bullshit about the space shuttle disaster, that the thing blew up because the astronauts were free-basing, well that just made me want to puke."

A prolonged sigh materialized from Dottie's end of the telephone line. Then she said, "Here's what I suggest. Make an audio tape of all your interviews from now on. Then listen to them. Listen to the way you sound and then try to—uh—try to do better."

So, with Doublewide now passed out after his intense session on the bike, I did as Dottie requested and listened to myself after that morning's appearance on *Good Morning, Wichita Falls*, a radio talk show where the listeners called in with questions and comments. They had me on because I'd just won the Smith and Wesson Open. The genial host of the program, Slim Wofford, did not come across as all that genial in my estimation.

Slim wanted to locate the role that sports plays in the big picture of modern social relevance. I thought the pursuit of that material died out with Howard Cosell and I said so on the radio. That's when Slim started getting huffy. He wanted to know why more Seniors golfers didn't articulate their political views.

"They don't articulate their political views because they're just like me. They don't have any," I said. That wasn't entirely correct. Quite a few Seniors golfers maintained a steadfast political position and it rested well to the right of General George Patton's.

Then Slim started hammering me. "How can a group of professional people who get all this media coverage be totally oblivious to what's going on around them?"

"I didn't say that we're oblivious. I said that we don't have political opinions. And let's be realistic. Should somebody who makes his living with a driver, a sand wedge, and a putter really be entitled to political opinions? Hell. I don't even think we should be allowed to vote."

"That attitude is irresponsible," Slim said.

"Why?" I said. "My mother is a person with strong political opinions. She's a life-long hater of Republicans. The reason for that was that her father—my grandfather—he was a big Republican and he had this attitude that you *can* take it with you. And so he did. When Grandpa Charlie died, back during the Depression, he had it written into his will that they bury his life savings with him. So they planted Grandpa with a big wad of cash in his casket, while the rest of the family survived by eating dandelions."

Slim Wofford had become impatient. "What's that got to do with your cavalier, uncaring attitude about American politics?"

"What I learned about people with strong political sympathies was that, if they're anything like my mother, then they're pissed off all the time. And who needs that?"

Slim, too exasperated to speak, took a call from a listener.

Darwin in Decatur. Darwin sounded like the typical, garden-variety backwoods barn burner and his ying-yang was all knotted up because his favorite linebacker had just gotten busted with a joint in his sock and Darwin wanted to know what ever happened to role models.

"Darwin, you impress me as somebody who can't tolerate folks who beat around the bush. So I'll give it to you straight," I said. "I don't think that people who get their names on the sports pages ought to be held out as role models. I don't care if it's John Elway or Mike Tyson. Jack Nicklaus or O. J. We're all just a bunch of trained seals and it's our job to show up on the television screen on Sunday afternoon and entertain a bunch of people who can't think of anything else to do. We're all just a bunch of little bitty people who live inside your TV set and other than that, we don't exist. So why should anybody even remotely care what we smoke and what we drink or who we screw when we're not performing on the television screen?"

Old Darwin. He didn't go along with that. He thought we needed to worry about setting a decent example for all the fucking Little Leaguers.

"Darwin," I said. "You're not listening. I said that athletes are people who live inside TV sets. The real role models are schoolteachers and preachers. Here's what gets me, Darwin. You can't pick up the morning paper and not see a story about some choir director who's been hauled in for buggering a bunch of little kids. When you read a story like that, how come you don't call the twenty-four-hour all-Jesus radio station just down the dial and bitch on one of *their* talk shows?"

Darwin hung up.

After the program, Slim Wofford told me off the air that while my opinions were not those of an enlightened man, in his estimation, that my ill-conceived, half-crazed meanderings, "Made for good radio." I made a mental note to pass that comment along to Dottie Ridge and discarded the recorded version of the program itself.

Once we finally arrived in Tulsa—fatigued, as usual, but still functional—Team Del split up for three days, which, as the cops say, had become more and more our modus operandi lately. Doublewide claimed that my incessant neuroses provided bad tonic for his stability-starved blood. So I would employ a rent-a-caddy for the pro-am action while Doublewide took a hiatus at what he had become certain would be Le Nest d'Amour at LouJeanne's house down in Broken Arrow.

Extended exposure to Caddy McBride qualified as a test of faith. Yet I didn't feel entirely comfortable when he was not around. The replacement caddy, Ray Bascombe, presented a sinister aspect that was not easy to define. Shaggy beard. Eyes that had beheld so much human misery that they seemed to be temporarily out of order. That, compounded by an obviously inferior nutritional game plan, and we received the portrait of a man who, at some point in his life, used to steal chickens. Combine that with the peculiar reality that I had absolutely nothing but poor results in life with people named Ray, and you got a partial picture, at least, as to why Ray made me feel ill at ease. The notion that he would soon be on his way was a source of relief.

What did not appear promising was the prospect of Team Del winning its fourth straight Seniors tournament there at the Weird Hills Country Club. That impressed me as one bad ass layout, an acreage littered with creek beds, caves, and ravines. All week, I would receive heavy media attention because nobody had ever won four Seniors events in a row.

We fired a mediocre round of 72 in the Wednesday version of the pro-am. Several players, including Bruno Pratt and Jonny Mitt, posted scores in the mid-60s. Just because I didn't feel comfortable at Weird Hills didn't mean those other boys couldn't chew this golf course to pieces. A member of the pro-am group happened to be my old basketball coach at Will Rogers State, Hoppie McBee. When I say "old," take that literally. I could tell that Hoppie didn't know me from Gene Autry. He kept calling me "Mel."

After the round, I was confronted by a cheerful soul who looked like he might have belonged to the seniors version of the 4-H Club, if they had one. He introduced himself as Marvin Somebody. The man presented the aura of someone with whom aluminum siding had played an important role in his life.

I'd seen better wardrobes on a scarecrow. But when Marvin said that he represented Waylon Biggs and that Waylon Biggs wanted to buy me a steak, even though I had never heard of any Waylon Biggs, that faraway instinctive whisper of Easy Tradin' Doyle said, "Go along with this character, meet Waylon Biggs and eat his steak." So I did.

Actually, I showed up as directed at the Top of the Cock Club, a very exclusive and uptown private dining and top shelf booze place up on the tallest structure in downtown Tulsa. The membership was confined to the swellest of the swells in Oklahoma, that underrated little province that included more per-capita rich fuckers than you'd ever hope to find in Kuwait City.

They directed me into this side room, a private room inside a private club, and that was where I met Waylon Biggs. Tan suit, maroon shirt, no necktie, short, fat, almost completely bald except for a ring of white fringe that appeared to have been professionally pasted on, that ran from ear to ear across the back of his head. Although most would have estimated Waylon Biggs at an even fifty, my hunch would have placed him at closer to his early forties. (I had a good intuition for that, remember.) Waylon wore a $25,000 wristwatch and a self-made smile, big as the state of Alaska, that covered his face from border to border.

Waylon was accompanied by two men, mid-thirtyish, who did not appear self-made but instead reflected that kind of speak-only-when-the-boss-asks-you-a-question oppression that the average person can't handle very long.

Surprisingly, I sat there for the better part of the first hour, sipped a magnificent (there's no other word for it) pinot noir while Waylon made one hell of a lot of small talk. In small pieces, Waylon let it be known that he had founded a company that manufactured useful items for useful folks and after his amusing account of a couple of naive misfires in dealing with the crafty cobras on Wall Street, he successfully took his company public and during the next decade, one-third of the babies in Oklahoma were being born in a hospital wing that was named after him.

I wondered if Waylon was testing me. I wondered if he was waiting to see if I would finally burst out, "Fer chrissakes, Waylon. When do I hear the punch line? When do I find out why you dragged my ass up here?"

But I didn't. That wasn't Team Del's style and shortly, of course, Team Del would be rewarded for its patience. Waylon said that he owned a factory around Wichita Falls and that he heard me talking on the radio the day before yesterday. "You said something that showed some insight," Waylon said. "That business about how all you jocks, for all intents and purposes, live inside a TV set."

Waylon laughed. "What's it like in there?"

"Not too bad, although the humidity kind of gets to me sometimes."

Waylon laughed again. "Well, as long as you're stuck in there, maybe I could find something else for you to do, so you won't have to be ignored six days out of the week."

One of his two flunkies handed me this small bound folder. TV commercial script, very similar in format to the one the Zombie people had shown me. Only this one featured Del Bonnet wearing work clothes and work boots. Then Del took a chain saw and revved the thing up. There was a laptop computer sitting on a tree stump and with one swoop, Del sawed the son of a bitch in half.

Then Del looked at the camera and said: "Chippewa Chain Saws. A reliable tool. A tool that works."

The folder contained about a half-dozen similar mini-dramas. Del Bonnet went to work on an automatic paging device with a Chippewa heavy duty hammer. Del attached a cell phone to an outhouse door with a Chippewa hand drill. Del dispensed with a fax machine, as he looked handy with his Chippewa jackhammer. Also, there was the one where Del chased a man with a briefcase down the courthouse steps while swinging a Chippewa garden hoe, again, a tool that worked.

And, at last, we saw Del striding through a door, beneath a sign that read Internal Revenue, and Del was carrying a Chippewa machete.

"Do you have any objections to this material?" said self-made Waylon.

"No."

"I designed the whole campaign myself," said Waylon. "I don't think it contains any mixed messages. The idea to use a Senior American is mine, too. The guy's hotter than a pissed off postal worker. At first, I wanted to use an ex-Green Bay Packers football player, from back when Vince Lombardi was coaching. I interviewed quite a few and Jesus—they were way too dissipated to look effective going after the lawyer with the hoe. So then I thought about using a character like you."

Waylon presented a document that contained the terms. Three years' worth of work. The numbers staggered me. Dottie would be thrilled. Carol DelHomme would be delighted. Even Easy Tradin' Doyle would have been impressed.

"When," asked Waylon, "is the USGA Seniors Open?"

"In three weeks," I said. "You need passes? I can arrange that."

"No," said Waylon. "I want you to win it. Otherwise, we ain't got no deal."

The Old Del, the one that I'd exiled up there on the ice floe, would have walked out of the Top of the Cock Club feelings as deflated as a three-dollar truck tire. The New Del simply looked at Waylon Biggs and said, "I'm getting you those passes anyway. I expect you to show up. And by the way. Bring your fuckin' checkbook."

The New Del Bravado Act, by the way, had about another twelve hours to live. Doublewide, back on the job, spoke in monosyllables about a meteorological phenomenon peculiar to the Cookson Hills region. He spoke about the prospect of rising barley prices in some nearby Kansas counties. He spoke about the influence of Far Eastern spiritual thought on Walt Whitman's *Leaves of Grass*. But Doublewide didn't utter a single word about his reunion with LouJeanne and his left eye was black and swollen shut.

All of this I naturally found quietly amusing. I would wait until the finish of the round to tell Doublewide about the deal with Waylon Biggs. After that, I figured he should be over LouJeanne forever.

We wandered out to the practice tee. Today I would be paired with Hale Irwin and Chi Chi Rodriguez. Team Del got better billing these days. We were marquee material on the Seniors Tour and suddenly even this rugged Weird Hills golf course didn't seem so intimidating.

After my customary little pre-practice ritual that included touching my toes ten times and scratching my balls, I unzipped the leather hood on my golf bag and looked inside.

Big Luther was gone.

22

After one of those tournaments in Arizona last winter, while Team Del could not yet even rate as space junk in the PGA Seniors constellation of touring stars, we took a quick side trip to Trinidad, Colorado. I had sensed that the grip was loosening on Big Luther. It was just a subtle hunch, almost microscopic, but I instinctively felt a very preliminary onset of glue failure.

So, through the heavyweight influence of a friend of a friend of a friend (the friend in the middle being Arnold Palmer), we succeeded in scheduling an appointment with America's preeminent grip specialist. Douglas Wimberly, a Brit, agreed to see us. Well. Not *us*. Just Big Luther and me. Doublewide McBride could not be categorized as an anglophile and I thought it best to keep him away from the clinic. I dispatched him off to the nearest junior high school to score me some tranquilizers because if my suspicions about the grip were well-founded, I'd need them.

How does one describe Douglas Wimberley? Despite standing at least six-foot-four, he presented a dwarflike quality. Every sentence that he uttered came accompanied with highly animated, almost frantic gestures. Wimberley represented a shining example of one of those individuals who crossed back-and-forth over the line that separated the genius from the insane with the frequency that most people looked up to see what time it was.

After using some precision instrument to extract a glue sample from beneath the grip, Wimberley performed a biopsy. His news was alarming. The problem area was localized, but almost certain to spread. Big Luther would require a complete grip replacement.

But, thanks to early detection, the odds were good (Wimberley spotted them at 90 percent) that Big Luther might anticipate a complete recovery. "A decade ago, this wouldn't have been (he pronounced it 'bean') possible, but thanks to recent discoveries . . ."

"With all due respect," I said, "shouldn't a case like this require a second opinion?"

Wimberley looked at me like I was a bug that had just crawled on top of his eggs Benedict. "To obtain a diagnosis even remotely as accurate as mine, you would have to fly to Stockholm," he said. "Do you really want to do that? I think n-a-u-g-h-t. Time is expedient. It's presently on our side and we don't wish to sacrifice that ad-vahn-tage." Yes. This was going to drain an unexpected chunk from what was then Team Del's modest operational budget. But there sure didn't seem to be any practical alternatives, or what Wimberley laconically termed "treatment options."

So I signed the consent form and the grip replacement took place. I paced around the parking lot for three hours during the procedure and muttered to myself like a lunatic. My life was at stake in there along with Big Luther's. That was a helpless feeling, the knowledge that you'd placed everything under the entire control of a virtual stranger, particularly some clinical oddball like Douglas Wimberley.

"I feel like I've been stabbed in the heart with a fireplace poker," I told Doublewide and slurred slightly as I spoke. If he hadn't located the downers, I wouldn't have said something that hokey. Since Doublewide felt that soap opera dialogue had become appropriate to the circumstances, he decided to top me.

"Grip specialist, huh? If anything happens to Big Luther, I'll kill that motherfucker with my bare hands."

Finally, Wimberley summoned me inside. Big Luther rested comfortably in the recovery room. Everything was cool. After a week of complete R and R, we'd be back out on the golf course.

I told the story of the grip replacement experience simply to illustrate how peculiarly people react to various manifestations of trauma. Strangely, after Big Luther disappeared, I didn't feel the same grinding anxiety that came with a less threatening circumstance. Rather than being racked with excruciating agitation, I was almost pleasantly numb.

Dottie. Doublewide. Carol. Even Jonny Mitt, who won the Weird Hills Open in a playoff against Harold Henning, and Waylon Biggs appeared more externally alarmed than me. Those were the only people who knew about Big Luther's being gone, other than those who snatched him and don't think I didn't have a prime suspect.

The key now was for me, at least, not to overreact. I had not anticipated being thrust into this unique position, that of the embattled, yet composed, skipper who issued rationally resolved determinations from his troubled helm. But I believed I was suited for the noble part.

Dottie Ridge flew directly to Tulsa when I informed her of the calamity. It was flattering to behold the extent of Dottie's concern. She was blowing off the NASCAR Possum Belly 600 at Arsenic Falls, North Carolina, in order to join up with Team Del in its hour of crisis. What made Dottie's arrival in Tulsa all the more gratifying was the notion that her genuine concern over the likely termination of a cash flow source was accompanied by the fear that with Big Luther gone, I wouldn't be able to muster a decent hard-on anymore.

We conducted an emergency summit conference at the EconoLodge East in Tulsa, a city that Team Del would remember with the same affection that John Dillinger remembered Chicago. Dottie appeared incredulous, really, at my apparent lack of panic. I'd actually gone through two rounds of the Weird Hills with a substitute driver, shot a couple of 71's and made the cut, barely.

What Dottie did not realize, and I didn't tell her, had to do with Carol DelHomme. Her makeshift therapy had succeeded in convincing me that Big Luther's place in the Big Scheme needed reevaluation. When my obit appeared, Big Luther needed to be listed as "meal ticket" rather than "next of kin."

Not that I wouldn't donate a testicle and a couple of toes in exchange for his safe return. Dottie wanted to call the cops. I vetoed that. "Dottie," I said, "I've watched enough *Columbo* to realize that in cases like this, experienced investigators, first and foremost, suspect an inside job.

"Given that reality, they would slap the cuffs on Doublewide faster than you can spell 'likely perpetrator.' So let's leave law enforcement out of this right now."

Doublewide said absolutely nothing, but nodded with an expression of grave concern. He realized that I was protecting his ass in two directions here. The cops would have wanted to know his whereabouts when Big Luther disappeared. A truthful explanation would have entailed whatever happened between Doublewide and LouJeanne over in Broken Arrow. If Doublewide had been reluctant to tell *me* about it, he damn sure couldn't have related it to the cops. Thus, no alibi.

"Then what *now*?" Dottie said. Something that I sensed right away about Dottie Ridge was the single facet of human existence that she could not abide was the absence of a plan. In consideration of Dottie's recent experiences with her NASCAR troops, we must assume that her tolerance levels in that regard had worn frightfully scant. And, because there was no *plan* right then, I decided to temporarily fall back on the phrase "logical course of action."

"The logical course of action," I said, "is to wait for them to come to us."

"Who is *them*?" Dottie's tone was not at all combative. Impatient, rather.

"Them is whoever took Big Luther."

"I know *that*." Now she sounded combative. I defused that right away.

"Dottie, here is what we do know. The videotape from the security cameras at Weird Hills Country Club show this temporary caddy that we used during the pro-am, his name is Ray Bascombe, leaving the locker room carrying a golf club. The tape is fuzzy but I know goddam good and well that it's Big Luther."

Dottie flashed me this sweetly conspiratorial "now we're getting somewhere" look that I had learned to love. What Doublewide also told me was that he thought he vaguely recognized the man who claimed his name was Ray Bascombe, but had no idea from where. We decided to withhold that news from Dottie because, as Doublewide expressed it, "If I do know this character, it might make me look kind of, uh, low rent."

"Before you get too optimistic," I told Dottie, "you have

to remember that Doublewide (Tracer of Lost Persons) McBride is a licensed private investigator, and his conventional methods have determined that Ray Bascombe, for the time being, has vanished. The more important consideration lies with the probability that he was working for somebody else. And that's who we have to identify."

"Who do you think that might be?" Dottie said.

"I don't know," I lied.

"How old is this Ray person, the caddy?" The gears of her thought processes had begun to mesh. I could hear the clicking sounds inside her head.

"About fifty-five," I said.

"All right," Dottie said. "I know the type. What we do now is simple. If this *is* the character who snatched Big Luther, then he's already been paid off. So Doublewide, I want you to visit every massage parlor within a hundred-mile radius of here and you'll find this Ray character within eight hours. Then bring him back here and we will tie him up and beat the dogshit out of him until he tells us who hired him."

"I believe that might be considered a violation of his constitutional civil rights," said Doublewide.

"What Doublewide is trying to say, Dottie," I cut in, "is that given his proclivities, if we send him on a tour of the massage parlors, we won't see him again for fifteen years. And—this is my big worry—if we do anything rash right now, then we push the risk that Big Luther will wind up on the bottom of Lake Chickasha." I didn't add that if whoever took Big Luther was actually who I thought it was, that was where he was, anyway.

The sound of the ringing telephone penetrated the stifling, frustrating atmosphere in that motel room. We had a FedEx delivery at the front desk. Doublewide went to fetch it.

Inside was the ransom note, fashioned old-style, the printed letters cut from the pages of a magazine and pasted onto a single letter-size sheet of white paper. I recognized the magazine from the familiar design of the type face: *Hustler*. More than ever, I felt like I was right about who took Big Luther.

"IF YOU WANT TO SEE YOU'RE [sic] DRIVER AGAIN, BE PREPARED TO DELIVER ONE HALF-MILLION CASH. DROP SIGHT [sic] DISCLOSED LATER."

"Half mill," I said. "Say so long to Big Luther. I might be willing to go fifty grand, but . . ."

"That settles it," said Dottie. "This confirms that it's kidnapping and we're calling in the FBI." When she said that, the color drained out of Doublewide's face so fast it almost made me seasick.

"I think that's the right plan now," I said. "Look. Somebody even printed a return address on the Fed-Ex. V. Foster. Chicago. The FBI crime lab can pinpoint shit that you can't believe. Come on, Doublewide. Didn't you watch that O. J. trial?"

"Yeah. You're probably right," Doublewide said. "And we're not trying to convict anybody. We just want our golf club back. But (and here Doublewide interjected a good point), does the FBI have jurisdiction in cases dealing with the kidnapping of . . . a golf club?"

Dottie and I both knew the answer to that but she let me articulate it. "Look at the wording of the letter," I told him. "It says, 'If you want to see your *driver* again . . . Well, for right now, we just tell them that the driver is Dottie's chauffeur, some guy named—"

"Luther," Dottie said. "Only he's *your* chauffeur. Not mine."

———

The next two weeks gave Team Del the payback for nearly an entire year's worth of cheap laughs. I would willingly trade away the entire Seniors tour experience, plus the Waterford crystal collection, to erase the grotesque memory of those next fourteen days.

Our FBI agent, Kelly Brabham, showed up within the hour at the EconoLodge. Back at Quantico, they must have trained those agents for at least two years to master that presentation when they first flip out the badge. It was all in the wrist. Agent Brabham, who was female, appeared skeptical right away.

"Do you have any photos of your missing driver?"

"No."

"Can you describe him?"

"Thin. Very thin. His head is large, at least in proportion to the rest of his body."

"Age, approximately?"

"With guys like Luther, it's impossible to tell."

"Color of his eyes? Hair?"

"No hair. Completely bald. Eyes? I'd have to say metallic."

"When did you last see him?"

"Wednesday. He didn't show up for work Thursday morning. But before we go any further, Agent Brabham, I have your leading suspect."

"Who's that?"

"Bruno Pratt. You can go arrest the little bastard right now and save the taxpayers the cost of an investigation. Just be careful, because I need to get that golf cl—I mean our driver—back in one piece."

"What makes you so certain that Bruno Pratt is involved?"

"Because in the National Chickenshit competition, Bruno Pratt has been awarded the buckle for All-Round Cowboy for last thirty years. But if you want hard physical evidence, you'll find it on that ransom note. The microscopes in your crime lab will locate cum stains all over that piece of the paper and the DNA will match up with Bruno Pratt and you can take that to the bank, Agent Brabham."

At first, it seemed, to the astonishment of Agent Brabham, that my suppositions proved flawless. The crime lab people located tiny deposits of sticky stuff (Doublewide said that LouJeanne used to call it Wigglejuice) in various spots around the ransom letter. Bruno Pratt was taken into custody.

Then the forensic experts determined that the substance on the paper was *not* Wigglejuice, but hair tonic. They even identified the brand—Wild Root Cream Oil—a product once derided as "greasy kid stuff" in television commercials back in the sixties. When Bruno Pratt was able to prove that his hair tonic of choice was Lucky Tiger, the FBI was forced to let him go.

Now the focus of the FBI kidnapping investigation became, in order of appearance: 1. Doublewide. 2. Me. 3. Dottie. 4. About 250 members of a paramilitary outfit known as the Oklahoma Musketeers Free Militia.

As the kidnapping investigation began to, if not flounder, then stagnate, Team Del participated in two Seniors tournaments that preceded the USGA Open. After I missed the cut at the Wayne Newton–Roy Clark Spandex Golf Classic at Branson, Missouri, using a conventional weapon as a driver with little success, the follow-up communication on the ransom demand arrived. That time, instead of FedEx, the material arrived in the form of an anonymous E-mail on the Team Del web site.

What the E-mail said was that if we had been willing to expend the $500,000 to get Big Luther back, we were to run a "personals" classified ad in the next Tuesday's edition of the *Philadelphia Inquirer*. The ad must simply have read: "A wet bird never flies at night."

We showed the E-mail to Agent Brabham, who, by now, smelled a rat the size of Rin Tin Tin. All parties agreed to run the ad. Get more clues, maybe. Stall for time.

The Seniors golf caravan moved to its next stop, the John Deere Golf Jamboree in Cairo, Illinois. The prevailing mood inside the Victory Wagon was not what I would have described as entirely festive. Team Del was considering the retention of the services of a criminal lawyer, since Agent Brabham was suggesting she might have a world of fun if we let her strap us onto the lie box.

Despite the overwhelming distractions and the distant but lingering shadows of Fort Leavenworth, I hit the ball better at the John Deere tournament than at any point probably since back in Orlando. Hit the fairways. Hit the greens. Made some putts. Still, without the added edge that we used to get from you-know-who, we finished in mid-pack.

Now the USGA Seniors Open, scheduled at the historic and storied Crankshaft Point Country Club, just outside Detroit, loomed as the next event on our calendar. Throughout the secret ordeal of Team Del (even Bruno Pratt was not exactly certain who got snatched, although he knew for sure that he wanted to sue somebody), my would-be sponsor, Waylon Biggs, had remained sympathetic. Waylon remained true to his word, too. If I won the Seniors Open, we proceeded with the Chippewa ad campaign. Otherwise . . .

Carol DelHomme had flown in for the weekend. Until then, Carol had only been told that Big Luther was missing. Upon her arrival, I sketched out the remaining details. About the FBI investigation and how, through an unfortunate misunderstanding on the part of Agent Brabham, the true identity of Big Luther had become a little, well, blurred.

Carol was stunned, at first. Then she brightened. Her job at the movie studio now stood in jeopardy. Unless Carol could locate a motion picture treatment—a rollicking epic— that grossed a half-jillion, she could call it quits. The story of the FBI investigation of the disappearing phallic golf stick with a multiple personality seemed like a natural.

Poor Carol. She was simply trying to elevate my spirits, just before I embarked on the disastrous inevitable.

"Don't give up yet," she said. "Don't you remember what happened in Texas? Big Luther went completely haywire, because you thought he was jealous, and you won the tournament, anyway. And you won it with your short game."

"Yeah. But that short game alone wouldn't have been enough. Big Luther sobered up on the last hole, before the playoff. Otherwise, we were fucked. I'm not looking for excuses. But under the circumstances, it's hard to be optimistic and realistic at the same time."

We sat up until about 11 o'clock. Then we went to bed. Or rather, I took the bed. Carol said that she preferred the sofa because she had a backache and the mattress in the bedroom was too soft.

I thought she actually shared what I perceived to be Dottie Ridge's concerns: That with Big Luther missing, I couldn't get it stiff anymore. I wanted to tell Carol about my new and refreshing attitude about Big Luther. Out of sight, out of mind.

The telephone woke me up. The clock on the TV read 2:59 A.M. Carol answered it, on the end table by the sofa.

"Yeah. He's right here." Carol cupped her hand over the phone, looked quite dismayed, and whispered, "It's the FBI. Agent Brabham."

We were both thinking the same thing. Good-bye golf tour. Hello, Leavenworth.

Agent Brabham apologized for the timing of the phone call, but she said, "We have a major break in the kidnaping case. That anonymous E-mail you received on the Team Del web site. We now have the technical capacity to trace some of those and in this instance, we were successful."

"Traced it where?"

"The source of the transmission was a business in Florida. Immokalee, Florida. Crossdresser Industries. We've arrested Billy Crossdresser and after some lengthy interrogation, he confessed and surrendered your missing driver."

"Really?"

"Yes, really. The driver is unharmed, but you might not recognize him. He doesn't look anything like the person you described."

23

A good likeness of Bruno Pratt, imperially hideous with that everlasting, diabolic white-lipped smirk of his, gazed upon me from the sports section of the *Detroit Free Press*. Guess that's why they call it *Free*—they sure couldn't hope to sell many if they keep running pictures of that little cretin. Then the headline: Pratt Oozes Confidence in Seniors Showdown.

Underneath the headline, in the story, the Big Ooze (my words, not theirs) predicted that he was going to win the Open, *my* Open, and in his mind, the only question was how easily and by how much. Listen to this quote: "I'm the alpha dog in this pack. The rest will just have to roll over and beg."

Now it's come to this, just like I knew it had to be back last winter, back there at the Seniors Q school. This was it, finally, the Seniors Open, my resurrection and my redemption, and over there stood the mocking nemesis, the hillbilly from hell, flapping his wings and dead set on scripting a twisted ending on what had been, up 'til now, a decent play. I tossed the paper over to Doublewide with my patented "I told you so" shrug.

"Just because Bruno's flapping his gums to some reporter. Just because it's in the paper doesn't mean it's true. *You*, of all people, oughtta realize that by now."

"Yeah, but the simple fact that he's even *in* the paper is a bad omen—the dreaded eclipse. If there was one player who'd screw this championship up, it was going to be Bruno. That's not a premonition. It's an honest to God fact. Like you dive off the high board, looking down, and notice that there's no water in the pool. You suspect that what happens next isn't going to feel very good. Doesn't take a fortune teller to figure that out."

We were climbing into the van for a twenty-minute drive over to Iron Hills where I was scheduled to tee off at 10:20 for the opening round of the Seniors Open—sans Big Luther, who was en route to Motown under special government protection—and probably sedated. He wouldn't arrive in time for Thursday's competition. No telling where his head would be when he finally showed up.

Doublewide sensed my agitation. I was about to attempt to win a tournament that would affect the scenery and landscape of the rest of my life, and deplorably suffering from what the motivation people call a state of total non-focus. The last thing I needed was a sermon from the caddy. But here it came. "The real champions had to be chin-deep in pig shit before they could ever think about bringing out their A-game."

I didn't say anything, knowing that a parable was coming up. "Take . . . take (now he was groping for a name) . . . the biggest American champion of all time. Charles Lindbergh. He took off into a hurricane. Why? 'Cause somebody tipped him off that the law was on the way to the airport with a fistful of warrants. Hot checks. Shoplifting. He had a choice. Thirty days in the cooler or crank that plane up and split. The constable chased him all the way down the runway, shootin' at him with a thirty-eight and yellin', 'Come back here, you sonuvabitch!' But he missed and that's why they called him Lucky Lindy."

"Did you hear that on Paul Harvey's 'The Rest of the Story' again?"

"Nah. History channel."

"Uh-huh. Well. Show me a hero and I'll show you a tragedy."

"Did you just make that up?"

"Not actually."

Compassionate was not how I would describe my overall feeling toward Doublewide over the past few months and particularly the last couple of weeks. Now we stood quivering on the brink of Zero Hero and he was chagrined about letting Big Luther get snatched and still concerned that he might get kicked off Team Del. Most of all, Doublewide remained terrified about the prospect of that FBI woman putting him in chains after the truth surfaced about the genuine identity of the kidnap victim. I was impressed by the sangfroid Doublewide was attempting to present under the circumstances, and told him so.

"What does 'sangfroid' mean?"

"It means appearing poised and cool while trying to explain to a deaf person that his pants are on fire."

In the process of attempting to provide me with quiet confidence before teeing off, Doublewide almost ran over the guy in the yellow helmet who was directing traffic at the entrance of the players' parking lot at Iron Hills. The area became suddenly alive with echoes of shouts and words that begin in "F." But, after being trapped in the locomotive of this runaway train for the past few months, an episode like that only served to pull me back into my comfort zone. I felt better.

Iron Hills provided a big departure from so many of those courses where they play most of the Seniors tournaments, the ones that had been built the day before yesterday as an adjunct to yet another gated community, golf courses festooned with more landscaping gimmicks than a Putt-Putt layout. Iron Hills offered some history and was built on the site of an ancient Mafia burial ground. They didn't plant them too deeply. There was a hump on the seventh green. A plaque near a sand trap identified it as the resting place of Lenny "the Maggot" Maziotto.

One of the people working in the clubhouse told me that Jimmy could be located right beneath the eighteenth tee. "All that stuff about Giants Stadium—that's pure New York hype. Typical East Coast crap. Jimmy was a home boy. The day he disappeared, the Detroit Tigers started a twenty-three-game losing streak," the clubhouse man swore. "That eighteenth tee—it's haunted. Strange stuff happens up there. Bad stuff."

"Such as?"

"Such as players, just about to begin their backswing, feel this cold, invisible hand, squeezing their nuts."

"Well, that might not be the ghost of Hoffa. That might be anybody."

"I can tell you worse stuff than that. A lot worse. When you get up to eighteen, just watch yourself." The clubhouse guy actually looked spooked. Watch myself? Tough assignment. How could you watch yourself and keep your eye on the ball at the same time?

We trudged over to the practice tee, passing a leader board en route. Bruno Pratt had teed off early and I saw his name up there in red numbers after about five holes. Yeah. Yeah. The idea was to ignore Bruno and concentrate on my own game, which would be the practical approach. However, given the compulsion I'd developed regarding my Lurking Rival, I could not suddenly pretend that he'd all of a sudden vanished off the planet. The size of the crowd assembled around the practice tee was almost startling—bigger than any final round gallery I'd seen at any other tournament on the Seniors tour. These old timers events usually harvested good TV ratings in front of a live audience that was practically nil. That wasn't the case today. I hadn't seen that many people gathered in one spot since this rooster fight that Crossdresser's people had staged back in the swamp. Now I pretended they were all out there to see me. At last, a positive omen. Team Del thrived on attention and now Team Del had suddenly become revved. Even my auxiliary driver, Big Luther's backup, the club that I called Vice President Ford because he'll bail your ass out in a pinch, seemed responsive to all the onlookers. After a dozen whacks, he seemed at least ten yards longer than normal. The short irons seemed ready for the task, and the putter, the Little Corporal, after demonstrating signs of tired blood for the past month, was relaxed, at least. Finally, it was just about showtime.

Eight minutes before tee time, I heard a snatch of conversation that rattled whatever composure I'd mustered. Some spectator guy, one of these guys who looks like he puts maple syrup *and* sour cream on his pancakes every morning, was arguing with his enormously significant other. "I don't give a crap what you say. It's him, godammit! It's Don Ameche!"

"Don Ameche's been dead for at least six years!" snapped back the significant other. "You need help, Ronnie. You've always needed help. Why don't you go off somewhere and get yourself some help?"

"Excuse me," I broke in. "Where is the gentleman who you think might be Don Ameche?"

Ronnie pointed toward a tall man wearing a pastel yellow blazer. "That guy. If that guy ain't Don Ameche, I'll kiss your . . ."

The man, of course, was Easy Tradin' Doyle, who had not changed a discernible iota in the almost four decades that had passed since I'd last seen him. He looked more like Don Ameche than Don Ameche. The woman clinging to his arm issued a certain star quality of her own. Her short white skirt was designed to best display a set of almost startlingly proportioned brown legs, accentuated by the kind of calves that are welcomed into the parlors of rich people everywhere. With less than five minutes until tee time, I approached the couple and said, "Hello, Doyle."

He grinned and said, "This is Coco. You've spoken to her on the phone."

"Coco. When I talked to you on the phone that time, I thought you'd said that Coco weighed about three-fifty."

"Did I say that? What I meant was that Coco is about thirty-five. But that's not right, either, is it Coco? It's closer to—uh . . ."

"Twenty-seven," said Coco.

"Yeah. Well. This is a helluva surprise, Doyle. And I gotta tell you, you look pretty damn fit. How have those tumors been treating you?"

"Tumors? Oh. Those. When the old green reaper, or whatever in the hell you call him, is gazing right down your tonsils, you're not afraid to listen to a third opinion. So I went to see this homeopathic neck popper over in Last Call, Vermont and guess what? He said those weren't tumors, they were undigested cabbage rolls . . ."

Doyle just stood there, wearing this look of serenity that I used to see three decades earlier, whenever he'd closed the sale on some used Dodge that was suffering with ulcers in the oil pan. My ex-stepfather looked about as terminal as Dick Clark. Coco sort of rolled her deliciously bovine eyes. Now they confronted me with the ultimate punch line. I had been scammed onto the Seniors tour by this old crocodile with his make-believe tumors. And it worked! If it hadn't been for this half-baked sob story, I'd still be trapped down in Caloosahatchee Pines, benignly gathering mildew. So what if Team Del had turned into something that resembled a Fattie Arbuckle revival act over the last month? That hadn't been Doyle's fault.

Finally, Team Del teed off and it wasn't until the fifth or sixth hole that I really began to concentrate entirely on the issue at hand, unable to shake the vision of the Green Reaper. That reeked of Big Box Office. Carol DelHomme needed to know. By the time I began to think about golf and the difficulty at hand, Team Del was two under. The substitute driver demonstrated absolutely no fear on the front nine and didn't choke until the thirteenth hole. At Iron Hills, any shot that landed beyond the perimeters of the fairway was destined for a mean-spirted purgatory. The golf ball appeared buried in a deep bowl of soggy Grape Nuts. Splat! I muscled the ball back into play and made bogey.

Team Del was not merely relieved but actually gratified to reach the eighteenth tee still one-under for the opening round. I remembered with some amusement about the legend of the haunted tee, when, "Fooof!" I actually fanned on the tee shot. The clubhead seemed to pass cleanly through the ball, and the ball somehow just sat there—motionless— with this stupid goddam grin on its ignorant-ass Max-fli face. A sympathetic gasp came from the gallery, the same sound you hear over the TV at the winter Olympics when the figure skater tries to make some fancy jump and falls on her skinny ass.

I took ten deep breaths and took another swing, realizing that if I missed again, I at least might wind up on *Good Morning America*. Whap. This time, the golf ball had the decency to go flying along the fairway like it was being paid to do. From there, Team Del got down in two, thanks to a successful thirty-foot putt. Apparently, the green was not haunted. Only the fuckin' tee. So what should have been a birdie was a par and what should have been a 70 had to be registered as a 71 on the scorecard. That left Team Del six shots behind the co-leaders, one of whom, naturally, was the wicked Bruno. Eighteen other Seniors golfers sat scattered between Team Del and the three leaders.

Considering the circumstances, Team Del was fortunate and I told Doublewide that on the drive back to the motel. He didn't want to talk about it. He didn't even ask me about the whiffed drive back on eighteen. Doublewide knew that Agent Brabham was awaiting our arrival and my teammate was petrified at the prospect of having to join the PMS sect of the brotherhood of caddies. PMS stood for the Printed and Mugged Society.

On the way to the golf course that morning, Doublewide had attempted to untie the half-hitches and square knots from all my synapses and on the way *back* from the golf course, it was time to reciprocate. "Suppose the Shit Creek scenario does, indeed, happen and we all go to jail," I reasoned. "Way back in college, at Will Rogers State, I had this philosophy professor who'd served some time for conspiracy to distribute hubris and he gave me the secret of survival behind bars."

"Whassat?" Doublewide hissed. He looked sick.

"He said that they put him in with this cell mate who

weighed about five hundred pounds and the cell mate liked to play a fantasy game that he called Ozzie and Harriet Behind Closed Doors. The big guy, of course, got to be Ozzie. But Harriet, she being the professor, said, 'The thing to do is to pretend that you like it.' And pretty soon, Ozzie lost interest."

Doublewide's face turned the color of cigar ashes. But his normal jack-o'-lantern glow returned in less than an hour, after Agent Brabham, to her eternal regret, confirmed that the U.S. Justice Department had decided not to render any charges against Team Del in the kidnapping fiasco. Thanks to a technicality—we'd said that our driver was missing but never used the word chauffeur—Team Del would skate. Agent Brabham did not actually articulate, but rather illustrated with some intense facial spasms, that back in the days of Eliot Ness and John Edgar Hoover, Team Del's outcome might not have been quite so merciful. "Those guys would have racked your balls like Minnesota Fats." That's what her overall demeanor said. Even Dottie Ridge, the former Rockette with her deep vault of sordid secrets, appeared to wish that she were anywhere but there in that motel room. Big Luther was over in a corner, in a lead-lined packing tube that was filled with those sadistic little styrofoam peanuts. I hoped that he was asleep.

Agent Brabham explained the processes that had been employed to crack the case. "We needed an actual confession from Crossdresser and brought down our interrogation specialists from FBI headquarters. They initiated the absolute latest in scientific technique—meaning that they beat the crap out of Crossdresser with a rubber hose for two full days, and he simply would not crack.

"But finally, they forced him to listen to Gordon Lightfoot's Christmas album a couple of times. Crossdresser caved in like a cardboard suitcase and spilled his guts. The kidnapping scheme, he admitted, wasn't for the ransom. He did it to win back Ms. Ridge. He said that without that driver, that you, Mister Bonnet, were just a . . . let's see how he put it . . . (the agent consulted a palm pilot) . . . just a 'silly old garden variety sack of hyena shit' and that when Ms. Ridge learned the truth, that she would drop you like a hot rock."

Here, Dottie appeared to be making direct eye contact with a brass lamp sitting on a nightstand across the room. Agent Brabham continued her narrative, a smooth monotone, no "uh's" or "er's" or pauses or punctuation marks. "The suspect, William Shakespeare Crossdresser, will *not* be charged with kidnapping." She could tell that I was startled. "The U.S. attorney for the Southern District of Florida believes that for a conviction, he would require the testimony of Big Luther, whom he feels would not make a convincing witness. Crossdresser has been indicted on federal charges of obstruction of good sportsmanship along with several accounts of reptile abuse. He'll serve at least ten years in maximum security, confined to a chat room."

"What about male fraud?" I interrupted. "Because if that fuckin' pervert's a real man, then I'm Eartha Kitt!" That was hurled out there as a backlash, because I was stinging from 'sack of hyena shit' slander. Dottie Ridge simply sighed.

"Poor Billy," she said.

On the morning of Round II of the Seniors, I had sent Doublewide off to Iron Hills early in a taxi. "Walk the entire course. Re-check all your distances. We've got to put the heat on today. And be careful," I'd told him. Several of the threesomes had been hijacked by masked guys with guns on the back nine the day before.

My motive in getting rid of Doublewide, and he realized this, had been to spend some quiet, getting re-acquainted time with Big Luther. Sometime in the middle in the night, I'd been yanked out of a sleep with the sudden panicky sensation that the golf club in that lead-lined packing tube was not Big Luther at all, but some imposter. Crossdresser, the maniac, was totally capable of slipping a counterfeit driver in on the Feds. At dawn's early light, I checked out the club and to my immense and eternal relief, Big Luther was genuine. See, he had this little birthmark on his shaft, about three and a half inches beneath the grip. You'd need a microscope to find it and I was the only person who knew that it was there.

After Doublewide left, I positioned Big Luther horizontally on the front seat of the Victory Wagon, segregating him from the other clubs. We needed to talk. I explained how bummed out we'd all been and how I accepted all of the blame for being careless enough to let him get snatched. I gave him all this "there's no me without you" horse crap. Big Luther was not listening.

On the practice tee, Big Luther only took three swings. No point in applying sensory overload. Those three cuts, though, made it evident that while Luther was not in top form, not yet, there were some definite signs that the old dynamo was still in there. Once play began, unfortunately, Big Luther's indifference turned to unbridled hostility. He dispatched me into that awful rough, which was like being lost in a dark cave, on two of the first four fairways. The Little Corporal bailed Team Del out with a couple of twenty footers for par. "Good," I whispered to Doublewide. "That's just a rebellion. It's understandable. It's healthy. The shrinks call it 'venting.' Let him get it out of his system and then we'll win this thing."

But the sonuvabitch did it again on the eighth, and again on the eleventh, way off to the right of the fairway, where the weeds came up to my eyebrows. While I was looking for my golf ball, I got attacked by a buzzard. Team Del was damn lucky to make bogey and now, instead of winning the Open, I was more concerned about just making the cut. Dottie Ridge's "poor Billy" was still on my mind. Poor Billy! Just when you think you've discovered a solitary pillar of logic among the maddened legions of the Female Nation, she turns out to be a goddam Indian groupie. So Dottie had transported me to the edge of the cliff and Big Luther seemed determined to pitch me over the side.

I clutched him around the neck, right below the club head, and screamed in his face. "You don't know it, but something happened while you were gone—I made a deal with the Chippewa people—you've heard of 'em, the tools that work—and they're going to make us all rich, but only (and by then I was really raising my voice) if we win this weekend. And now you're trying to queer the deal. So go ahead, but if you do . . . you know what? I'm going to make my own commercial. I'm gonna take this Chippewa bolt cutter and *snap off your fuckin' head!!*"

Doublewide gave me this look that suggested more fear than amazement.

"What the hell's going on?"

"Tough love," said the pro.

Big Luther maintained his "up yours" attitude for the remainder of the round, but at least he didn't send me back into the Black Forest, not even on eighteen, where every day is Halloween on that tee box. Team Del finished thirty-six holes exactly eleven strokes behind the leader, Bruno Pratt. At least, we made the cut. I'd finally learned to identify the positives.

Carol DelHomme, after much indecision, decided to fly back for the final two rounds. I'd practically begged her to come. We sneaked over to a quiet bistro, the all-you-can-eat Pork Chop Palace in Windsor and started slamming down martinis. That was a clear deviation from my season-long M.O., the clear thinking and straight shooting agenda was no longer gaining desirable results.

I told Carol that I was glad she'd changed her mind. "If you're worried about being a distraction, don't," I said. "I'm actually trying to collect distractions. One or two more and I can set a PGA record."

"That's not why I didn't want to come. It's just that when you go to a travel agent in Hollywood to buy a plane ticket to Detroit, they look at you like you've got leprosy. I can't take any more of the crap. All the LA restaurants have bottled water stewards now. They make you sample it before they'll sell you the bottle. And then I ordered lasagna— just plain old lasagna, for God's sake, and the guy said, 'Do you want grapefruit slices with that?' So it's official. I'm leaving."

"What do you mean?" That's what I said. "Oh great. Another distraction," was what I was actually thinking.

"I quit the studio this week. By mutual agreement. I'm going on the road for the *Ripley's Believe It Or Not* show. I go coast-to-coast, finding freaks and mutations and getting them to go on the air and talk about their out-of-body death experiences. This job doesn't really pay shit, but I meet some interesting people."

"Huh. You could find all the freaks and crackpots you need just following the Seniors tour around."

"I know. That's how I got the job."

"I'm glad you're leaving. My game's all shot because I think you're still chasing around with Chandler King."

"You've lost your fuckin' mind," Carol said, although I hadn't, really. I was just drunk.

"If not him, then somebody. Probably a stunt man with some name like . . . Ian."

"Jesus. I can't believe you think I've gotta put up with this kind of dog crap from some closet sex addict who's shacked up with a hundred-and-fifty-year-old hoochie-coochie girl!"

People at the next table appeared amused. "I wish my tee shots carried like your voice does," I said. Good. Our first public scene. My guess was that things were about to get real ugly. And I was right.

Saturday's round began beneath an Oakland Raiders sky. Silver, black, and menacing.

The operational part of Team Del—me—arrived on the course with six minutes to spare before we were to tee off. No time to practice. Doublewide looked seasick. "Your eyes look like road kill! Where in the *hell* have you been?"

"Just got married at Reverend Smeel's wedding chapel. Got the $59.95 Saturday Morning Special."

The caddy was agitated. "Got married? No shit? Who to?"

"Carol."

Doublewide seemed relieved. "Wudja? Knock her up?"

I ignored the caddy and teed off. Big Luther was in exceptionally good form. We birdied three of the first four holes. "Shit, I need to go to chapel more often," I told Doublewide.

The sky took on this genuine Doomsday look, like it did in that Chuck Heston Bible movie where all of the Israelites escaped for New Jersey through this hole in the ocean. Team Del was rolling, although everything seemed spooky when we reached that eighteenth tee. As I swung the club, a sudden huge gust of wind almost knocked me over. The golf ball flew all the way to the edge of the green and we made the putt for an eagle. That gave Team Del a 62 for the round, a course record at Iron Hills. Most of the field was still out there and the weather really started to deteriorate while I signed my scorecard. The wind created havoc and a lot of those guys were fighting to just break 90. Ha! By the end of the day, Team Del had passed fifty-five golfers and was tied with Jonny Mitt in second place, three shots behind Bruno Pratt.

Before the sun had even thought about rising on the morning of the day that would determine whether it was my destiny to walk through life wearing real or synthetic alligator shoes, I woke up in the middle of one of those anxiety dreams. The dream seemed dreadfully real, set right here in Detroit. The final round of the Open was about to happen and I couldn't get to the course, trapped in a Marvin Gaye music video.

The perils of sleep seemed even less promising than the price I might pay for getting up before five o'clock—against the law in civilized countries—but the decision was to get up and prepare the traditional Team Del Sunday breakfast. An emu egg, two mangoes, five desiccated liver tablets, six tablespoons of barley flakes, and two cups of liquid bean curd thoroughly mixed in my Hamilton Beach blender. The result was a stamina-boosting concoction with an appearance unlikely to be tabbed as the hot new color in the Fall Fashions catalogue.

Our newest member of Team Del, via matrimony, was awakened by the racket from the blender. She gazed upon my pre-tournament meal. "What in God's name . . . ؟"

"Breakfast of champions."

"Then what do the losers eat؟"

We killed the next three hours watching PBS, a program about the history of picture frames. Team Del was shooting its 62 over on an *ESPN* replay. My tactic, on the morning of the round that promised to be one of those gut-grinders, was to think about anything *but* golf. That was not easy to accomplish when we approached the clubhouse in our rented honeymoon Oldsmobile. The weather seemed perfect. Everywhere you looked, droves of people. Iron Hills had become like a Kmart on Christmas eve.

Team Del and its playing partner, an ex-undertaker named Laughing Bob Banowitz, had been slotted to tee off next-to-last, eight minutes before the final pair, Jonny Mitt and Bruno Pratt. A crowd of about twenty people were circled around Bruno near the practice range. As usual, Bruno had gone out to the wino farm and paid these guys five dollars apiece to come out to the course and ask him for his autograph.

Soon, we were standing not ten feet from each other, swatting practice balls. I felt uneasy. I'd tried to explain to Carol that my fixation on this Pratt fucker really worked to fuel my furnace—and that like almost all pro golfers, the abominable prospect of losing outweighed the passion to win. Carol thought that was stupid. Now the predicament. The ultimate showdown lingered minutes away and suddenly and strangely, I felt as if I didn't hate the guy enough.

Fortunately, Bruno rallied to the rescue. "Ya know, no

matter how hard I try, I just can't seem to catch a goddam break." That was Bruno addressing me, the first time either had spoken.

"How's that?"

"Because I'm going to win the Seniors Open and you'll be getting all of the media attention. Ain't that a fuckin' shame? I mean, where's the justice?"

"Gimme the punch line, Bruno."

"Well, the thing is, as a professional golfer, I've got an obligation to, uh—well, as they used to teach down on the plantation—when you know the truth, you've got to tell it. So when I walk into that media center after we finish this round, I don't have any choice but to tell all those people how y'all concocted this Marx Brothers scheme to have your driver kidnapped and then had every government cop in the U.S. out chasing after this—golf club! The PGA will boot your ass off the tour—for the good of the game and all. And the USGA. And the SPCA. The whole country'll be pissed off. (Bruno was having a ball.) But look at the bright side. After all these years, you're a celebrity again! Y'all probably still ain't kinky enough for Letterman, but Jerry Springer'll goddam sure let you fuckers on!"

The man was amazing. Even though I was actually visualizing my endorsement contract being run through a Chippewa paper shredder, I had to laugh. "Bruno—how did you happen to learn of this—uh—this late-breaking story?"

"You know that FBI agent named Brabham? Hell, of course you know her. As a sheer coincidence, for the last month, I've been screwing her sister."

Bruno Pratt must have still been cackling on the first green or, otherwise, he might not have missed his foot-and-a-half par putt. And he'd been too busy rehearsing his media room presentation or else he would not have double-bogeyed the fourth hole. Team Del finished the front nine with nine pars. The skies had become dark again and Team Del was tied for the lead with Bruno. Mitt, and my partner, the jolly undertaker, had been practically camping out in that sadistic rough and were non-factors. Nobody down the pack was producing any hot moves. It was Bruno and Team Del, jaw to jaw. And now, I didn't care.

Doublewide started jumping around like an interior decorator at a Judy Garland concert when Team Del knocked down three straight birdies to open the back nine. Of course, he hadn't been in on my practice range exchange with Bruno the Terrible. Finally, some noise from the crowd behind me confirmed that Pratt had finally done something. He'd knocked one into the cup from a sand trap on a tough par five for eagle.

Big Luther appeared to take it personally. He launched back-to-back Atlas missiles at sixteen *and* seventeen and I couldn't help but make birdie. If Pratt was firing back, his gallery would have told me so. But I couldn't be totally certain, because most of the people had begun fleeing the golf course. The sky was so dark, we could barely see the pin from the middle of the fairway.

The ghost of Jimmy Hoffa had apparently surveyed the heavens and abandoned the premises on the eighteenth tee. Big Luther's final effort was routinely majestic and my 9-iron dropped three feet from the hole. I checked the leader board. Team Del remained three shots on top of Pratt. The hay was in the barn.

Then, back toward the eighteenth tee, a noise like a sonic boom seemed to shake the entire golf course. Through the dark, I could see people running, some toward the tee; others away from the tee.

"Gimmee the Little Corporal and trot back down there

and find out what the fuck's happening." I told Doublewide. He didn't take long. While I lined that last little putt, not only for this closing round of the Open but maybe forever, Doublewide trotted up, grinning like a cocker spaniel on an Alpo can.

"Bruno Pratt," he reported. "He got hit by lightning."

"He'll do anything to get some ink. Is he . . . is he OK.? I mean, is he going to be able finish the round.?"

Doublewide just shook his head. "Shit no, man. Bruno's deader than John Wayne."

Epilogue

Christmas morning in the Rockies. We'd bought a place here in Lake City, former home town of a distinguished cannibal named Packer, specifically so that Carol could experience a personal first, that being a White Christmas. And guess what? No snow. According to the paper, it was colder in Caloosahatchee Pines than it was here, meaning that people in both places would be pissed off. Carol remained un-bummed about the outdoor conditions. "Never get agitated about things you can't control." That was what she said as she walked from the redwood deck and went to work on the *New York Times* Sunday crossword.

Five minutes later: "Goddammit! They ought to take the lunatic who makes up this puzzle and ship his ass back to the nut house. What kind of person sits up all night figuring out ways to torment people? What did I ever do to *him*?"

"Why don't you just call the paper and do that?" I said. "Tell 'em to ship him back to the nut house. Or otherwise, just calm down. You're the one who says not to get bent out of shape about things you're not in charge of."

"Shut up." So this was married life. Then, "Haystack. A seven letter word for haystack that starts with 'c.' There's no such thing."

"Calhoun," I said. "Haystack Calhoun. He was a professional wrestler. Back in the fifties, I think. Weighed about eight hundred pounds."

"That's what I mean. No normal, half-way intelligent human being would know something as fucked up as that."

We had been confined within the same walls for about five months now. Really, it hasn't been that bad, probably about a B or a B-plus. Carol sucker punched me one night after we'd bought this place, during an argument over whether Big Luther should have his own bedroom. Took four stitches in my top lip. But overall . . . well, things could have been a hell of a lot worse. Not just our marriage. Anybody's. Everybody was eccentric in his or her own way, which was why matrimony's such an unnatural damn institution. The biggest adjustment for me involved coping with Carol's bedtime routine, rubbing Preparation H around her eyes because it was supposed to be a wrinkle retardant.

The much larger challenge to this marriage would emerge when we embarked on our second season of the Seniors tour. We'd hired Conrad, Carol's goofy brother, to work as my new caddy.

"Conrad needs some fresh air. He spends too much time in the garage, making model airplanes."

"Yes, dear."

See, Team Del finally split up. Now it's just Del and we liked it better that way. I now willingly concede what happened immediately after I'd won the Seniors Open in Detroit would forever stand out as the shock of my life. I'd gone to tell Dottie Ridge about Carol and me sneaking off to the wedding chapel, trying to break it to her gently, and Dottie laughed in my face—said that she and Doublewide were engaged! They'd been gettin' it on ever since that week when I'd gone down and played in that Yucatán Open. Had I felt like a fuckin' fool? Hell, yeah, and Carol didn't stop laughing for the next three weeks.

They still haven't gotten married but Doublewide, the man with balls the size of Cincinnati, said he wants me to be best man. When and if they do marry, it can't possibly last. Doublewide sounds like a steam locomotive when he's asleep.

The, uh, awkwardness of that whole, tawdry turn of events was mitigated by the overwhelming public reaction to our ad campaign for Chippewa, the tools that work. I'd become a quasi-celebrity. The ad came off just like we'd planned back in Tulsa that day that Big Luther had disappeared. Simple concept. Hard drive conked out and I hauled out the trusty Chippewa chain saw, and shouted, "OK! Download *this!*" Then, R-R-R-R-R-R-R! sliced the fuckin' PC in half.

Well, not only did Chippewa start selling a shit pot full of chain saws, the ad generated what *U.S. News & World Report* called the anti-tech backlash. People were going off-line in droves. Dot com stocks took to the basement. Some chairman at Microsoft took a job in a shoe factory.

Now we had to go back to LA to tape yet another commercial, one that was scheduled to run during the Super Bowl. In this one, they have two actors who play a geek and a nerd, looking young, rich, and arrogant, and the geek is telling the nerd that "our company now offers unique Internet applications that accelerate the extraction of raw data into searchable information." Then Del appears and seals the guy's lips together with a Chippewa staple gun.

It shaped up as an active and probably hectic week. After the commercial, we had to fly to Chicago to participate in a deposition. Bunny Pratt, Bruno's happy widow, sued the

PGA for sending him out to play in a thunderstorm. Bunny's lawyer, Harvey Weinglass, contended that due to the overall nature of Bruno's persona, that if God were going to select somebody to be zapped, then Bruno would have been the one. This put me on shaky territory. The PGA wouldn't be happy and we'd probably be looking at some kind of sanctions, but, under oath, how could I testify that Mr. Weinglass didn't have a valid argument?

It was astonishing to consider that this time one year ago, I had spent an entire morning cautioning Mrs. Cornelia Vandercrack that undergoing hip replacement surgery simply because it might help her break 90 might not be the wisest choice, and devoting the afternoon to refereeing the Caloosahatcee Pines croquet tournament. What had happened next worked as a profound lesson to me and all of the other recent AARP initiates, the children of bewilderment: Just when you think you've seen it all, think again.

From across the room, I heard a gurgling sound. It was Carol, still struggling with the puzzle. "O—My—Gawd! Seventy-nine down. 'Golfer Bonnet.' Three letters. Starts with 'D'."

Clearly an omen. Good or bad, no telling. Our lone certainty was that there would be no turning back—not after Doublewide McBride phoned about an hour later to say that he'd just been hired to fill the vacancy as the teaching professional at Caloosahatchee Pines.